The Last Seven

The Ninth Century
Book 7

M J Porter

M J Publishing

Cover design and map by Flintlock Covers

ISBN 978-1-914332-44-9 (ebook)

ISBN 978-1-914332-43-2 (paperback)

ISBN 978-1-914332-42-5 (hardback)

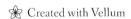 Created with Vellum

For the two J's and the one C. Thank you for always supporting me.

Contents

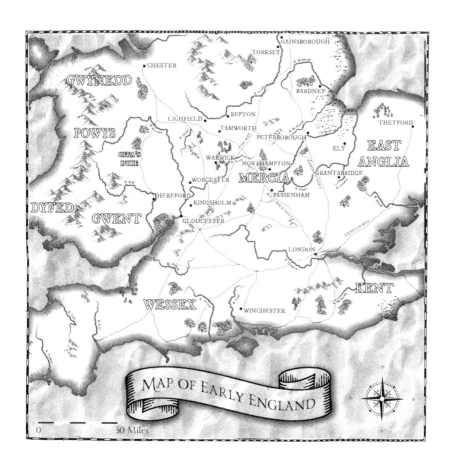

MAP OF EARLY ENGLAND

0   50 Miles

Prologue

Grantabridge, AD875

'They've caged our fucking men,' Sæbald growls, moving forwards without thought.

'Wait,' I urge him. The cage, because that's what it certainly is, is halfway down a row of what must be workshops. The tang of fire and worked metal is ripe in the air, and I wonder why there'd be a cage amongst the workshops. Wouldn't they have been better served to keep my men prisoner alongside my aunt?

'It'll be for the moneyer,' Wærwulf informs me in his gruff voice, his words coming from behind me. Slowly I begin to understand. We must be in the trade section of Grantabridge, and my warriors, or at least Beornstan, have been kept captive in the cage usually reserved for precious metals and goods. I must assume, as I glower at it, that the building isn't yet complete. It lacks a roof of thatch and enclosing sides of wood, and it's open to the elements. For now, it's merely a cage of crossed wooden beams and posts, and no good to anyone, unless they want to keep good fucking Mercian men captive.

'We have to rescue him,' Sæbald urges me, advancing as though to do just that. His usually clean-shaven face is fuzzy, and he scratches at it irritably. We've not had the time of late to look to tend to our personal needs.

I'm not going to argue with him, but first, first, we need to ensure my aunt makes it to safety from her captivity, and only then can I return for the rest of my men.

'We'll come back for him,' I advise Sæbald in a harsh whisper. But he shakes his head, eyes wild, unheeding of the danger we're in, here, inside the bloody Viking raider settlement of Grantabridge, with its tall wooden walls cutting off all chance of escape until we reach the riverside gate.

'I'm not fucking leaving him,' Sæbald responds in an angry growl, aware that if he speaks too loudly, he might just give away our location to the prowling men of Jarl Guthrum. Leonath has returned to our side to determine the delay. His eyes peer at me in the darkness, his empty hand urging me to hurry up, his lips open to reveal his missing front tooth.

'Beornstan,' Sæbald murmurs to Leonath before I can order him back to the rest of my men. 'Caged,' Sæbald snarls furiously. I know then that I'll be unable to force him onwards towards our chance of escape. I'm far from surprised. If I wasn't trying to protect my aunt, I wouldn't leave my men either, and certainly not if they were fucking caged.

But there is the matter of my aunt. She can't fight her way out of here, unlike my warriors, and she's been a captive for too long already.

'Go and release them,' I urge the pair. It's better if I fucking order it than they just go off on their own. 'I'll send two more back to help you.'

'No need, my lord,' Leonath bows slightly. 'It's just a matter of opening the cage, and then we'll follow. Take Lady Cyneswith to safety. That must be your priority.' I hate to hear my decisions laid bare before me, but Leonath's right in what he says. It's not as though I've not just been thinking about it.

I bite my lip and look again at the chaos we've caused inside

Grantabridge. There are buildings ablaze, flames leaping high into the black night sky from thatch roofs and wooden-built buildings. The sky is lit so brightly now that it could be daytime. The screams of those still trapped by the advancing flames, and those desperate in their attempts to escape, can be heard over and above the shouts of Jarl Guthrum's men, seeking out whoever rescued Lady Cyneswith from her captivity. Those shouts are coming closer, the screams as well, and even the flames aren't taking their time in forging a path through so much combustible material. For a moment, I'm reminded of the fire at Torksey, of the grey-shrouded men appearing from the aftermath. I shake the image clear from my mind. Now isn't the time to relieve old memories. Now is the time to move and get my aunt free from Grantabridge and fucking Jarl Guthrum.

'Do it, and be quick about it,' I encourage them. 'Remember, the river gate.' Sæbald is already advancing towards the cage, dashing from the shadows of one building to another. 'Follow him,' I order Leonath and resolutely turn my back on them, even though it goes against everything I believe. I hope all of my missing men are held inside that cage. It's bad enough that I've lost two men already beneath Viking raider blades. I don't plan on allowing more to fall to their bloody harvest.

Hastily, I angle towards where the remainder of my men have gone, slipping between the rear of buildings that have so far not been engulfed in the encroaching conflagration, with the settlement-enclosing wall at their backs. Goda furiously beckons me on as he waits for me. His eyes are red-rimmed in the terrible light, and his beard is filled with ash as he batters at it, adding yet more dust to the cloud that envelopes us.

'What is it now?' Goda demands to know as I sprint to his side, mindful of where I place my feet over the uneven surface, but his gaze stays behind me. He must be seeking out Leonath and Sæbald.

'They've found Beornstan.'

His lips compress unhappily. 'And the others?'

3

'I don't know. Sæbald and Leonath will release him and check for the others.'

'You won't aid them?' There's a sharpness to his tone I don't appreciate. I feel stung into replying.

'I said we'd return when my aunt was safely out of Grantabridge, but Sæbald was having fucking none of it.'

'Stubborn bastard,' Goda confirms, but whether he agrees with my decision or not, I'm unsure. And then, I realise, I don't know if he means bloody Sæbald or me. But, together, we resume our escape route, following the retreating backs of the rest of my warriors.

As we move further and further around the edge of the settlement, it grows quieter and quieter until I realise I can hear the stone I kick tumbling into the darkness around me. My breathing's grown ragged, my breaths shallower as I try not to take in too much of the cloying smoke. In an effort to calm myself, I take a deep breath, hand over my mouth to keep as much of the smoke out as possible. Anyone left on guard duty will surely hear me if I don't get myself under control or burst into a fit of coughing. Ahead, the gloom is more complete; behind, all is still chaos, with the horizon glowing bright with the reds and yellows of leaping flames.

We pass the wooden walls and posts of buildings, and it's impossible to know if Viking raider men, women and children rest inside, content that their homes are in no danger of falling prey to the flames. Abruptly, we're at a different building, this one shallower and longer, and I can hear the movements of agitated horses. This time, I'm the one to stop abruptly.

Ahead, I've caught sight of the comforting shapes of Icel and Hereman, escorting my aunt between them, and I know she's as safe as possible while inside an enemy encampment. Those horses, I know, will belong to my men, and more importantly, they're Mercian horses. I want them sodding back. I think of Haden. I'd rescue him. I have bloody rescued him from the ministrations of my enemy, and I'll do so again. I'll do the same for my men's horses. Hopefully, I'll even discover my aunt's horse amongst them.

4

'The horses,' I urge Goda, and he nods quickly, just stopping himself from colliding with me, understanding before I need to say anything else. I'm glad he holds his tongue and doesn't berate me for thinking of the horses but leaving Sæbald and Leonath to rescue my missing men.

'This way,' and I begin to creep along the side of the stable, avoiding the jutting-out wooden poles that support the building's walls and roof. The roof here doesn't hang low to the ground as elsewhere but stops just above where I can reach my arm. The thatch smells damp, and I appreciate, all over again, just how fierce the raging fire must be to ignite such damp material in the east of the settlement. We've been bloody lucky so far. The fire has caught, we've found my aunt, and now we need to find a means of escape. I just need my luck to last a little longer.

I pause at the open doorway, hand on my seax, ready should one of the bastards try and stop me from retrieving my stolen horses. I can hear hooves moving over the wooden floorboards and the outraged nickers of one horse to another, for while the fire might feel as though it's distant, the smell of smoke is present. Every so often, a swirl of smoke-filled air covers everything, and the air is hazy and filled with a strange glow. The horses know they're in danger, even if none of the Viking raiders has realised just yet.

'Follow me,' I urge Goda.

'Aye, I will,' he confirms, gripping his seax, his face set in a line of determination. I know he's thinking of his horse, Magic, safe on the far side of the River Granta. He knows he'd risk his life for the animal. The horses are just as much a part of our fighting force as our fellow warriors.

As one, we step into the stables, looking everywhere to ensure no one guards the animals. It's dark inside, making it just about impossible to see anything beyond the frightened eyes of the horses as one kicks a stable door. They know we're there.

I rush forward, eyeing my aunt's mount with relief. The animal looks at me, head back, preparing to offer a shrill neigh, but I stop her, reaching out to run my hand over her long nose.

'Hello, girl,' I murmur softly, and her fear subsides. 'Are the others here?' I query softly, but Goda has made his way along the row of half-doors and doesn't hear me. The place smells only faintly of horse manure. Our enemy has chosen to care for the animals they stole in the raid that netted them more than just my aunt and warriors.

'There's Beornstan's horse.' I tell myself, moving away from my aunt's horse. 'And those of my dead men.' I growl softly, revenge and vengeance on my mind. From somewhere far away, I hear the Viking raiders shouting one to another, their cries harsh and guttural. I could dash from here and satisfy my need for retribution. But no. I must rescue the horses, just as much as I must rescue my men and my aunt. 'Ah, hello there, Cuthbert,' Goda murmurs, making his way towards me.

How I've missed Wulfred, Cuthbert's rider, and his foul mouth. Now there's a man who knows how to swear his way out of anything. He'd have made short work of our current predicament, his words cutting to the bone, laying bare all that we faced, and doing it with a wry smirk. His faith in what we do has never dimmed. I hope it hasn't now that he's been held as a captive by our enemy.

'The horses are all here,' I query, taking a quick count of those I can see.

'Aye, my lord, they are,' Goda confirms. These horses all belong to my warriors and my aunt. There are no unknown mounts that I can see, and now they follow my every movement as I reach to open stable doors and encourage them to exit their confinement. Not that they need much encouragement, as they eagerly walk free.

And then, from outside, I hear rushing footsteps, where before, there was only angry shouting, and look to Goda. He's also heard; that much is evident in the way he stills, pushing between two horses to free himself should he need to fight. On silent feet, the two of us merge into the shadows close to the door, hoping we won't be seen before we can kill the fuckers.

If I wouldn't stop for my men, I shouldn't have stopped for the bloody horses, but I have, and now, with just the two of us, we need to fight off our enemy and rescue the horses as well. And, I realise, not only that, but we need to find a way to corral the horses from the stables without being seen by more of the jarl's men who are specifically searching for us. Quite how we're going to bloody accomplish that is beyond me.

'In here,' I hear a voice that's almost quieter than a whisper and grin, and not just because they speak in the language of the Saxons.

'Beornstan,' I quickly step from the shadows as Sæbald and Leonath pull their seaxes from weapons' belts, only to visibly relax their warriors' stance as they sight me,

'Fuck's sake, Coelwulf, you nearly got stabbed through the neck,' Sæbald complains, his words a harsh whisper, showing more his relief at not stabbing me than anything else.

I glimpse Beornstan, hoping to find a smile on his face for being rescued, but his face lacks such an expression, and I realise, as I glance behind him, that there's only him. Where I consider are the rest of my warriors?

Beornstan stinks of shit, and his face is a welter of bruises and two black eyes, the wound on the side of his face, gained on the Welsh borderlands earlier in the year, had only just healed, and now it bleeds freely once more. What have the fuckers done to him?

'My lord king,' his tone is formal, although his words are lisped through a split lip and perhaps a swollen tongue as well. Chocolate noses his way forwards, and Beornstan does reach out to run his hand along his horse's shoulder; more of a welcome than I receive. I should have gone for him. I should have been the one to release him from that bastard cage.

'It's fucking good to see you,' I mutter, wanting to embrace him but aware that he's not going to appreciate it. He's as prickly as a boar.

'Aye, let's get the bastard horses and get out of here,' Leonath confirms, something in his voice assuring me that now isn't the time for a reunion between Beornstan and me. I consider what's passed between them. What words have they shared? But there's really no time.

'The other men?' I ask, just to be sure, as Sæbald moves amongst the horses with Goda at his side.

'Not with Beornstan. He tried to escape. The fuckers caged him with no food or water for the last week, but only after a hard beating. He doesn't know where the others are. But he says that Osmod and Ingwald definitely still live. The others, he's not so sure about as he was blindfolded en route, slung over his horse like a sack of flour. He thinks the same happened to the others.'

'Fuck,' I curse, reaching for my aunt's horse again. 'We can't sneak ten horses out of the stables,' I murmur, unease creeping along my spine.

'No, we can't. We'll just have to be brazened about it and ride them. If anyone asks, then we gallop for it.' Sæbald offers his advice, and I find myself meeting his wide grin.

'That's even more shit than my idea to get inside Grantabridge,' I argue, just because it feels good to hear my men's voices.

'Aye, my lord,' his lips turn upwards as he speaks. The flicker of his eyes illuminates a well-worn face, complete with its own scars won in battle. 'And we can all see how fucking well that's going.'

I shake my head, smirking all the same. None of this is going as I planned. My force is split. My aunt is hopefully somewhere ahead of us, perhaps even already through the river gate and over the bridge the bastards have built over the River Granta. And while I've found Beornstan and my aunt, and the horses, I've lost Rudolf and Cuth-walh, so I've really gained very fucking little. Apart from the bloody horses.

'Right, we could do with Wærwulf to speak his magic and ease our passage, but as he's not here, we just fucking go for it. I'll lead on my aunt's mount and take Jaspar as well. You should all have two horses each. Ride one, and lead the other. If someone questions us, just ignore them and head for the gateway over the Granta. If it gets nasty, I want Beornstan and Sæbald to make a run for it to the gate. The riderless horses should follow, and the rest of us will defend your backs.'

As plans go, it's fucking poor. We need to hope that people are either sleeping or too consumed with what's happening with the fire to think much of ten horses being led away in a place where horses are a rarity. I can't see that we'll escape without a bloody fight. If we're seen then, Jarl Guthrum is bound to put my other men under a stricter guard, but I'll have to think about that when it happens. For now, I need to free my aunt's horse and hope that Icel, Hereman and my other warriors can do the same for my aunt.

Emerging into the greyness of the night, dawn seems to be chasing our heels as I urge my aunt's horse onwards towards the west, Jaspar eager to follow her, his reins in my hands. I know it's far too quiet here after the noise and panic closer to the fire. I understand that the sound of hooves passing over the clearly marked street, lined with its wooden drainage system, will arouse suspicion, but I hope not enough that someone will actually fucking stand before us and bar our passage.

At least from the back of my aunt's horse, I can see more. Not enough to see over roofs but enough that should someone emerge with a sharpened blade, flashing in the moonlight, from a door or street, I'll see them before they can attack.

Beornstan still hasn't said anything to me. He rides just behind me. Goda has the task of coming last, but it doesn't really matter where we are. All of us could be easily threatened by someone walking from their home or just running up or down the street in search of more buckets for water. I did notice, with a wry smile, that all the buckets in the stable had gone. Someone was tasked with guarding the animals, but they must have abandoned their post to help contain the fire. They'll be in the shit when they get back, and all the horses are missing.

I'd quite like to see that, but not as much as I'd like to escape from behind Grantabridge's walls. My men, left behind with the horses on the other side of the Granta, must be wondering what's kept us. I certainly didn't consider we'd be gone for so long or that we'd need to find a new means of escape different to the one we used to get inside.

The sound of the horse's hooves echoes in the smoke-hazed air, yet no one comes to question us. There's no hint of iron emerging through the smoky air. Ahead, I finally manage to catch sight of the gateway we've been looking for. And beyond it, I can sense, rather than see, that my kingdom of Mercia is waiting for me if I can just get through the bloody gateway, and over the sodding bridge, without being seen.

The closer we get, the more I tense, my aunt's horse trying to fight me as my instructions for her to walk slowly confuse her. The smell of the smoke is getting ever stronger, and she wants nothing more than to gallop from the place.

This is too easy. I can't see that fucking Jarl Guthrum will have given up his hunt for us so soon, and yet I can't hear the shouts of his men anymore. The Viking raiders must realise there are Mercians here, inside Grantabridge, come to rescue my aunt. Surely? How else would she have managed to escape and kill the seven guards tasked with protecting her?

On seeing the gate ahead, a break in the darkness of the encircling wall, I spot something that makes my heart leap. Icel and Hereman, with my aunt between them, scuttle through the open gateway, Ordlaf and Gardulf, standing with bloodied seaxes, no doubt having killed the men on guard duty there. My aunt's horse nickers in welcome, my aunt pausing to look back at us, and I'm just about to spur the animal on when a mass of heavily armed Viking raiders swarms across my path, emerging from behind two abandoned carts to either side of the main thoroughfare.

The horse bucks and twists, and while I fight her, I'm forced to relax my grip on Jaspar. He ploughs through the mass of Viking raiders at a gallop as though they weren't there. I watch from the corner of my eye as he forces the Viking raiders to jump aside, one of my foemen falling beneath the hooves with a wet crack. It seems that Jaspar has taken the first kill in this fresh encounter. I'd smirk if the situation weren't so fucking dire.

By the time I have my aunt's horse again under control, Jaspar has followed my aunt and most of my warriors through the unguarded gate beating any of Jarl Guthrum's men who think to intervene. No doubt, Edmund and the Mercian ealdormen are there to ensure they're not apprehended again by the Viking raider warriors.

But now my heart stills, my breaths shallow, for none other than that pestilent bastard Jarl Guthrum leers at me from beneath his distinctive warriors' helm, the sharp beak of an owl mirrored in the flame-shimmering nose guard, his exposed arms flashing with their owl inkings. In his hands, he holds both a seax and a dirty and ash-covered Rudolf, who'd twist free from such a tight grip; only the bastard holds a similarly engraved seax settled against Rudolf's exposed pale throat. The blade's edge reflects the flames that leap from roof to roof behind my head, as though the flames are as eager to reach the westward-facing gate as I've been.

Fuck.

So close, and yet it seems I must fight my way to bastard freedom and, in the process, ensure that Rudolf lives against all of the bloody odds stacked against me and my few men and horses.

Chapter One

Easter AD875

'My lord king.' I growl at the fucking whinging tone and then try to smooth my face. It doesn't come easily, and I can see my aunt watching me carefully. Her expression is severe, and for her, the clothing she's donned is elaborate. I fiddle with a loose thread that runs from the embellishments on my tunic. It's so stiff I can hardly move. If I was a man given to flights of fancy, I could almost say the bloody thing is strangling me as I sit, listening and pretending to show some concern.

'Where the fuck's Pybba?' The words roll around my head, and there's almost no space for anything else. Yet the bishop is bleating, and the ealdormen are watching me with careful expressions on their faces, as though they, too, know that I might lose all composure at any moment.

I don't say the words aloud, but I must think them loudly enough that Edmund winces at me. He's on edge, I can tell from the grimace on his face, which remains handsome despite the loss of an eye. His clothes, like mine, are for ceremony and ritual, and I could laugh at how uncomfortable he is if only I didn't feel the same.

I think he fears I'll lash out. I might just do that. I'd sooner face seven shiploads of fucking Viking raiders than my loyal Mercians at the moment. I need something, or rather, someone to kill. Diplomacy dictates that it shouldn't be one of my warriors, one of my ealdormen, or even one of my bishops.

My gaze falters, and suddenly I don't see the men and women of the witan, seated and surrounding me, attentive expressions on their faces, but instead that moment I realised my warrior was missing, just when success had been snatched from our enemy, and the river thundered at our backs. I remember my words. They fall easily into my mind now.

'But first, tell me, where the fuck is Pybba because he's not here?' I'd lifted my hands to either side, indicating to my attentive warriors that everyone else had been accounted for.

I'd look to Rudolf first of all, my warriors. He'd done me the courtesy of looking down at his mud-splattered feet, water pooling down his neck, his shoulders low, entirely deflated even after such a victory against the Viking raiders. He'd not wanted to tell me, and I'd not wanted to bloody hear it. Fucking Pybba.

Damn it.

'My lord king?' I fix a perplexed expression on my face, look to my aunt, who now glowers at me, alongside Edmund, and I'm grateful when Bishop Wærferth comes to my aid with his keen intelligence and sprightly demeanour.

'My lord king,' his words are as smooth as always. I admire him with such poise in the face of my obvious distraction and belligerence. 'Bishop Deorlaf raises some concerns regarding the defence of the settlement of Hereford. We did discuss this matter quite recently, my lord king. Perhaps, something similar to that which now protects Northampton?' Bishop Wærferth assists me a great deal. I should be more grateful for his patience.

I nod. I know we did. But just the mention of the name Hereford has sent my thoughts spiralling towards Pybba. When I find him, I'm going to fucking kill him.

'Defences need to be built. I have men from Northampton who

can discuss matters with the local carpenters. I'll also ensure funds are directed your way. As with Bishop Wærferth and Worcester, I can exempt you from the burden of feeding the kings' horses and their servants for the next four years, and in that time, you can oversee the construction of walls to protect the inhabitants of the local area.' All of a sudden, I remember our previous discussions enough to make such a decision without having to think for too long.

Bishop Deorlaf's face clears of confusion at my obvious disinterest while he spoke, he bows low to show his gratitude. He shouldn't be grateful for such actions. I'm the bloody king of Mercia. This is my role. To protect my people. All of them. Even the whining bishops.

But see how easy it is to please my bishops? Just determine a means whereby they have the available coin to do what they desire. Ah coin. I know what's coming next, tempering my frustration once more. First, Bishop Deorlaf retakes his seat, and I wait for the next demand on my time. I know I agreed to this witan, and I know I said I'd wear Mercia's warrior helm of shimmering gold and silver, but I'd rather be elbow deep amongst the Viking raiders, fighting to the death, than here, in the great hall of Worcester, with all eyes on me. I'm not a man for clever words. And certainly not for honeyed words.

'And the new coinage?' Bishop Wærferth queries, one busy eyebrow high, as he indicates to the scribe beside him that something should be noted for future reference. Bishop Wærferth will assign the deeds discussed here today to vellum with ink. My decisions will be recorded for all time or thrown back into my face when I renege on one of my promises.

'Ah, the coinage,' I think. It's an issue that needs solving.

'Have the new coin dies been prepared?' I ask, again, once more recalling previous conversations, trying to banish the sounds of the thundering river from my memories.

'Not yet, my lord king. It's necessary to first decide on a design. Will it show your head, as your predecessors?' Bishop Wærferth's tone manages to convey respect even while he chastises me for forgetting one of the many details I should be able to recall. And indeed, one of the decisions I should have made a long time ago.

'Why would people need to see my head?' I blurt aloud. 'Is it so they know whose head they need to sever when we meet in battle?'

A sharp intake of breath greets my words, and I puff through my cheeks. Fuck it. I keep forgetting that I'm not standing on the battlefield, seax in hand, ready to slaughter my enemy and potentially give my life for my warriors or for Mercia, but amongst men and women of administrative tasks. They have, potentially, never felt the weight of a seax in their hands or the blood of an enemy filling their mouth. I try not to eye the women who look as though they might faint if I don't stop, and even some of the men, the bishops and abbots, look equally horrified.

Bishop Wærferth surprises me by grinning in response. He wears clothes as rich as mine, but the wider sleeves that cover his lined hands allow him far more freedom of movement than my tightly stitched collars.

'My lord king, your head on the coins is merely the means of ensuring that people know the coinage is legitimate and issued with your standing behind it. I can't see that anyone will come seeking your head. If not for the royal helm, that head on the coins could represent almost anyone. The likeness, alas, will be merely that.'

I flash him a grateful smile for removing the roiling tension from the room. I act as though I've never seen a Mercian coin before, and of course, I have, but I usually consign to my aunt's competent hands such matters as paying my men and suppliers. It's not that I don't possess coins. I just prefer to barter with my seax and sword than with actual coins.

'Then yes, let's determine a design and have the dies distributed?' This is half a question. I'm sure I know the process, but these things are better left to someone more knowledgeable.

'And the weight?'

'Is Mercia in desperate need of money?' Again, I recall my aunt's words to me before the witan convened. She spoke to me at length about the matter. She knew I wasn't paying enough attention, and now, it seems, she's to be proved right, as I embarrass myself with the constant questions.

'Not at this time, no. The Viking raiders have caused some problems, but they've not made huge financial demands on the inhabitants of Mercia. Her warriors, yes, but not her money.' Bishop Wærferth consults one of the many documents his scribe has arranged around him before answering. I notice that the male scribe might be responsible for assisting the bishop with his memory, but it's a woman, a nun, who assiduously makes notes. I watch her quill flowing over the hard surface of the vellum—such skill. I'm impressed. I've never had the patience to learn more than how to write my name on vellum, and even then, it's far from in a firm hand.

'Then we keep the current weight of the coins. It's a means of showing our strength. A weak coinage leans towards a weak king. Perhaps, we should even increase the weight?' I shake my head, dismissing my suggestion. 'No, we leave the weights as standard. And the cost for exchanging the coins?' I'm more than aware that some of my ealdormen and nobles look uneasy at the thought of new coins. I'm not surprised. The process of having the old coins melted down and restruck isn't for free. There are always costs incurred. Even I resent them. But, it has been many years since the last coins were struck, and they can't continue with that traitor, Burgred's head, stamped upon them.

'A minimal fee,' Bishop Deorlaf concurs. 'The moneyers will be told of this, as well. The dies will be for a small fee, and the conversion process will merely cover the cost of labour and resources. As you said, the people of Mercia shouldn't be punished for declaiming a new king on their coins.'

I nod. This pleases me. I know King Burgred was a bugger for extracting huge sums of money from Mercia for such a process. Fuck knows what he spent it all on. It certainly wasn't Mercia's defences.

'And now, my lord king.' Once more, Bishop Deorlaf speaks. 'The matter of Wessex.'

'I'll take advice,' I confirm, refusing to meet the eager expression on Bishop Smithwulf's face. That little worm is too keen to ally with the Wessex king. Perhaps I should send him to Wessex and get him out of the bloody way.

'I have it on good authority that King Alfred of Wessex would welcome an alliance with Mercia; to rekindle the bonds that once stretched over the River Thames,' of course, it's Bishop Smithwulf who speaks, standing and bowing his head for his movements lack any sincerity. I am not a lover of these holy men who've made it their life's work not to pray for the souls of Mercians but rather to advance as high as they can in the church's hierarchy, leaving the business of actually praying to their priests.

Those bonds between Mercia and Wessex were ones of family; King Alfred's sister married King Burgred. King Alfred married a woman of Mercia, Ealhswith. They say she was a member of the royal family, but she's certainly not a member of my family. A fat lot of good this shadowy royal family did Mercia. But, they were evidently enough for the Wessex royal family, which does intrigue me. What did they know that I don't, or did King Burgred trick them into accepting a woman as wife who was less royal than many thought?

'And how precisely does King Alfred think this might happen?' I press.

'A marriage union between you and a prominent Wessex bride. And a Mercian bride for a prominent Wessex nobleman?' So not as good a settlement as King Burgred received. I imagine I shouldn't have suspected it would be. 'Alas, the king has only a small daughter at this time.' The implication is clear. She's young, and I won't live long enough to marry her. Bloody charming. It's hardly a good basis for reaching an accord. If I were to marry, and a child be born, only for me to die in battle, then that child would become merely a victim in the wars with the Viking raiders and Wessex. It's not a life I've enjoyed. I won't place it on the head of my unborn children.

'I don't believe a marriage union is in Mercia's best interests at this time.' My aunt speaks, standing and inclining her head towards me rather than bending low into a curtsey. Like other women in the room, she can speak her mind before the witan. I wouldn't follow the way the Wessex kings conduct their business. Lady Ealhswith isn't even proclaimed as Wessex's queen. She's merely the king's wife. 'The king has no children with which to reciprocate.' We've argued about this. She wants me to marry. I don't see how I can have the time to be a husband. I barely have time to sit here and listen to these bloody tedious arguments about a union.

'I agree. No marriage union. It'll need to be something else.' I confirm quickly, keen to dismiss the notion that I need a woman in my bed to complain at me for my long absences and ruined clothes.

'Mutual support?' Bishop Smithwulf presses, his words too insistent. What has the bastard promised the Wessex king?

'Like before?' Ealdorman Ælhun scoffs at the suggestion, standing and bowing his head as well as he speaks. He's correct. Wessex was about as much use as a mud bank in a flood when the Viking raiders attacked during King Burgred's reign. I meet the ealdorman's eyes. His gaze is clear, and he speaks well, and I notice that he has the ability to swing his arms from side to side in his tunic. I wish my aunt had offered me the same amount of freedom in her choice of clothing for me. I even admire how the pale blue of the tunic sets off the shimmering frost of his beard. I can't see that my clothing, so richly embellished with gold and silver thread, will be quite so forgiving on my frame.

The ealdorman's words are greeted with a murmur of approval, and I note Kyred nodding along. I'm keen to promote him at the royal court, but as of yet, he remains Bishop Wærferth's, oath-sworn man. I'm sure the bishop will allow Kyred to become one of my thegns, but again, I just need the time to make the advancement.

The Wessex-favouring Bishop Smithwulf's expression is enough to have me laughing out loud. I hold my amusement in check. Ridiculing Bishop Smithwulf in such a public gathering isn't the way to win support from the man with his feet so firmly ensconced behind

London's ancient crumbling walls, with the threat of Wessex only a river away. And the even greater threat of the bastard Viking raiders from the River Thames on that sodding river.

I look around the room, but this time note the view that greets me. The bishop's hall is a long building, essentially little different to the longhouses in which most of my people live, only here, there are colourful tapestries along the walls, and where these don't cover the wooden walls, bright colours festoon the place. It's a cheerful place; I can't deny it, even if some of the tapestries are a little too religious for my liking. And, of course, behind my head is a Mercian shield depicting the twin-headed eagle that's my family's emblem. I move my fingers as though I might drum them on the table before me, then stop myself. I can't show any emotion while the discussion of Alfred of Wessex takes place. Perhaps, I think, I should just be grateful that Alfred's father by marriage, Ealdorman Æthelred Mucel, and his wife, Eadburh, are no longer alive to bleat at me about the alliance, in the same vein as Bishop Smithwulf.

'No, it needs to be something different,' I confirm. Silence falls in the bishop's hall in Worcester. That surprises me. I thought everyone would have ideas on how everything could be solved. But it seems not. Now I risk glancing at Bishop Smithwulf, and there's disappointment on his face. He thinks I should marry some worthless member of Wessex's royal family. I just can't see it being of any benefit to Mercia. The twisted histories of our two kingdoms are entirely that, twisted, and truly, bringing little of benefit to either of us.

King Alfred is the last of four brothers to survive. He has two young nephews, one of whom should be king in his place. Still, Alfred clings to his kingship, and as far as I know, or even care, there are no notable women to speak of, not even the woman who wed not only Alfred's father but his brother as well, after their father's death, before returning to Flanders and finally, wedding, it's said, for love, after the brother died as well. Poor woman. To be widowed twice. Although, well, perhaps it is a relief for her to be free from the Wessex ruling family.

The ruling Wessex family have no one, such as my aunt, who holds any position of power. The Wessex men are a funny breed. Their reticence to allow women to rule as they should never fails to surprise me, although rumour has it, it's the fault of a good Mercian woman in the past that has made the Wessex men squirm and refuse the honour. That, at least, I can bloody believe. It's good to know that Mercians have been bedevilling them for many long years.

'Perhaps some more thought,' I suggest, keen to move on to the next topic. I want to be gone from here. I have a missing warrior to find, and while the Viking raiders hold their peace a little longer, I want to take advantage of that to hunt him down, and fucking kill him.

'My lord king,' Bishop Wærferth bows his head in agreement. I take in a deep breath. I'm sure this torture must be nearly over—my neck aches from the weight of Mercia's warrior helm. I've not worn it since my coronation when I was dabbed with touches of oil and somehow made more holy than my fellow men and women. I shudder at the memory of that tedious ceremony. The events which immediately followed it hold warmer memories for me.

We have a feast prepared for us, and I'll be glad when I can fill my aching belly. Here, in Worcester, at the witan summoned for the Easter celebration, I've been forced to temper my appetite and eat the things prescribed by the bishop and the holy men and women in the run-up to the holiest celebration that is Easter. I'm bloody starving. Fighting men have no time for making themselves weak through a lack of nourishing food by fasting. It might be all well and good for the monks and nuns who need to do little more than spend the day on their knees praying. But, it's not the sort of life I need. Far from it. I need more than fish to fill my belly.

Just as I believe I might escape from here with no more than four wasted days, I hear a commotion from outside. Edmund quickly leaves my aunt's side, who has retaken her seat at last and hastens to find out what's happening. Not that he's the first to know. No, Rudolf has already slipped from the hall, sliding his way through the barely open gates that keep the settlement secure. I listen to incomprehensible conversation impatiently. I consider marching outside myself when time stretches too long, but my aunt shakes her head at me, lips tight, and even Icel seems to imply with his wide stance, almost blocking the doorway, that I should bide my time. Even Icel, I notice, has been given a new tunic to wear. My aunt's women must have been sewing non-stop since I announced my intention to hold a crown-wearing ceremony at the Easter witan.

Bollocks to this, I think, moving to stand, only for the doors to open wide and for Rudolf to hurry inside, Edmund practically stepping on his heels in his haste to reach my side. I consider who'll speak first, but neither of them does. Instead, another strides into the hall.

I grimace. Bad enough that Ealdorman Aldred was late to my witan, even worse now he comes dressed for war. I flick a look to Rudolf, and his young face carries a grimace. It's not a good sign.

'My lord king,' the younger man sweeps dramatically to his knee, but I bid him rise immediately. What news does he have? It can't be good.

'My lord king,' he swallows as though reconsidering the wisdom of his actions, his neck white above the rim of his collar and the fur of his cloak. With a sour thought, I notice that he still festoons himself with trinkets and baubles. He should really learn the worth of people as opposed to jewels and gems. 'News from Northumbria. Jarl Halfdan lives and has gifted land within Northumbria to his comrades.' I've heard rumours of this. I'm not sure if it's good or bad for Mercia. I mean, it's not good for bloody Northumbria, but I'm Mercia's king, not Northumbria's. What happens to the far side of the mighty Humber estuary is not really of prime concern to me.

'He travels north to battle the Pictish kingdom.' Again, this can only be good for me. If Jarl Halfdan has decided that his best chance of staying alive is to fight the blood-thirsty Pictish warriors, then he's welcome to it. I know them to be wrathful and fierce. Hopefully, they'll finish the job of killing Jarl Halfdan that I've started more than once. Why won't the plague-ridden bastard just fucking die?

'The king of Northumbria bids you assist him in reclaiming his kingdom.' I groan then. I've no intention of doing so. Northumbrian kings have fallen beneath the blade of the Viking raiders with increasing regularity. If Jarl Halfdan claims Northumbria, then I don't know how I can aid King Ricsige in his endeavours to hold the kingdom. But it seems the damn fool won't take no for an answer.

Behind Ealdorman Aldred trails a man I'd hoped not to see again. Archbishop Wulfhere of York. What does the bloody pestilent man want now?

Chapter Two

'**M**y lord king,' Archbishop Wulfhere is travel-stained, although he's taken some time to clean the muck from his face and hands, even in his haste to present himself before the witan. He's older than I am and, I think, has allowed himself to become a little too fat and rounded from good wine and food. I pity the horse he's ridden here.

I know he's allied with the Viking raiders before now when they claimed York, or Jorvik as they call it. It seems he might regret that. I can't see that his bloody guilt should become my problem, though.

I call a servant close, and they rush away to find wine for the missing ealdorman and the man he's brought with him. It would have been nice to know of this upset. I would berate the ealdorman for it, but the words would fall on deaf ears. Ealdorman Aldred thinks he knows better than I do, even though I've shown him that he doesn't, as have the Viking raiders.

I seek out Bishop Burgheard of Lindsey amongst the holy men and see he's glowering at the archbishop from his place on the front row of chairs. That brings me some consolation. I imagine that Bishop Burgheard had some prior knowledge of the archbishop's arrival, or perhaps he thought he'd put him off. Either way, I don't blame Bishop Burgheard. He's far from as gullible as Ealdorman Aldred. As far as I'm concerned, the ealdorman has yet to realise that he's both lucky to be alive and still hold his position after what happened at Gainsborough.

'Archbishop. You're most welcome in Worcester and at Mercia's witan.' I keep my tone even. Better to not show my true thoughts until I've heard him out.

'Thank you, my lord king. You're indeed gracious to once more extend Mercia's hospitality to me.' I bite down on my initial reply. He makes it sound like he's staying forever, and he's bloody not. My predecessor may have allowed Archbishop Wulfhere and Northumbria's king to shelter in Mercia. I don't know if I'm minded to do the same. If they'd just bloody killed Jarl Halfdan in the first place, then Repton and Mercia wouldn't have been overrun, and I wouldn't have the Grantabridge jarls waiting to strike once more on my eastern borders.

A seat is brought for the archbishop as he stands from bowing before me. He perches to the side of the seated row of bishops, jutting into the aisle space. Bishop Wæferth inclines his head to the archbishop in greeting, although they don't speak, and then the line of men mirror the movement, Bishop Deorlaf of Worcester, Bishop Smithwulf of London, Bishop Burgheard, Bishop Eadberht of Lichfield and finally, Bishop Ceobred of Leicester. They look to me like brightly headed summer flowers bobbing in the breeze.

There's a shuffle of vellum on vellum, and some quiet conversation exchanged between Bishop Wærferth and his scribes as they're forced to move around to find room to write, as the archbishop expansively encroaches into the area set aside for them. I watch as a small wooden writing desk is moved to one side with a wince of pain for legs too long held in one position. The bishop holds a bottle of ink carefully while the woman shuffles into a more comfortable position, only to hand it back to her. I know I'm not the only one to watch this comedy taking place before me with disbelief. This is the fucking witan!

I finally sigh, the shuffle of noise and murmur of conversation brought to an end only for the archbishop to stand again. Bloody fool. He doesn't even wait to be addressed. I hear a soft exclamation of complaint, I think, from my aunt. Or if not her, then from Edmund.

'I come from York with news of our usurper king.' The archbishop's tone is filled with loathing. I scrutinise the man. Beneath the road's grime, I can tell he has expensive tastes. Even his boots are trimmed with fur at the ankles, and around his neck lies a huge silver cross, flickering in the light that streams through the high-up open window.

'Ealdorman Aldred informs us that Jarl Halfdan has travelled north to attack the Pictish kingdom.'

'He has, my lord king, yes, so now is the perfect time to reclaim York from the usurper and replace him with Northumbria's rightful, anointed king.' The archbishop's tone is filled with conviction.

'And whose army is going to do that?' I demand. Northumbria has been as riven with battle and bloodshed as Mercia has been. I wouldn't be sure that Northumbria could rouse enough to take on the might of the Viking raiders, especially when they have settled the land and now have families in whose name they fight.

'Why yours, my lord king,' Archbishop Wulfhere announces, as though it's evident to everyone in the room, and my heart stills. Fuck that, I think. I'm not about to risk my Mercians in Northumbria. If I don't want to ally with King Alfred of Wessex, who at least nearly has an entire kingdom at his back and the attendant warriors as well, then why would I want to bloody ally with Archbishop Wulfhere and Northumbria's virtually kingdom-less king?

I can feel my aunt's warning eyes on me. Fuck, I can feel every single person's gaze on me in that room. I'm aghast at Ealdorman Aldred for placing me in such a position. I'm astounded that Archbishop Wulfhere will travel here without any prior warning and demand such from me. But more importantly, how can I respond, here and now, to such a request? I've just told everyone I wouldn't make an alliance with Wessex because such an act has nothing to offer Mercia. To turn that on its head and align with Northumbria when there's nothing but the promise of bloodshed is, frankly, bloody mad. But the archbishop watches me intently while Ealdorman Aldred waits expectantly, and I begin to realise that my fucking reputation is a bastard curse.

'Archbishop Wulfhere,' I begin. My words are heated, and I hear someone cough loudly—no doubt Edmund, at my aunt's insistence. Or perhaps Icel's. I wish Pybba were here. He'd keep me right.

I try again. 'Archbishop Wulfhere, you present an interesting idea, which isn't without appeal, but now isn't the time to discuss such. We were about to conclude the witan and partake of our Easter feast. You'll join us?'

I hear someone's audible exhalation at my reasoned words while I note the flash of confusion on the archbishop's face. At least he's not angry, I think to myself.

'But, my lord king, now is the perfect time to,' he persists. I override him.

'Alas. You've missed the Easter Mass, and no doubt, you need to pray. I'm sure that Bishop Wærferth will be able to assist you with monks to offer your prayers on this most holy of days.' I look to Bishop Wærferth, who inclines his head respectfully, gesturing for one of his clerics to attend to the archbishop, the faintest smirk on his lips. The cleric hastens to the bishop's side, bows low to listen to the whispered instructions, his head angled away from the archbishop so that he looks to the wall, not the flustered archbishop and dashes from the hall, his footsteps loud in the stillness of the room, despite everyone's shuffling. We've all been sat still for far too long.

'You're most kind, my lord king,' Archbishop Wulfhere begins, and I rise, cutting him off before he can attempt to remonstrate with me. Everyone in the hall hastens to their feet in imitation of me and bows low. Archbishop Wulfhere is left with no option but to do the same.

'Well done,' my aunt murmurs as I wait to escort her from the bishop's hall. Outside, the day is cold but bright. In the fields, lambs are beginning to appear, and the promise of a new fighting season stirs my steps. Although, first, I must find bloody Pybba.

'He'll pressure you, though.' She confides in me as we walk together, her arm looped through mine. My aunt undoubtedly has more experience with the archbishop than I do. This isn't the first time Archbishop Wulfhere has run to Mercia for assistance. It's a shame it won't be his bloody last.

'What would he have me do?' I demand from her, stepping into the courtyard. I can see where horses have left their tribute and where stable hands are trying to clear it away before everyone erupts from the bishop's hall. I slow my steps. No one will risk overtaking me just yet. I wave them on, and the lads hasten to scrape away the stinking shit. Another carries a bucket of water, no doubt to sluice away the stream of piss as well.

'Resurrect the dead? I don't have the men. I have the Grantabridge jarls and the problems on the borders with the Welsh kingdoms.'

'I doubt he expects you to resurrect the dead,' my aunt confirms, her lips barely moving. 'You're right to be wary. You can only do so much.' Now I stop, turn to peer at her, and she quirks an eyebrow at me. She must know how much I'd like to scupper Jarl Halfdan, how I yearn for his death. I'm trying to be sensible, and it seems she means to goad me.

'What would you have me do?'

'Listen to him, little more. He, like King Burgred, has lived with the Viking raiders, as opposed to you, who merely kills them whenever you find them. It might be that there's a middle ground between giving them everything they want and draining their lifeblood from their bodies.' I detect a flicker of amusement in her words as she sums up my attitude to the bastards quite so succinctly.

'You'd sooner Northumbria than Wessex?' This shouldn't surprise me.

She grimaces. I know how much my aunt despises King Alfred and his three long-dead brothers, Æthelbald, Æthelberht and Æthelred. All kings in their own right before they died and left Alfred as the last surviving branch of that family. It's almost a pity he's proved to be so much longer lived than the others.

'I'd sooner no alliance was necessary. But King Alfred seeks you out, and now Archbishop Wulfhere does the same. It seems to me, nephew dear, that you must be the saviour of the Saxon kingdoms, although how you're to do that, other than with bloody intent, is beyond me.' Gently, she disentangles her arm from mine and moves to walk away. I can see where Edmund is waiting for her, respectfully, some distance away, his eyes on the stablehands as they rush away, their duty complete. Does Edmund have more news to share with her? Or will she merely relay our conversation to him?

I pause, considering her words, only to stride onwards in the wake of the scampering stablehands, to where I can hear the horses in the stable, one above all others. I'm dressed as Mercia's king, but Haden doesn't give a shit about that. And neither do I.

Chapter Three

'What is it, you bloody irksome beast?'

Rudolf has caught up with me, Hiltiberht as well. Both of them run to match my steps, although Rudolf is less out of puff than Hiltiberht. The boy has grown. Again. He needs new shoes, trews and tunics more often than I eat. My stomach growls angrily. The smell of the feast is enough to drive a hungry man away from his techy horse, but well, Haden is Haden. He must need something to be making such a bloody racket.

Over the top of the stable door, I spy a too familiar white and black nose. Haden watches me with scathing eyes, giving the door a final kick just to make his point.

'What is it?' I ask once more, moving to run my hand along his long nose. It smells of hay and oats. The lads do a good job of keeping the animals clean and watered.

'My lord king?' Hiltiberht squeaks at my side. I turn to meet his eyes sharply, a scathing retort on my lips for reminding me that I'm the sodding king.

'Your helm, my lord,' he gasps quickly. Damn, I'd forgotten I still wore the bloody thing. I bend my head, slip it forwards and then backwards, and then repeat the movement. It's a tight fit. Without ceremony, I dump it in Hiltiberht's waiting hands, and he fumbles to hold the weight of the gold and silver. It's a relief to be free of the bloody thing.

'If I have to put it on my head, you can hold it with your two hands,' I inform him, but not without sympathy. It is a heavy piece of equipment. No doubt, Bishop Wærferth's cleric is looking for the helm to lock it away inside its wooden box, which sits inside a hidden compartment inside the bishop's hall. The poor man should have been quicker to find me if he didn't want it to carry the aroma of a horse.

'What is it, you foul brute?' Unheeding my fine clothes, I open the stable door and sidle close to Haden. He's not settled on my appearance, and that worries me. He's mostly recovered from his injuries, but sometimes, he's uncomfortable, and today is one of those days as he moves around me as though he doesn't want me here, even though he summoned me. Think of that. Mercia's king beholden to his bloody horse.

I press my hands into his side while Rudolf consoles him, and I sigh to hear how he speaks to Mercia's finest mount but hold my tongue. Haden is calmer now, and I can take my time without fear of having my foot stamped on or being crushed against the side of the stable.

His skin feels hot, and I speak to Rudolf over Haden's body.

'A mild infection?' I suggest, although his healed wound seems well enough, even his coat has grown back to cover the marks of it. I'm not really sure of these things. I move to check Haden's hooves and legs, running my hands down the rear two first and picking up the hooves with only some minor disagreements. Then I circle Haden and come once more to the front, but the left and right legs seem fine, and there's no swelling or tenderness on his hoofs.

'I'll take a look,' Rudolf assures me. I realise then that Icel has joined our small collection. He's spoken to his mount, Samson, and now comes to assess Haden.

'His eyes are a little red-rimmed,' Icel offers. I peer at Haden. I'd not noticed, but yes, they're not as clear as usual.

Rudolf's words are muffled.

'It's an old stitch,' he confirms. 'It's not dissolved, and now it's pink and sore. I can cure him,' he promises me, already half out of the stable. But I shake my head. I don't think that's what troubles my horse. It might make him uncomfortable, but not enough to have him kicking the stable door and bellowing for my attention. Even Haden, as bull-headed as he can be, must realise that Worcester is filled with men, women and children, and their horses as well. It's easier to find room to stable a mount than find somewhere to lay down your head.

I look around the stable, peering at the wooden struts and posts of the building, perplexed. There's something else here. I'm sure of it. I turn to Icel and nod him towards the right while I go left. He moves smoothly, quickly and quietly, despite his size. I can do the same without my helm and weapons at my waist.

I eye Samson and Cinder, both watching what's happening, although more focused on the hay they're eating, pulling long strands with their even longer tongues. I move on to Dever and Poppy. Dever glances at me with some unease, and I open his stable door and peer down into the hay. I hold my breath, not that it's much help, and then I bend down and look beneath Dever's legs and reach out.

'Who are you?' I demand from the startling green eyes that meet mine from inside a dirty face.

'My, my lord,' a small voice squeals and I shake my head.

'My lord king,' Icel rumbles menacingly, appearing behind my shoulder, his feet making a thud, thud noise as he settles, his stance wide, ready to fight.

'My lord king,' the voice repeats, wide eyes glancing between Icel and me. I see the boy take a deep breath and swallow his fear before speaking.

'My lord king. My name's Æthelred, and I've come to seek your protection.'

I feel my forehead furrow at this. Now, it seems, even small boys seek me out. I really need to do something about my bastard reputation.

'Well, Dever doesn't appreciate you hiding over there. Come out and tell me all about yourself.'

The boy peers from me to the hulking menace of Icel and swallows again. I'm not surprised. When he stands and slowly walks toward us, I'm impressed by his confidence. If I were no more than nine or ten and faced with a giant such as Icel, or even myself, I'd probably stay hiding behind the horse.

When Æthelred stands before me, Dever whiffles into his blond hair, parting it. It seems Dever wasn't that concerned by his young friend. It was just Haden that felt the whole world needed to know there was someone else in the stables who shouldn't be there. I'm surprised. I would have expected Haden to be used to small children patting his nose. Oh, how I make myself fucking laugh.

'Come out here,' I instruct him. Rudolf stands to my side, watching Æthelred. I'd ask him if he knew who the boy was, but it's evident he doesn't

I close Dever's stable door and peer down at the youngster.

'How did you get in here?'

'Through the door,' and he points to the doorway. More of my warriors have gathered there now. Lyfing is to the front, his hand hovering over his weapons belt. At least one of the fuckers came bloody prepared.

'And so, you live in Worcester?' I ask. I should really be making my way to the feast, but for a moment, my curiosity outweighs my hunger.

'No, my lord king. Not from Worcester.'

'Then how did you get here?' This is more painful than getting Icel to speak about his past.

'My mother told me to seek out the king if I was ever left alone, and now that she's dead, I'm alone, and so I've come to seek my king.'

'Ah, lad. I'm sorry to hear about your mother.' I never knew mine.

Instantly, I feel both jealous and sad for him. Perhaps it was better for me that my mother's name is merely that, to me, a name.

A huge tear falls from both eyes and drips down thin cheeks to land in the hay at his feet.

'Come on, let's get you something to eat,' I announce. I have many questions, but for now, I want Æthelred to feel safe. If that means we have to feed him up for a month, then that's what we'll have to do. Certainly, beneath his thin cloak, I can see all of his bones. There's no flesh to him. It's been a hard winter. I hope he's not been forced to fend for himself all winter long.

'Hiltiberht,' I summon my squire, who appears quickly, my helm missing from his hands. The cleric must have found him. Or, I imagine, Hiltiberht has taken it to him. The lad is too kind-hearted. Hiltiberht's eyes flash from me to Æthelred, and he earns my regard by speaking first.

'My lord king. I'll tend to him while you attend your feast. I'll find him somewhere to sleep and a warmer cloak.' Hiltiberht smiles at the youngster, and I nod, pleased with the resolution. My stomach growls again, and I move away, only for a small voice to call me again.

'My lord king. Will you? Will you care for me? I have no family. She told me to seek the king. She said that you'd care for me. Will you?'

'Aye, lad. We'll look after you,' I assure him, seeing in his eyes a proud and brave boy, but one who's scared and alone. I imagine all of my warriors can see themselves in his thin frame and terror. Not every warrior comes from a good family who fed them enough to reach their full potential. No, many of my warriors were once just as ragged and abandoned as Æthelred. It seems, no matter my best intentions, there are always those with nothing and those who are bereaved. It saddens me.

And then I stride away. There'll be time for such thoughts later. For now, I have bishops and a bloody pesky archbishop to feast and listen to. It's not exactly a fucking delight for me.

Chapter Four

'What will you do?' Bishop Wærferth sits beside me on the raised dais, looking out towards the rest of the members of the witan, along with their wives and, often, children as well. Apart from the monks and nuns. They have nieces and nephews, mostly not children. If they do have children, it behoves them to pretend they're nieces or nephews rather than risk the displeasure of their religious house, abbot or bishop.

I know to what the bishop's referring, and yet I raise an eyebrow at him as though unsure what he means. The meal before me is huge and well-cooked and seasoned. The baked fish has been a particular delight, the garlic infused in the crust of the bread will be enough to keep most of my petitioners away if they think to get too close. But, it seems, not the bishop who helped me become Mercia's king. Sometimes, I'm not sure that I'm entirely grateful to him. I probably should be. But well? Am I?

'With the archbishop,' Wærferth elucidates without even a soft sigh of frustration. He really is a very calm individual. I admire him for that.

'What can I do? Our fight with Jarl Halfdan doesn't extend to wanting to traipse north and throw him out of York. If he'd just sod off and stay on the other side of the River Humber, I'd be happy enough.'

Bishop Wærferth nods. He's eaten his fill and now sits, wine goblet in hand, watching those around us and trying not to gaze at the archbishop, who's been seated close to my aunt. I imagine Wulfhere's far from pleased about that. But, to be honest, the archbishop will get more sympathy from her than he will from me, despite the fact my aunt knows him of old. I didn't have time to ask her about him. I will soon enough.

Not for the first time, I feel frustrated about my refusal to attend upon King Burgred in his royal palaces and for being largely absent from all politics while my brother was the ealdorman of the Hwicce. There are things I should know but don't. Well, things that some think I should know. Maybe it's better for some people to come to me without preconceptions.

'Jarl Halfdan is a particular problem.'

'Yes, he is.'

'If not for Halfdan, we wouldn't have the Grantabridge jarls on our borders.'

'No, we bloody wouldn't,' I growl. I might have beaten them back from Northampton, but they've hardly gone home. I'd like to set Grantabridge ablaze so that they've no choice but to leave this island. I try just to say 'bloody' in the bishop's presence. I'd sooner say something else, but my aunt's complaints have finally started to work on me. Not everyone is a warrior.

'What if he's victorious over the people of the Pictish kingdom?' Bishop Wærferth muses as though the thought has only just occurred to him.

I smirk. 'Really, you think to try that one on me?' Wærferth meets my gaze evenly, grins, and looks much younger then. I almost wish I'd known Wærferth before he became a man of God. We might have got into some interesting scrapes.

'I was just testing you to see how far you were prepared to extend the vendetta.'

'Had Icel not returned to me, I'd have been very bloody keen. The jarl should be pleased that Icel didn't die from his wounds. Then I might be more eager, shall we say.'

'What if the archbishop approaches King Alfred?'

I shake my head. I'm actually enjoying sparing with the bishop. He speaks as plainly to me as Edmund, Icel or Pybba. There, I've annoyed myself once more—bloody Pybba. I need to find him. I won't countenance the fear that he might be dead. The canny bastard will be alive, somewhere. He better be.

'Do you think King Alfred will send his warriors to the north? I just can't see it. Wessex have hardly clothed themselves in glory with their attempts to aid Mercia. In fact, if the archbishop can get King Alfred to look that far north, then he's welcome to it.'

'So, you'd be content with the Wessex king surrounding Mercia?'

'I'd be content if I thought the Wessex king capable of it.' I reply quickly. 'He doesn't have the men. Mercia doesn't have the men. Wessex doesn't have the men. It's not as though we can call on a hoard of warriors from over the sea, unlike the Viking raiders.'

'But if every kingdom worked together?'

'Then what? The Viking raiders would just attack somewhere else.' I hold Bishop Wærferth's eyes now. I want him to understand my reasoning.

'The Viking raiders aren't a cohesive force, unlike the Mercian or even the Wessex warriors. No one man commands them. No one man determines where they'll attack and where they won't. You have only to look at the men from Repton. Jarl Halfdan is in the north. The other jarls are in the east. And we also have men on the west, while others turn their eyes to Wessex. How are we to know where they'll go next? If they fail at one endeavour, they merely go somewhere else. And our island isn't alone in this. I know, and so do you, that quick; raiding parties are a problem everywhere. Look at Frankia. Look at Dublin. I believe Jarl Halfdan will go there next. He can't proclaim himself a king of Northumbria, for he doesn't hold all of Northumbria, Bamburgh and its fastness holds against him, but he can be king of Dublin if he wishes to be named a king in his lifetime.'

The jovial mood of the feast has drained from Bishop Wærferth's face. He doesn't look scared, but he does look worried.

'So, there's no hope?'

'There's always hope,' I counter. 'But we need to be careful, and we need to be clever. We can't go running to help others when Mercia is already so threatened. Other than today, and perhaps the last month, I've rarely stayed in one place since I became king. I've killed my enemy in Repton, Torksey, Gainsborough, Northampton and on the border with the Welsh. The Viking raiders almost made it to Kingsholm.' I sigh heavily. Even I'm depressing the fuck out of myself now.

'So, King Alfred and Archbishop Wulfhere?' Bishop Wærferth presses softly, his gaze unwavering.

'We need to make all the right noises but without any of the commitment,' I confirm, nodding quickly. I've not asked any of my ealdormen for their opinion, or even my aunt, Edmund, Icel or Rudolf. And I can't ask bloody Pybba, but all the same, I know it's the correct answer.

'No one can see Mercia in its entirety other than me. And you must try and do the same, bishop. If we fall into defending only certain areas, then Mercia will fail. And the Viking raiders need only feel settled in one place, and they'll attempt to impose their control over the whole kingdom. To keep Mercia whole, Mercia must fight as a whole. We have no resources to help other kings and their efforts. If we spread ourselves too thinly, we'll fail.'

'And so, to walls?' Bishop Wærferth asks.

'Yes, walls and ditches. The Mercians need to do what they can to protect themselves until my warriors, or their ealdorman's warriors, can relieve them. We need strong walls and men and women who can stab and slice with any weapon they have to hand. We can't continue with King Burgred's ploy of trying to ignore the problem. It isn't going away, not any time soon, and no matter how much you and your monks and nuns might pray, it will.'

'I'll handle the archbishop,' Wærferth confirms, confidently, resolve on his face, as he places his wine goblet, without having taken a single sip, back on the table. 'I know how to speak to a man such as him. I'll do the same with Bishop Smithwulf of London. If I have your permission, I'll convene a gathering of the holy men and women, just like the witan. I'll allow discussion and ensure that they understand the limitations and their own parts in what you plan.'

I sigh deeply at his words, gazing out at those enjoying themselves at this Easter feast. I would sooner wipe every single bastard Viking raider from the face of the Earth, but I can't do that. I can defeat three hundred men, but three thousand, or thirty thousand, or however many of the fuckers there are, isn't the work of one man. I can lead by example, though, and I mean to do a bloody good job of that.

Chapter Five

The following day

'Aunt.'

'Nephew.' She replies as curtly as I address her. A smile plays around my lips, but one she doesn't return.

'Where are you going?' she demands instead, her eyes flashing at the activity taking place around us. She wears a thick cloak, the hood pulled up over her hair, and she wears good boots on her feet.

'To find Pybba.' Haden is saddled and ready in the crowded forecourt. So are the majority of the rest of my warriors. Icel has Samson ready to go. Rudolf and Dever are also eager to depart, so eager that Rudolf is already mounted. Wærwulf talks hurriedly to one of the stable hands, and I consider that Cinder may be injured, but then Wærwulf nods and continues with his preparations. Perhaps not, then.

The other horses shimmer with good health. There are almost too many to name, and yet I try all the same. Kermit, Simba, Keira, Storm, only then I consider Edmund.

Edmund and Jethson are taking their time, and I narrow my eyes at my warrior. Surely he must have told my aunt of our intentions. Why then does she question me?

'What of larger matters?' She doesn't name the archbishop or King Alfred, but I know it's the pair of them that consume her thoughts.

'Those matters will wait. Pybba has waited long enough.'

'Pybba is one man.'

'He's my bloody warrior,' I cut her off before she says something that will forever taint our relationship. She needs to understand that Pybba might only be one man, but he is much more than that to me. 'He's my friend. You and the bishop expect me to rule with an iron fist and ensure Mercia is safe from her enemies. To do so, I need friends and warriors at my back that I trust with my life.'

She opens and then snaps shut her mouth, her face settling in an uneasy frown. I'm grateful she doesn't mention that Pybba has only one hand or that he might be dead, for all we know. I know all that. I don't need to be reminded of it.

'I'll leave my warriors with you for you to command and ensure your safety. They'll work with Turhtredus, and you can all return to Kingsholm and remain there.' Those men that I've determined should stay with my aunt have accepted their assignment with some unease. It's an honour to be tasked with protecting my aunt, and yet, some of them would rather be hunting Pybba. But I can't allow that. Kingsholm would benefit from my men being there for a while. And so Hiltiberht, Ordheah, Ælgar, Osmod, Cuthwalh, Gardulf, Eadfrith, Beornstan, Eadulf, Oda, Wulfred, Eahric, Ordlaf, Wulfstan, Cealwin, Siric, Osbert and Eadberht, alongside their horses, will remain with my aunt.

'And what would you have me do with your latest waif and stray?' She counters, not even thanking me for such attention to her safety. I probably shouldn't expect it.

I look to where young Æthelred is watching everything, mouth open in shock at witnessing my war band preparing to ride out. Luckily, he's found himself a place out of the way, settled high on a cart waiting to be unloaded once my men and horses have moved out of Worcester.

'What you always do?' I offer with a shrug. I don't want to admit that I'd forgotten all about him. 'Take him to Kingsholm. Ensure he has some learning, and assign him a trade or have him trained with a blade.'

'But who is he?' my aunt persists.

'I've no bloody idea. His mother told him to seek out Mercia's king. I know little more than that. It's not as though he's a burden. He's good with the horses.'

'Hum,' she stands, hands on her hips, eyeing Æthelred. I've had him fed while Hiltiberht has found him a warmer cloak, for all the day is bright and filled with the promise of the coming better weather. I'm just pleased it's not sodding raining. I've spent far too much of the winter in my saddle, drenched and fighting, shivering and praying for the warmer weather.

'I'll do as you ask. But I'd sooner know more about him. I don't even know where he came from?'

'Neither do I,' I confirm. 'Find out what you can. It would be good to know who his mother was. I'm going to assume that he's the son of one of Kingsholm's warriors. But who, I have no idea?' Once more, her lips purse. I can see I've caught her interest now.

'Fine. I'll do what I can for him. And now, you must return as soon as possible and not place yourself in too much danger. Mercia has no heir, remember that.' I wince at the reminder of my refusal to arrange a marriage alliance with Wessex. Her tone surprises me. I wouldn't have thought she'd welcome a Wessex bitch to Kingsholm. Perhaps she'd welcome any child born from the union. But no. I've no interest in marrying and having a child to follow me. What will happen to Mercia after my death isn't my current worry. A man can only do so much with his one life.

There are too many enemies to even think of taking my pleasure.

'I will, and thank you,' I confirm, turning Haden's head towards the gateway that gives access over the River Severn and then mounting up. We're journeying to Hereford. Not with Bishop Deor-laf. He'll be too slow with his entourage. I plan on travelling far more quickly and ensuring I arrive before he can attempt to convince me to help in the building of the earthworks he wishes to construct around his church and the larger settlement. But mostly around his bloody church.

I turn to eye Edmund. He's waiting impatiently some distance behind me. Jethson tugging at his bit and generally being a pain in the arse, although at least he's not worrying Haden. For once, Haden is surprisingly pliant beneath me. When I pulled him from his stable, he came eagerly, happy to be leaving his confinement. I agree with him. Better to ride to battle than to face the cloying men and women of the witan with their tedious demands. I consider just what Edmund did say to my aunt, for certainly, she's not glaring at him as she does at me.

Rudolf is beside me, Dever as eager as I've ever seen him to leave the comfort of the stables. When I gifted Dever to Rudolf, I didn't believe I was doing him any great favour, but the pair of them are good together.

Rudolf's face is lined with worry, his usual good cheer missing. When Pybba convinced my warriors to leave him behind, to the west of the River Wye, he promised to be back within one month. That was two months ago. His failure to return has caused Rudolf to question his decision to agree to Pybba's plan. He blames himself, even though there were more than him who had to agree.

Bloody Pybba. Always thinking he knows better than everyone else, and now look, the bloody king of Mercia is forced to ride out, fully armed, to rescue him, or retrieve him, or find his cold body, although it better fucking not be that. I'll be bloody fuming if Pybba's dead. I won't so much give money for prayers to be offered for his soul, but rather for them to be sent his way, chastising him for being a bloody arse. I'll make sure he knows my true feelings on the matter, even if he is dead.

'Come on, men,' I call over my shoulder. 'Let's get bloody going.' And with no more fanfare, I ride from Worcester. I have to find Pybba, and then, well, I need to decide where the greatest menace lies, the Grantabridge jarls, King Alfred of Wessex, or bloody Jarl Halfdan in the north.

* * *

I've been at Worcester for no more than a week, and yet I feel a weight lift from my shoulders as soon as I'm free from its newly built walls. I imagine Bishop Wærferth would be devastated to know Worcester feels like a prison to me. But I can't help that. The people of Mercia might crave walls behind which to shelter from our enemy, but I need open spaces, and so does Haden.

He springs forward as soon as we've argued about crossing the bridge over the Severn. He really is a stubborn bastard. Ahead lies a wilderness of land just waking from its winter slumber. Much of it has been washed by the terrible flooding we endured following the deep snow storms. I pity the farmers whose crops might have been borne away on a wave of dirty water. Mind, some have already told me that it'll do the soil some good. I think back to my days when I would bend double and harvest the grains, anything for a few coins to drink away. I shudder. I've not been that man for a long time, although, well, I can't say it's not made me the man I am today.

Rudolf is the first to speak as we follow the tracks towards the west.

'He said he'd be fine and that he'd return within a month.' There's tightly controlled fury in Rudolf's words. He's said this to me many times before in the last month, and I'd tell him to hold his tongue, but Rudolf needs to speak the words again. The repetition is the only way he can make sense of his part in losing Pybba.

'He's a stubborn fool,' Icel rumbles from his saddle. I'd not realised he was so close. The thunder of hooves makes it difficult to know where anyone is. Ahead, Leonath and Goda are scouts, just to ensure no one attempts to attack us. 'He'll be well. We just need to bloody find him.'

I think back to when we travelled into the Welsh kingdoms, or rather, half of my warriors did, to assist an old ally. Only, we'd been played for fools. My warriors and I had almost lost our lives, first in the woodlands and then trying to escape the wrathful River Severn over a bridge that was held together more with hope than any feat of bloody engineering. The fact we'd survived owed a lot more to chance than skill than I'm comfortable admitting. Ever.

'But he said,' Rudolf persists.

I turn to Rudolf. His face flashes with fury, and I suppress a smirk. The lad is far too much like me. I can't see that's a good thing for him. Look at what's fucking happened to me? But there's not much I can do about it. Not now.

'What will you do when we find him?' I tilt Rudolf's thoughts slightly.

'Tie him up and have him bound at Kingsholm so he can never bloody leave again.' I laugh at that. It seems Rudolf has given the matter as much thought as I have.

'I'd send him to forge a pact with King Alfred,' Icel counters, his voice booming over the clatter of hooves. I turn to look at him, surprised. I can't deny there's some logic there. But would it be a punishment? Pybba might just enjoy meddling in matters of politics.

'I'd send him to the north,' Edmund counters, but I shake my head. 'Then I'd force him to speak to the archbishop. He's an old whinge bag.' I chuckle darkly at Edmund's tone. Edmund has more experience with Archbishop Wulfhere than I do. Under my brother's command, Edmund and the warriors who served him spent more time at King Burgred's court than I ever did.

'He makes himself an ally of the bastard Viking raiders and then expects Mercia to help him when he senses an opportunity. That man should have stayed well away from York if he wanted to earn himself my respect.'

'I think we can all agree that there's any number of unenviable tasks we can assign Pybba for his singular thinking,' I confirm. I don't want an argument, and I don't want to bring the politics of Worcester on my journey.

'Well, what will you do with him?' Rudolf demands hotly.

'I'll hold him in my arms and tell him I've missed him,' I confirm, not at all embarrassed by the knowledge I know I speak the fucking truth.

'And then I'll punch him and give him bloody what for.' I murmur

'Aye, my lord. I might do that as well,' Rudolf concedes eventually. We fall silent then. The sound of the hooves over the landscape fluctuates between loud, soft, and downright wet. It must have rained during the night, and all the puddles from the long-ago storms that still linger in the dips and hollows of the land, have overflowed once more. There's just too much water, just like the bastard Viking raiders. It's impossible to predict where will be flooded and where won't correctly; where will be attacked and where won't.

We pass people tending to the fields as we skirt through small settlements and by-pass farms, where cattle graze in the damp fields, and the bleat of newborn lambs can be heard. It fills me with firm resolution. This time last year, I wasn't a king; the Viking raiders weren't even hunting me. But, I was hunting the Viking raiders and ensuring the borders of the land under my control were safe from the Viking raiders and from any bastards from Wessex who might have thought to try their luck. How much has changed in the last year, and also how little. My horse is still a stubborn bastard, and Icel is a firm menace at my shoulder. Even Edmund is little changed. He persists in hating the Welsh, although I'd sooner have them as an ally than any other. I know he thirsts for what may happen if we're forced to travel into the Welsh kingdoms to find Pybba.

Perhaps we all need a good fucking fight, and then we might feel more ourselves. As the day advances, and we only stop every so often to allow the horses to drink and ourselves to piss, I know that my enemy stalks me, even here, even now, and I bloody relish that knowledge.

Chapter Six

We reach Hereford within the day, and I'm afforded lodgings by Bishop Deorlaf's servants in his absence. They rush around us, trying to offer all sorts of comfort, but all we need is a hot meal and somewhere to sleep. Tomorrow, we must ride once more, ever westward.

Edmund sits and stares moodily into the fire while Rudolf and Icel indulge in one of their usual circular conversations. I listen with half an ear. My warriors have been in good cheer, riding to hunt down Pybba, but it's been a bloody long day, all the same.

'Tell me of when you beat the Wessex warriors? It can't have been far from here?'

'On which occasion?' Icel startles me by almost answering the question. Rudolf looks at me, surprise written into his features, and I offer a shrug. He should have given more thought to his question.

'The first time?' Rudolf says with more surety than he must feel.

But Icel shakes his head and glowers into the fire. I notice that his hand reaches for his neck. A flash of something catches my eye, but I turn away from him. Icel is a changed man since his terrible injury, yet he's also not. Still, the flash of sorrow on his face is something new to me. Icel is a bastard warrior. I've never seen him sob for anyone. I've never known him to bend his head and pray for anyone other than my long-dead brother. Or maybe I have. I consider what I know of him, even as he rumbles to conversation.

'I'll tell you of when I killed Wessex warriors, but not the first time I did so.' Again, Icel is being unusually specific. I'm aware that I'm not the only one to have ceased all activity and cocked an ear to this conversation. Even Hereman is listening. Gardulf stills, his beaker half to his mouth. None of us can believe that we're about to hear something about Icel's past.

'I was younger than you,' Icel confirms, his eyes still focused on the fire, his hands held lightly on his lap. He shows no sign of being distressed by the memory. 'And on that occasion, I was alone, all alone, behind an enemy fortification, and I killed to stay alive. I killed a dying man, and I killed men who weren't dying as well. And I did it all for Mercia.'

Icel's gaze suddenly spears me, and I swallow down a sudden wave of fear. Icel is a mean bastard, as I said. I can see that he's turned Rudolf's simple question to his own ends. While Edmund is never backward in ranting against the bastard Welsh, as he terms them, Icel has always been more reserved. Until now. Talk of this proposed alliance with Wessex has upset him. Fuck, it's upset me as well.

Rudolf hangs on every word, as always. If Hiltiberht were here, he'd be doing the same, but I sent him with my aunt. This expedition might get nasty, and I don't want to put Hiltiberht off fighting. Not this time. I'm always happy to show the lads the truth of the scops tales and allow the youngsters the decision. Not everyone can be a warrior.

Icel finally looks aside. His hands are still loose. Whatever he tells us about him and his past, he's long since made peace with those actions he describes.

'The Wessex warriors are men, just like you and I, but their kings. Well, their kings and ealdormen are nothing compared to a true

Mercian. They might have fought the Viking raiders, but really, all they ever wanted was to take control of Mercia, and I've watched too many fucking Mercian men die for that to happen.'

Silence fills the hall. Even those who aren't members of my warband have stilled at Icel's barely suppressed rage. The servants stand, holding jugs or cups or even a trencher filled with fresh pork, but no one moves. No one. We don't want to break the spell Icel has woven over us.

'Without their kings and ealdormen, the Wessex men and women would be good allies for the Mercians, but their kings?' Icel shakes his head in disgust and stares into the dancing flames. Even they seem to have quietened in the face of Icel's fury. They don't dance as they might usually do. But they do glow blue at their core. I tear my eyes away and note that Icel now rubs the palm of his right hand with his left hand. I can't see what's there, but I've seen the mess of his scared hand before. He prefers to keep it hidden from prying eyes, but you can't live cheek by jowl with someone and not know some of their secrets.

'And so, I was alone, in enemy territory, with nothing but my wits to keep me alive. That and a blunt Wessex seax.'

I've never heard this story before. It's missing all of Icel's usual boasting. This, I realise, truly happened to him. He's not speaking of some fancy. He's not filling his words with bluff and exaggeration to belittle one of my accomplishments. No, he speaks of his past. And that's a rare thing from Icel.

'It was coming on time for winter. It was cold, and I was alone. And the Wessex leaders showed themselves for what they were. Craven bastards, all of them. They abandoned their men. Left them to be killed.' Icel's words fall like a stone into the silence. He tells me of the past, but equally, he tells me of something more important. I don't believe I'm the only one to pick up on this. We might be grouchy, complaining, and calling Pybba every foul name under the sun, but Icel approves of what I'm doing. No man should be left behind. Ever. Even if it's their bloody choice.

I expect Icel to say more, but he doesn't, and even Rudolf doesn't have the temerity to ask for additional information. Instead, the men slowly resume their tasks, eating, drinking, and cleaning weapons again that they believe have somehow become dirty, sheathed on their weapons belts all day. The servants leave us alone, a jug of ale to every four of my men. I fear we may become maudlin if we should drink it all. Not that I will. I'm content with water.

And then Edmund speaks, his scop song filling the silence, and suddenly, we're mourning all the men who've died in the last year since the Viking raiders came for me, and instead, we chased them from Repton, those that lived.

'A man of the Hwicce,
He gulped mead at midnight feasts.
Slew Viking raiders, night and day.
Brave Athelstan, long will his valour endure.'

I'm not alone in mumbling along with the words. I know them once Edmund speaks them, but ask me to say them without his voice as a counterpart, and I'd be bloody lost. I'd know my dead warriors' names, but little more.

'Beornberht, son of the Magonsæte.
A proud man, a wise man, a strong man.
He fought and pierced with spears.
Above the blood, he slew with swords.'

I look to Hemming as the scop song continues. Tears glisten in his eyes, and I can see how he holds his body tight, to fend off more blows. He's a brave boy. His father would be proud of him.

'A man fought for Mercia.
Against Viking raiders and foes.
Shield flashing red,
Brave Oslac, slew Viking raiders each seven-day.'

All of my warriors have been brave men. Oslac is much missed, for all, on occasion, he was a right shit.

"Hereberht was at the forefront, brave in battle.
He stained his spear, and splashed with blood

A thousand and more before Halfdan's men
His bravery cut short his life."

Hereberht died at Torksey, battling the bastard Viking raiders there. His death pained Eoppa, but I don't blame Hereberht for Eoppa's death. Eoppa knew what he was doing.

"A friend I have lost, faithful he was,
After joy, there was silence
Red his sword, let it never be cleansed
A friend I have lost, brave Eoppa."

Still, the loss of Eoppa burns, for all he died valiantly.

'Sturdy and strong, it would be wrong not to praise them.
Amid blood-red blades, in black sockets.
The war-hounds fought fiercely, tight formation.
Of the war band of Coelwulf, I would think it a burden,
To leave any in the shape of man alive.'

It takes time for any of us to return to the here and now. Icel and then Edmund have taken us to places we might sooner not travel. I look at my men, all of them, Rudolf, Edmund, Icel, Hereman, Lyfing, Goda, Gyrth, Wulfhere, Hemming, Leonath, and Wærwulf. They're all brave. Most of them carry some scar or other, even if it's little more than a missing tooth or the more serious loss of a finger, toe, or even hand, as in Pybba's case. Many of them are far from fair to look upon. And yet, we all fight on, for Mercia, for one another, and our families.

I consider my wounds, running my fingers around the lumpy scar on my neck that shows where I nearly had my head severed. My aunt thought the scar would heal smoothly, but I'm grateful it hasn't. It's a reminder for me and also a threat for those who think of killing me. It speaks for itself. 'Look at my wounds, and see that I still fucking live.'

'Let's hope we find fucking Pybba alive and don't have to add another droning verse to that particular travesty,' Icel offers. Icel's face is in the shadows of the fire, and it's not possible to tell whether he tries to speak in jest or not. My warriors. Daft fuckers, the lot of them, all raise their tankards and beakers and then turn in for the night. I'm sure not to be the only one desperate to be on my way the next day.

We leave before the sun has risen in the morning. Dawn is a watery promise on the distant horizon. It's a cold day, the wind blowing from the hills, and I'm grateful once more for my winter cloak and the heat from Haden's body. He doesn't feel the cold and is content to trot onwards.

My men are subdued. I try to consider how I can bouy them, but the insight into Icel's hatred of Wessex, and Edmund's reminder of our lost men, has prompted us all to realise that Pybba might be lost and that we have more enemies than just the Viking raiders. I'm always happy to fight the Welsh, although I'd sooner be their ally. Certainly, I'd rather help them against the Viking raiders than bloody King Alfred of Wessex.

In no time at all, I'm aware that we must almost be in the Welsh kingdoms. Last time we travelled so far west, I was unprepared to risk myself, and in fact, none of my warriors or my aunt would have been pleased with me if I'd crossed the border defined by the old dyke. But this is entirely different.

'Where did you leave him?' I demand from Rudolf.

'Where he asked to be fucking left,' Edmund retorts. He's fed up with my criticism about Pybba.

'Then you better fucking lead on,' I urge him, but Edmund looks to Hereman.

Billy picks his way forwards, his warm breath pooling in the cold air, and the pair of them examine the way ahead. I look down, trying not to smile, as the two so closely mirror one another.

'This way,' Hereman confirms, but I think he's following Billy's lead as Billy's already moving slightly south.

'Are you bloody sure?' Edmund growls. I shake my head. Edmund's in a foul mood today.

'Yes, I'm bloody sure. I mean, do you know where to fucking go?' Hereman calls over his shoulder, his good humour easy to hear. Hereman's not allowing himself to be too sentimental.

I wait and pull Haden next to Icel's Samson. Icel notes me but says nothing as Samson rumbles to a trot. I have to ask him about his thoughts towards Wessex. I'm curious about his story. There's so much about Icel I don't know. He's long been almost part of the furniture at Kingsholm. It's easy to forget that he wasn't always there and that he wasn't always an oath-sworn member of the war band based at Kingsholm, older men being replaced by young men, who then become old and are in turn replaced. The graveyard at Kingsholm, surrounding the church there, is filled with men who've fought for Mercia, as well as their families.

'My lord,' Icel eventually breaks the silence. 'I don't trust the Wessex king,' he prevents me from asking my questions. I'm grateful. 'I've never trusted the bastard Wessex king and his nobility. The Wessex warriors; they're another matter entirely. They used to be lethal; now, they have weak men to rule them and so fall beneath Viking raider blades with too much bloody frequency.'

'So, you don't think it wise to ally with them?'

Icel shakes his silvered head but keeps his eyes on the road ahead.

'The kingdom of Wessex has been seeking a means to overrule Mercia ever since that bastard King Ecgberht was crowned her king. He hated the Mercians. He wanted to show that animosity by taking control of the kingdom. And, for a time, he succeeded, but not for long.'

'Sometimes, I forget how bloody old you are,' I apologise. Icel speaks of events before I was even born.

'Sometimes, I forget how bloody young you used to be,' Icel counters, and I growl. Talk about a fucking half-arsed compliment. 'And Rudolf, well, he's young enough to be my grandson.' His words stir a memory in me. Has Icel ever been a father? I don't think he has. Certainly, not in the recent past.

'I would leave Wessex well alone. They won't aid Mercia in any helpful way. King Alfred merely means to have the better, Mercian warriors at his beck and call so that his own men don't pay the ultimate price. He knows that his brothers and father before him weren't far-thinking enough to ensure Wessex could counter the Viking raiders. Even now, he holds onto Wessex by his fingernails.'

I nod. I'm relieved to hear Icel's words. I know my aunt will share them. Yes, there'll be some keen to forge an alliance, but right now, I can only think of Bishop Smithwulf, who truly wants it. He's poised, on Mercia's southern border, in a perilous situation. The Viking raiders have long been fascinated with London and the ancient walls surrounding the older parts of the settlement, the mighty River Thames too much of an invitation for men and women who travel by ship. Perhaps those walls need extending? Maybe, like at Worcester and Northampton, there need to be walls around the twin parts of London, separated by the River Fleet.

But the Wessex kingship is just as obsessed with London as the Viking raiders. The River Thames is a physical boundary along much of its path, but in places, Mercia certainly reaches further into land Wessex thinks to hold than they might like.

'Ware,' the cry ripples through the air, and I sigh heavily. Not even a day out of sodding Hereford, and there's some new catastrophe with which to contend. I just hope it's nothing to do with bloody Pybba.

Chapter Seven

I t's Edmund who gives the cry. He's been riding to the front, keen to be away from everyone else, forcing his path through Goda and Leonath, their two mounts allowing it with less fuss than their riders. Edmund's a moody git when he wants to be. Now I ride to join him, where he sits, Jethson still beneath him, peering forwards. I grimace. Already I realise what he sees. The smell, despite the cold, is enough to alert me that people have died here and recently enough that they stink.

'Poor bastards,' I exclaim, already attempting to dismount. Edmund turns and shakes his head, fury in his flashing green eye.

'You're the bloody king. Stay in your damn saddle,' he orders me as Hereman dismounts from Billy. Not one of us is unprepared. We all have hands reaching for our weapons belts. I can feel the handle of my seax as I flex my fingers over it. It's a comfort despite the scene before me.

There's a gentle incline, and Hereman's boots squelch as he hits the ground.

'Bloody bollocks,' he exclaims. I glance down. Dark brown mud has been kicked up over his feet and ankles. He's not alone; Lyfing and Goda join him on the ground. The three have their seaxes drawn, their horses remaining with the rest of us. All of them are ready for what might come as they prowl forwards.

I can see three bodies, pale flesh beneath the flashing sun. There I was enjoying the coming warmer weather, the promise of new growth and here, these people were already dead and rotting. The smell is unpleasant but bearable for now.

I watch Hereman. I'm aware that Icel, Leonath and Rudolf have turned their horses, eyes raking in the area we've ridden over and where anyone might think to ambush us. There's an open expanse behind us, but trees crowd the slopes. Anyone could be hiding out there. But we all know the ambush happened some time ago. There's no one here. Not bloody alive, anyway.

'Four of them,' Hereman confirms, standing from where he's been bent over the broken bodies. 'They had a cart. It must have contained supplies, and some bastard's run off with whatever they had to trade and taken the horse with them as well. You can see the tracks.'

'Mercians?' I ask. I'm hoping they were, although how I expect Hereman and the others to know this, I'm not sure.

'Well, they were probably going towards the border,' he muses. I ignore Edmund's incredulous look flashed my way. His brother doesn't think the bloody question's stupid.

'They put up a fight,' Hereman continues, as though he's speaking of the mundane, not the death of his fellow men and women. 'There are some marks on their bodies, and I also think they wounded someone. I'm sure there's a patch of blood trailing away in that direction.' He points towards a dip in the land.

'So, we go after them?' Goda demands, fury in his voice.

This I'm not sure about. We came for Pybba. Why then should I become distracted by this terrible scene? But fuck it. Goda's right. I can't allow this to go unavenged.

'We're going that way anyway? Aren't we?' I turn to Edmund. He nods just once. His expression remains sullen as he gnaws at his lower lip. Bad enough to know there are Viking raiders out there, perhaps, but now it seems that someone is killing my Mercians. Is it Viking raiders, or is it the bloody Welsh? Or is it their fellow Mercians? I'm fucking sure there are enough enemies without turning on one another.

'Then once we've buried the dead, we'll lead on.' Now, I jump from Haden. I'm not going to leave these people to rot further. I grimace as I note the staring eye sockets of the first body. It's of an older man, grey hair blowing softly around a lined face. His left eye missing, no doubt pecked away by a hungry crow or some such. He lies, on his back, legs crumpled beneath him. I can see the wound that killed him, just below where his heart should beat. A bloody wound, but the red of his blood has faded to a dirty brown. His body has been further disturbed. If he had a weapons belt, it's missing, and so is any purse filled with coins he might have had. But he wears his tunic, despite the bloody hollow in him. It's of good, thick cloth. I take him to be a trader.

I walk to the next body then. This is of a younger man. I can see the similarity between the two, even in death and even with both eyes missing. His belly has been opened, his pale guts trailing over the floor. Well, some of his guts are. Here and there, pieces are missing so that the idea of them being one is an illusion through which I can see the hardness of the ground. Perhaps the wolves or some other scavenger.

Next, there's a young boy, no older than young Æthelred, discovered in the stables at Worcester. His eyes remain and reveal a startled look. I shake my head. Such a fucking terrible waste. But then I come to the woman, and of course, whoever robbed these people of their possessions and lives, has done even worse to her. She's naked, and I turn aside from the horror of her wounds. They are many.

'What the fuck?' Lyfing growls, pulling what he can of her remaining ripped clothes over her nakedness. I mean, it doesn't matter; she's dead, poor woman. But all the same, I bend and assist him. It'll take us some time to find a means of burying her. None of my warriors will want to expose her in such a way.

Lyfing continues to mutter to himself. I appreciate what's enraged him. I've never understood the desire to rape an enemy's woman. What good does it do? Other than to show that, really, if a man can do that to someone he's supposed to hate, what does it say about him when he does it to someone he allegedly loves?

'Over here,' Hemming has been scouting the vicinity, and he appears, face flushed, from the far end of the slope. 'There's some loose soil that's fairly easy to move aside.' I see then that he's been employing his shield as a shovel. Light soil clings to the bottom of the shield rim.

'Rudolf and Wulfhere, help Hemming,' I command, and now Rudolf's muttering at me as well. I know, and he knows, that I've asked the party's youngest members to fulfil this task because any of the others will bloody bellyache about it, even though they want the dead buried. I can't be fucking arsed with the complaining.

While the three youngsters disappear down the slope, Wærwulf accompanies them, eyes keen, and I turn to Icel, who stands at my side.

'Help me with him.' The horses are milling around, far enough away from the dead bodies that I don't object to them cropping the short winter grass.

'Aye, my lord,' Icel rumbles, and between us, we manage to hook the body of the older man. It's disgustingly slick and soft beneath my hands, but it's easier to do by hand than by dragging the body over one of the saddles. I'd get far more covered in gore if I attempted that.

It's uncomfortable, walking the body away from where the man died, his body swaying between the two of us, but I refuse to complain. I'm not the dead one after all, and if one day I fall beneath an enemy blade and die like this, I'd hope someone else would do the same.

'Very kingly,' Rudolf attempts to quip, from where he's resting on his arse, sweat beading his face, his shield covered in light-coloured mud.

'Aye, this is what it means to be a bloody king,' I try and find some humour in the situation. 'A good king buries his dead and kills their killers,' I continue. My tone is off; even I can hear that.

With more luck than care, we place the man into the shallow grave Hemming, Wulfhere and Rudolf have forced from the softer soil. I'm slightly concerned that the bodies might be easily disturbed by prey animals, but it's the best we can do for now. I might have to send others to do a better job at a later date.

Leonath and Wærwulf bring the other man, Hereman the boy, cradled in his arms, and then it falls to Goda and Lyfing to gather the woman. I don't turn aside but watch as she's lowered into the long, shallow grave, besides people I must assume were her father, husband, and son. I'm reminded fiercely of our visit to the settlement close to the River Stour where Lady Eadburh ruled and the Viking raiders killed the children. They have no compunction in killing and raping those without the means to defend themselves.

'I hope it was the bloody Viking raiders,' Goda growls as we lift our heads from where they've been bowed over the grave. There's no priest here to offer the right words, but I think having my warriors bent on vengeance should be enough to please our Lord God.

'Right, back on your horses,' I call to my men. I'll not allow them more time to brood on what's happened here. We need to hunt down Pybba and, hopefully, the damn bastards who killed my Mercians.

We're solemn as we resume the journey. Hereman is at the front, alongside his brother, Goda and Leonath just behind them. Hereman has his eyes down on the slick of blood he thinks will lead us to the killers while Edmund watches the forward path, a perpetual scowl on his drawn face.

'Well, he's a bloody bundle of joy today,' Wærwulf murmurs. I shake my head, finding my lips quirking all the same.

'He's getting worse, not better,' I confirm. Edmund has been a member of the ealdorman of the Hwicce's warband for many more years than I have. In fact, I'd find it difficult to determine who'd ridden in it for the longest. I want to say Icel, but perhaps it's not him. It might be Cealwin or Cuthwahl. Or maybe Icel, after all. I've never thought of finding out before. I was bequeathed these men on my brother's death. I've never thought to question how they came to be oath sworn to the ealdorman of Hwicce. But, I assume that even the most violent of men must eventually tire of fighting.

'It takes men like that,' Wærwulf cautions me, and I realise he's trying to tell me something else. I meet his frank eyes, noting that his nose looks wonky from a wound taken fighting Jarl Halfdan. I don't think it's actually wonky, but the thin-white scar that dissects it is far from straight and makes his face seem out of proportion on the left-hand side.

'What does?' I demand.

'When they've had enough but haven't realised yet. He's been fighting since he was younger than Rudolf. He might well have bloody had enough.' I startle. Edmund? Had enough of fighting for Mercia? I can't see it.

'I'm sure he's just his usual grouchy self, but I'll keep an eye on him and my thanks.'

'Aye, my lord. Sometimes, it takes someone else's perspective to tell a man what he needs.' With that, he gathers Cinder's reins and knees her forward to join Hereman and Edmund. I quirk a smile. The bugger chides Edmund.

'Put a fucking smile on it, you miserable sod,' Wærwulf calls to him. Hereman looks up, his upper body rocking with his humour, but Edmund hunches more miserably than before in his saddle.

'Fuck off, Wærwulf,' Edmund counters angrily, and now we all laugh. Edmund might as well have just told Wærwulf he's right to call him out for his ill-humour than respond in such a way.

Only then, Hereman stops again, Edmund continuing beyond him, and I raise my voice. 'Edmund, get fucking back,' I urge him, not above reminding him that he berated me for being inattentive. Ahead, there's a dip in the land, thick trees stretch to either side, divided by the cleft of the roadway, and between them, a ragged collection of warriors stands.

'Fuck. We've found the bastards,' I growl.

Chapter Eight

We've found the bastard killers. There are more of them than there are us.

They're not mounted, but they have enough iron to compensate for the lack of snapping teeth and kicking hooves.

'Wonderful,' I huff.

'Who the fuck are you?' Hereman growls while Edmund forces Jethson to reverse, not an easy feat to accomplish with any horse, especially not Jethson, but better to back up than turn a back on our enemy.

There's no response to the cry. I consider whether the men understand or not. I wish I knew if they were Viking raiders or from the Welsh kingdoms, but it's impossible to tell. Not until one of them speaks.

The men, I count them, smirking to be so like Rudolf in needing to know exact numbers and realise that there are twenty-one of them. But we have the horses, so our number is doubled.

'Oye, I'm talking to you,' Hereman jabs again. His words echo through the damp space between the trees.

I try and peer into those depths to see if there's more of this force hiding inside the tree line, but the tree trunks are so densely packed together that it's impossible to tell. Maybe there are. Maybe there aren't. There's bugger all I can do about it now.

'Now, Hereman, be fucking polite?' I caution, but there's no amusement in my voice.

I turn to Wærwulf. He inclines his head, and a harsh sentence filled with the words of Viking raiders thrums through the air. There's still no response, but there doesn't need to be. The way a handful of the men jolt with understanding is telling enough.

'Right, Viking raiders,' I sigh, reaching for my seax and shield, preparing to dismount from Haden's back while cramming my linen cap and iron helm onto my head. I'm grateful this is my helm, not Mercia's ceremonial one. I'd be unable to move my neck, let alone fight, with that on my head.

The enemy, realising that they've given themselves away, mirrors my actions.

'Hemming, Wulfhere, Rudolf, to the back,' I command them. I hear their complaints, even as they obey me. I leap from Haden's back, only for my left foot to slip on the slick, moss-covered surface. I don't fall, but that's more thanks to Haden's steadying presence than any great skill.

I grimace. They've chosen a good place to face us. I consider if they have dry land to fight on, but it's irrelevant. I'll have to battle them even if we're arse-deep in mud.

'Mercians,' the single word is filled with disdain as Hereman, Wærwulf and Edmund dismount and dismiss their mounts with a slap to rumps. In no particular rush, the horses amble past me to join Haden, Dever and the rest of their comrades. They've one job to do, and that's to stay out of the way until we might need them.

'Aye, you bastards. We're the Mercians. And you can bugger off our land, or die,' Edmund's ill-temper is directed at the line of men. His voice hums with more than menace. It seems Edmund's been spoiling for a fight, and now he's going to get one. It must have been, what, nearly two months since he took the life of an enemy. He's clearly been fucking missing it.

'Come on, men,' I urge my warriors. I can see more than just me eyeing our surroundings rather than our enemy. The enemy has prior knowledge of this place, and we don't. They currently have the upper hand, and we need to make some snap decisions.

For now, I'm prepared to accept they're alone and that no others wait to reinforce them. Why they're here is beyond me. A small force. It's certainly not enough to crew a ship. I can't hear a river nearby, but there is no doubt one. Maybe they're all that's left of a ship's crew. Or maybe it's something else.

Our enemy also prepares. There are some shields, but not, I notice, enough for every man to carry one. They do, however, all seem to have long spears. The majority also wear helms, apart from one man with shocking red hair, which dances in the stiffening breeze. He carries not one but two war axes, and when he smirks at me, I can see no teeth, only a black maw.

Others catch my attention. One carries a shield in his right hand, not his left, the blackened image of something obscured on the wood of the shield. All of the shields appear to show something different. I consider whether these men are survivors of a larger force or if they've just decided there's no need to broadcast the identity of the jarl who has their oath.

Not that any of the men look like a jarl. Well. Perhaps one of them does, but the figure is of a slimmer build than the majority, the clothes in slightly better condition. I dismiss the idea of that person being a man. They're either a youth or a woman. If it's a woman, then she's done well to exert control over these bastards, which makes me think she must be the wife of a jarl. Has someone come to seek vengeance against me? It wouldn't be the first bloody time.

'King Coelwulf,' the voice that speaks is rough and stumbles over the unfamiliar words.

'Aye,' Icel calls in response.

A flicker of confusion on the face, and then the eyes turn to Icel.

Icel stands battle-ready, his shield in one hand, his seax in the other. His build speaks of his prowess, his long, grey beard, of his skill. Poor fuckers.

'King Coelwulf?' comes again, confusion in the words. No doubt, they know that I'm a younger man than Icel.

'Aye,' now it's Lyfing who responds. The eyes of every one of our enemies flicker to where Lyfing stands at the far end of my short line of warriors. Lyfing's helm has long been repaired, and yet, beneath the light of the sun, I detect where the dent has been beaten from it. I'm not sure he looks kingly enough, but fuck it, I hardly festoon myself in jewels and fine battle gear. I utilise equipment I've had for over a decade. It's serviceable and lethal but not at all ceremonial. I'm always amazed that this tactic is so damn effective.

'I seek the wergild payment for my husband and my son.' Once more, the words are spoken with care. Someone has taught this person those words.

So, my deduction was correct. It's a woman who faces me. She looks fierce in all her battle equipment, but I imagine much of it is for show. Whether she can fight or not remains to be seen. Certainly, I wouldn't risk wearing so many arm rings and amulets around my neck. She's just looking for someone to use them to strangle her.

'Jarl Sigurd,' she continues. I look from Wærwulf at my right to Leonath at my left. I've no idea whom she's talking about, and immediately, I can see the fury on her face as all of my warriors look blank.

'He was killed. By Lord Coelwulf, at Repton. My son as well.'

Then I hear Wærwulf chuckle, and a memory finally comes to the fore.

Another flood of words from Wærwulf. I hope he'll translate those words without me having to ask. That would give our ruse away.

'I told the bitch he didn't die at Repton. He died in a forest, far from Repton. At Repton, I wore his armour and gained admittance into the jarls stronghold.'

I realise now that the shields are intended to be black. Jarl Sigurd was the man who menaced in blackened armour, his shields, his helm, and his byrnie. We fought him at Warwick, or close to Warwick. He was the man who allied with the deceitful Ealdorman Wulfstan. The bastard.

Again, Wærwulf speaks in their tongue, the words spoken with more fluency than she can manage in my language.

'I told her he died in battle. There's no wergild to pay,' Wærwulf shares with us all. And yet, she's come to demand payment for her dead husband and son. I consider why she didn't just send one of her warriors. Equally, I'm confused as to why she thought to find me here, almost inside the Welsh kingdom of Powys. Surely, she'd have done better to find me at Worcester or Repton? Although, well, she wouldn't have gotten that far, not if she'd come onto Mercian land here.

Again, Wærwulf speaks to the woman. The woman, jaw clenched with anger beneath her warriors' helm, answers in half shrieked words.

'She says her men killed the traders. They were supposed to bring them to the king but turned on them.'

'A likely story,' I mumble, but at least we know who killed the Mercians we buried on the hill. No doubt, they forced them against their will. Or perhaps not. The cart was definitely facing away from the central parts of Mercia, not the other way round.

'Are we going to kill 'em or offer them a pot of fucking mead?' Edmund growls. He makes a fair point.

I raise my shield to cover my mouth.

'Tell them that if they leave here now and pay the wergild for the dead Mercians, I'll allow five of them to live. But not the jarl's wife.' Wærwulf's eyes bulge at my words, but he grins and relays my message all the same.

I watch with interest to see how the words are interpreted. The woman is incensed as she reaches for her seax. I note that she handles it with some prior knowledge of the blade. But it's one thing to hold a weapon threateningly and quite another to be able to kill with it.

Some of her warriors shuffle with unease. There are a few who glance into the woodlands as though devising a means of escaping. At least six of them glower as meanly as Edmund must be doing.

It'll be a fucking fight then. That pleases me. And no doubt Edmund.

The woman shrieks her response. Wærwulf listens carefully, but halfway through her rant, he begins to speak.

'The mean bitch will have none of it. She'd rather all her men died, and that suits me. How about you, Edmund?'

'Aye. A fight. It'll clear my head,' he confirms, his voice devoid of its usual pre-battle terror. I don't think Edmund has ever needed to fight as much as he does now. What's eating him is impossible to know, but something is.

'Advance,' I say softly, pleased when Wærwulf repeats my words much louder. I don't believe the enemy thinks Wærwulf is King Coelwulf, but it's good to persist with the misdirection. The enemy wouldn't agree to my terms, and I didn't want them to anyway. I have no intention of allowing even one Viking raider to return to their home just so they can gather a new force and attack Mercia again. In that, I know I differ from my predecessor. King Burgred's tactics failed. In fact, they were woeful. Different might not be better, but it's fucking satisfying whenever I take the life of one of the bastards.

As one, we amble to a slight run, shields before us. I have my eyes focused on the woman.

'I'll take her,' Wærwulf growls.

'You can have the first attack,' I confirm. 'If that fails, then I'll bloody kill her.' And then there's no more time for conversation. We come at them with a unified front, but not with our shields overlapping. This will be more of a one-on-one battle. I clash with one of the fiercer warriors, no doubt one of the men with special command of the jarl's wife.

He's a broad man, his shield perhaps better than some others, and he benefits from a helm and a byrnie. He also has a war axe. All the same, he's barely prepared for my attack, his shield smashing into his body because the hold is weak as I make my first forceful strike with my seax, ramming my shield into his at the same time.

I wince at the sound of the poorly held shield hitting his chin. When he opens his mouth, blood dribbles from the corners of his thick lips—damn bastard. I thrust my shield against him again, hoping to repeat the action, and it works. This time, the shield hits higher, just below his nose guard, and blood blooms there as well. But he finally makes a move against me, his war axe clashing with my shield as I take one step back. I need more room to swing my seax.

There's a tremendous amount of force in his blow. I absorb it while tightening the hold on my shield. He smirks the fool, thinking he can beat me so easily. I dash to his side, slicing my seax down his byrnie as I go, and then back up again, nicking his chin as a final flourish. He shrieks in pain, but I eye the next of my foemen.

This man is the opposite. Thin and slight, with an evil glint in a hazel eye. Below his helm, a thick black moustache and beard almost cover his mouth. He has a spear in his right hand and a shield in the other. He jabs it at me, thinking of skewering my leg below the knee. I drop my shield low to counter the move and dart towards him so that his spear, extended towards me, can't get anywhere close, held at bay by my shield. I see him try and withdraw it, but it can't retract quickly enough and gets hooked on my shield as well. I have my seax at his throat.

'Fucking fool,' I huff into his face, seax slicing open his throat, severing his beard simultaneously. Confused eyes watch me for a moment, but I focus on the first man. I cut him across his forearm but not mortally, his eyes flickering from the dead man to me. I risk a glance to Wærwulf. He and the woman are still fighting, but it's nearly over. Mind, I'm impressed by how long she's prevailed.

'Hakon,' the first man cries, watching his ally thud to the floor.

'Was a shit warrior,' I counter, deciding how to kill the man. He has his shield held firmly against his body, his war axe hidden as well. He might, I consider, have exchanged hands while I was occupied with this Hakon. If so, he'll come at me from a different direction this time. Yet, I'm not convinced he's thought that far ahead. And now, rage has taken him. He won't have long to grieve.

He lurches at me. I hold firm. His arm lifts to fling his war axe towards me. I grasp my shield aloft, counter that blow, and twist beneath my arm so that he runs onto my seax. He huffs, a loud farting noise filling the air. I twist the blade in an attempt to free it. He howls like a wolf on a full moon before sliding from my blade.

I suck in a deep breath and eye the rest of the battle.

Hereman is at the centre of a maelstrom. Four men have decided to attack him with a variety of weapons. Even as I watch, one of the men takes a slicing blow to his chin and veers with the shock of the scarlet flood down his face. Another thinks to press home an advantage, but Hereman glowers at him, feinting to one side and then cracking him across the side of the head with the hilt of his seax. One of the remaining two men shrieks fearfully while Hereman rounds on him and immediately rushes away. Hereman menaces the final man. It won't be long. All of them will die, even the one who thought to run away.

I look to Rudolf and Hemming. Rudolf is used to battling with Pybba, but he's doing well enough against the blond-haired man who thinks Rudolf will be an easy kill. Hemming isn't coping as well alone, but already, Icel is alert to the danger and angles himself so that he and his two foemen will collide with the fight taking place.

I hear a half-strangled cry from close by. Wærwulf roars his triumph at killing the jarl's woman, who collapsed to the ground, while one of the other Viking raiders hammers on his back. I reach out and flick my blade across the wide shoulder blades of the guard. He turns from Wærwulf, howling with pain, and I incline my head to my warrior. Wærwulf grins his thanks and stabs into the man's chest. The sound of the blade scraping over bone makes me wince.

I spy a group of four warriors running into the woodlands. I speed my steps to follow them.

'Edmund,' I roar. 'To me,' and I leave it at that. I'll have to hope he follows or that someone does.

The last of the four men risk a glance over his shoulder at my cry and hurries his pace. Already, the two men in front of him have disappeared beneath the fir trees. I reach out and just miss grabbing his byrnie. Overhead, day turns to night. Bloody bollocks. It's dark beneath the trees. Not that the four slow their steps. It's evident that they know where they're going. I risk turning and checking on my warriors.

The fight is all but over. Edmund is rushing my way while Icel is helping Hemming to his feet. The lad limps, but I can see nothing more serious from where I am. Quickly, I count my warriors and, assured they all still stand, I march back beneath the spreading boughs of the trees.

Where have those four men gone? It must be something important if they're prepared to abandon their jarl's wife in such a way. Or, perhaps, they're simply craven and too scared to meet their deaths.

Certainly, they're far from quiet under the trees. Beneath my feet, the ground feels spongy and also damp in other places. The scent of ripeness hangs in the air, but it's not the smell of the dead. It's almost pleasant.

Behind me, I hear Edmund crash through the branches.

'What the fuck?' he demands, his breathing harsh.

'Four of them went this way. I want to know why?'

Edmund swallows down his scowl and spreads out beside me. Together, we begin to make our way through the trees. Not all the branches are low hanging, but there's enough that I quickly lose sight of Edmund, only to round another tree and find him again.

He looks at me, his eye flashing in the gloom.

'We should bloody get the others,' he berates me, jerking his head back the way we've come.

'There are only four of the bastards,' I argue. I fear if one of us goes back, that we'll lose the men. Every so often, I see a back or a leg disappearing around another tree trunk or branch.

'On your fucking head,' Edmund huffs. Ahead, voices drift back to us, angry voices. I can't make out the words, but the intent is easy enough to decipher.

'What's all this about,' I murmur to Edmund. His expression has lost its anger, and now he just looks perplexed. A waft of smoke assures me that we're heading to the camp of our foemen, but when I emerge into a larger space, I don't expect to be faced with what I find there. Not at all.

Chapter Nine

'What the fuck?' Edmund explodes, dashing forwards. I understand why he's so incensed.

Sitting there, with his ankles and knees bound, is none other than Pybba. His face is a violent shade of green and black, one huge bruise from beginning to end. As his hand is missing, his guards have tied his one hand behind him. And he's not alone. There are five other people underneath those trees, and the four Viking raider warriors who thought to run away turn startled eyes my way as they realise they're not alone, and neither of those left to guard the prisoners. One of them quickly slips away between the trees, and I let him go. The other three are caught between me, Edmund and the six captives. If they want to run, they should have bloody done it by now.

'Pybba,' I roar, diving past the foemen to pull the gag from his mouth. Pybba coughs and bucks as I slice through the hempen rope at his ankles and knees and release his hand. He stinks. I dread to think for how long he's been captive.

His wrist is a giant purple bruise. I reach for the next captive; only one of the warriors has found some stones and stands in my way.

He shakes his shaved head. I rise and thrust the hilt of my seax against his nose, following up with a crash of my shield against his neck so that he gasps for air, arms flailing. The life leaves him, and he thuds to the ground, only just missing Pybba's legs.

'My thanks,' Pybba spits. His voice is thick with lack of use, cracking. He coughs again. I scour the campsite and reach for an abandoned drinking skin. I knock the lid aside, sniff it suspiciously and then hand it to Pybba when I'm sure it's nothing more potent than water.

He drinks thirstily, but my eyes are on Edmund. He's engaged the three remaining men, and the clash of iron-on-iron rings through the quiet place. I dip and slice through the hemp rope on a younger woman's hands and legs, and then content she can free the other captives with an abandoned knife I hand to her, I race to Edmund's side.

Edmund doesn't need my help, but fury burbles through my body. I slide next to Edmund, wary of his lethal seax, which batters aside a largish man with frightened eyes. I leave him to Edmund and smirk at the remaining two men. They're a similar height, they might even be half-decent warriors, but I don't give them the fucking chance to show me their skills.

Lashing out with my seax, I land a cut on the chin of the closest man, dancing into the next opponent. He has his hand on a war axe and moves toward me. I counter it with my seax, the uncomfortable sensation of the two pieces of iron meeting shuddering up my arm. I tighten my grip and, noticing that the first man, blood pouring from his chin, has finally found some stones, lash out with my left fist, cutting across my body to land the blow. He staggers again but keeps his feet.

The second man, in my mind, I call him skinny, smirks at my failure to down his ally. Daft fuck. Quickly, I move my seax, and it swipes across his face, severing the tip of his nose so that he howls in pain. He really shouldn't have removed his helm if he ever had one. Not one to put a good strike to waste, my arm continues to fall, seax pointing, and it slashes open the first man's byrnie. The padded material gives with a soft shush, and now he has no helm and no byrnie. I'd stab him, but Edmund beats me to it. The man looks down at the blade that's pierced his chest and dies like that. Head hanging low. I can well imagine the look of surprise on his face.

The second man shrieks in rage, and I think he'll attempt an escape, but Pybba's found a weapon. Unbeknown to our enemy, he stands to his side. With careful aim, and a very sharp seax, Pybba severs the man's left hand, and it thuds to the floor, a torrent of blood following it.

The man turns, war axe in hand, and I promptly step between him and Pybba. Pybba's swaying alarmingly, breathing too heavily. While Pybba might have killed the man, he doesn't have the strength to battle him until the inevitable outcome is achieved.

Rage and pain mingle on the dying man's face, his missing nose tip, sheeting blood down his chest, while blood from his wrist grows in intensity. I shake my head at him, but his eyes are reddened with fury, and he launches at me, even now.

As he careers into my chest, the smell of him is overwhelming. The sharp metallic smell of blood, the scent of too much ale and not enough water, the fact his clothes have been unwashed for days if not weeks. And still, I stumble beneath him, my seax going wildly to the side, only just missing Pybba, who manages to jump aside.

'Shit,' I mumble, holding my neck rigid so as not to hit it on the hard floor. The man's head is just below my chest, and I punch him, first with my left fist and then with my right one, although it feels weak from knocking it upon the ground. I feel the man buckle on top of me, and then he stills. I look up and meet Edmund's eyes.

He smirks at me.

'You all right there?' he queries. His face is clear from all blood. He could have just risen from bathing.

'Fine, thanks,' I huff. The dead man is becoming heavier and heavier on me, and the stink of his blood is thick in the air.

'Get the bastard off me,' I demand, shuffling around on the

ground but unable to dislodge the man. My arse hurts, and tomorrow, I might not be able to sit in my saddle. Damn cunt.

'Aye, give me a moment,' Edmund huffs. I see his balance change and the body turn to one side, but still, it doesn't free me.

'Use your bloody hands,' I urge him. 'Kicking is going to do fuck all.'

'If you think you can do better, then do it your bloody self,' Edmund sulks, turning his back on me.

'Edmund, get the fuck back here,' I entreat him, but the affronted shit has gone on his way. I fight with the body, trying to roll, first one way and then another, digging my heels into the hard surface.

'Fuck, he's a heavy bastard,' I huff. I can feel my trews growing damp with blood, and I wrinkle my nose. Bad enough to smell the fucker now. I don't want to stink of him all bloody day long.

And I'm still making no progress. Eventually, I feel the weight dislodge and look into the eyes of a woman and a youth. I know who they are, of course, but I'm just grateful to be free from the weight and able to move clear from the vast pool of maroon fluid. It reaches the stone circle of the fire, and I can hear it sizzling as it encounters the residual heat.

I want to jump to my feet, berate Edmund for being a fucking cock, as usual, but he's down on one knee, back to me.

'My thanks,' I exclaim, accepting the hand of the woman and staggering to my feet. I look down and kick the handless man. His body moves with the motion, but there's no life left in him.

'Are you well?' I demand of the woman, Pybba's daughter.

'I am now,' she exclaims, but her shocked voice betrays those words.

'What's the matter with Pybba?' I've realised what Edmund's doing, and the words are flung over my shoulder as I walk towards the two of them.

'He was sick. That's why he lingered. We were all sick. And then they apprehended us, and he shouldn't have been out in all weathers but tended to at home.'

I shake my head. Now that I get a good look at Pybba, I can see that he's not just bruised and beaten. He looks weak, and his eyes are feverish as he lies on the ground, looking up at Edmund, who checks his body for other visible wounds. Around us, the small collection of captives move around, seeking food and water and adding more fuel to the fire. I note Pybba's daughter. Her dress is filthy; the hem looks like it's been dragged through a pile of horse shit on more than one occasion. But I don't see her husband, although I do see her son. He's older than I think he should be, but everyone's children are. Somewhere, in the last ten years, I've lost track of how old everyone should be, and now the children are as old as I believe the parents to be.

I want to ask her where her husband is and where her daughter is, but the words stick in my throat. Those aren't the first questions I should ask her. It's all too easy to determine what's befallen them. I realise then that two of the other people are older, as old as Pybba. The man is entirely bald, his small eyes making him look mole-like. The woman has short-cropped grey hair, and her dress is in a much better condition than Penna's, Pybba's daughter.

The other two people are youngsters. I don't recognise them, but my concern is for Pybba.

'He needs rest,' Penna urges. 'And somewhere safe to recover.' For someone captive only moments ago, she seems remarkably recovered.

'We'll take him to Kingsholm,' I decide. 'My aunt will care for him.'

I suddenly remember the rest of my warriors and turn, facing where I think we entered the woodland, only they've found me, not vice versa.

Rudolf skips into the clearing, his eyes alert, jaw clenched. His eyes turn from me to Penna and down to the ground, where Edmund tends to Pybba. He rushes forwards, no thought to anyone else, his seax slack in his hand.

'Pybba,' his single word is filled with relief and worry combined.

'They're all dead,' Icel rears up next, his eyes quickly assessing what's happened here. Hereman, Goda and Wærwulf follow him. The others, it appears, have remained to tend to the horses and the dying.

'What happened?' I finally think to ask.

'The Viking raider bastards attacked us,' a gruff voice responds. I imagine this is perhaps Penna's father-in-law. 'They knew who Pybba was. That Norse bitch thought it would be a way of getting to you, my lord king.' There's respect in his words, but they roll with the accent of the Welsh. There's a language that likes to use long words for things I might name more easily.

I nod. This, then, is all my fault.

'If Pybba had stayed out of it, none of this would have happened.' The man's words are rimmed with ice. I startle at his fury.

'Now, Higuel. It's not his fault.'

'He led them straight to us,' Higuel's voice is strained with fury. 'If it weren't for him, my son would still be alive.' I wince to hear those words, turning to Penna with sympathy on my face. But she scowls.

'We don't know he's dead. Or Beca. They might yet live.'

'I don't see how,' Higuel dismisses her words. I sense that all is not well here. Edmund helps Pybba to sit and then to stand once more, Rudolf on the other side of him. Pybba looks to Rudolf, a strained expression on his face.

'Brimman,' Pybba whispers, and I swallow my grief to know his horse is lost to him.

'She's not here,' Penna murmurs. 'They took her, or rather another man did. He was to go somewhere, but I don't know where.'

'He was to go to their ship and get the rest of them,' Higuel interjects. 'I heard them discussing it.'

'So, this isn't all of them?' I demand from him. He meets my eyes squarely.

'No, this is some of them. The rest were waiting, and now they'll be coming.' I peer into the trees as though they might be preparing to attack even now. Suddenly, I feel eyes everywhere.

'We need to leave this place, and then I can return with more of my warriors.' I didn't bring everyone with me. I'd not truly expected to encounter more Viking raiders, not after we succeeded in killing so many at the turn of the year. I curse my stupidity now. It'll take time, and all I want to do is find Brimman and kill the bastards.

'They'll only be a day or two behind,' Higuel insists. The older woman is bending to riffle through the bags and sacks that must contain all of the Viking raiders' supplies. She hungrily pulls forth days-old bread and bites into it, only to wince. It must be hard as nails.

'We have bread and cheese and dried meat,' I inform her. 'With the horses. Come, we should leave here.' In that, I include all of them. Higuel stands before me, defiant, his barrel chest puffed out, his bald head shimmering with his rage.

'What of my son and granddaughter?' I want to say that he said they were dead, but I hold my tongue.

'We'll seek them when we hunt down our enemy.' I confirm. Icel is moving through the treeline; perhaps, like me, he fears an imminent attack. Wærwulf has joined him.

'They could be dead by then,' Higuel counters. Penna rounds on the man.

'You said they were dead anyway. A day or two will make little difference if that's the case.' The words are harsh, filled with grief, and Pybba staggers towards his daughter, Edmund and Rudolf close to him.

'I'm sorry, my dear,' he says, his words filled with the remorse of ages. I shudder to hear Pybba so weak, as though even those words exhaust him.

'It wasn't your fault,' she snaps, but there's no sympathy in them.

I turn to face the group.

'When did this happen?'

'Two months ago,' the older woman offers. I don't yet know her name.

'Have you been here for all that time?' I counter.

'No. They've been in hiding, waiting for better weather. They took Penna's home and made it their own for some of that time. We've only been on the road for two weeks, moving at night time.' She sounds exhausted. I'm unsurprised. Still, I'm relieved their captors kept them alive. To my mind, it would have been easier to kill them all apart from Pybba. But then, Pybba no doubt needed his daughter and grandson as a reason to lead them to me and perhaps to aid him following his illness.

'Then they know caution. That should give us the time we need.' But I'm already thinking, and I can tell the others are as well. Rudolf fixes me with a furious gaze. We need to stay here, and yet we also need to protect Pybba and his extended family.

I look to Icel. He stands, just in sight, back to us, glaring into the near distance.

'We need to get moving,' I announce. If I can get them away from here, even if it means giving up some of the horses, then it's only two days ride to Hereford at a steady enough pace that they'll be able to manage. At Hereford, Bishop Deorlaf can provide assistance, send for the rest of my warriors, and order his warriors this way as well. Then I'll have the numbers to counter this new attack. I don't allow my mind to consider the problems of Northumbria or Wessex. This is about Mercia, and I am Mercia's king.

'Come, we'll carry Pybba.'

'You bloody won't,' Pybba snaps, swaying as he reaches out to embrace his daughter. She doesn't welcome the affection, although she does clasp his remaining hand. Her son is wide-eyed and fearful, standing close to the older woman. She's moved on from hunting for food to seeking treasures from the dead men.

'Rudolf, that one there took my wealth,' Pybba points to the man whose hand he severed. 'Get it back for me.'

Rudolf, so used to following Pybba's order, does as he's asked, scampering from his side, although he gives him a sideways look to ensure he'll stay on his feet.

I eye Pybba then. He's going to argue with me about my plans. But then, he should have obeyed my last set of fucking orders rather than rushing off in the Welsh borderlands. He'll just have to bloody put up with it.

Chapter Ten

Pybba's cries reach me for some time after I've sent him back to Hereford on Haden. My horse, for once, has obeyed my command. I hope he continues to do so. Likewise, Penna is mounted on Dever, her father-in-law on Billy, her son on Samson, alongside Jethson, Stilton, Keira as well as Sæbald and Lyfing's mount, who take people or their few remaining possessions. I've also sent Goda and Wærwulf with them to ensure they arrive in Hereford in one piece.

That leaves me with too few horses and too many of my men.

I don't think Goda appreciated the command to return to Hereford, eyeing Hemming meaningfully, but if there's a battle, I'd rather he was there to protect the abductees than young Hemming. And Perry, his mount, is young. If I need someone to flee back to Hereford should something befall us, then Perry and Hemming are the ideal pair. Aside from Perry, I've also kept Leonath's, Petre. If Perry is quick and fleet of foot, Petre is determined and steadfast. He could be bleeding and would still limp home. He's a stubborn shit.

Edmund glowers at me.

'This is a fucking stupid idea,' he informs, with all the tact of shit on his boot.

'Why thank you,' I half-bow towards him. I hear what he's saying, though. It more than likely is a shit idea, but with the jarl's wife and her warriors dead, we need to ensure the rest of the bastards die as well.

'It would have been better to take them back to Hereford?' he continues to glower.

'How?' I ask, my voice quiet. I'm not angry with him, not really. I'm curious as to how he thinks I could have arranged this better.

'They could have walked?' he menaces. His eye flashes danger-ously. I have a feeling he knows he's being a stupid shit but can't stop himself now. Beside him, Hereman rumbles. It's not a word, just a counterpart. Edmund meets his gaze, turning away from my scrutiny.

'What?' There's more bite to Edmund's tone.

'This might be a fucking stupid idea, but yours is ten times worse.' Edmund's lips settle in a thin line. I think this might get violent for a brief moment, but Edmund shakes his head and subsides.

'We're more vulnerable here than we ever have been. We can't run without horses, and Perry and Petre can hardly take half of us each, not when two of them are Icel and Hereman.' Edmund once more holds my gaze with his single, piercing eye. I shrug.

'Aye, I know that. But it would have taken time to return to Here-ford and then get back here. We'll find Brimman, so then there'll be three horses.' It's hardly comforting, and Edmund rolls his eye at me, disgust written into the lines of his face. I consider then if I'm the cause of those lines. Before we met, was he a happier man? Did he smile and cavort? Did he joke and laugh with my brother? I'd ask, but I don't want to know the answer.

We've moved the dead men from their campsite. I'm expecting the one who escaped to return at any moment or to bring with him the rest of the Viking raiders. At least that'll make it easier for us than trying to hunt them down.

The dead from the slaughter field have been left well alone. One of Wærwulf's tasks is to bring people from Hereford who can bury those dead. I don't have the men to perform such a task, and our focus remains the enemy.

Rudolf is almost silent as he stirs whatever's cooking in the pot. It smells meaty, but it'll probably be more oats than meat. The Viking raiders had supplies taken from Penna's home. There aren't huge quantities, but enough to feed them for some time to come.

'Will he be all right?' Rudolf eventually asks. I know he's been brooding on this since assisting Pybba into Haden's saddle, having spoken to Haden for some time beforehand. Rudolf was taking no chances. I didn't find the need to add my caution. I'm sure Haden will behave for Pybba. He wouldn't bloody do it for me.

'Pybba should recover. He's just weak from the fever,' Icel rouses himself to reassure the youngster. I appreciate the words. Icel has a fair knowledge of some healing techniques. Every so often, he does something I don't think he should know how to do. I'd ask him about it, but Icel is reticent about some areas of his long life. Healing is one of them. If I asked him to treat a wound, he'd deny it, but sometimes, his sense overpowers his decision to forget that part of his life.

Rudolf nods, continuing to stir the pot. Lyfing and Leonath have taken the first watch. Lyfing stands just inside the treeline, able to see the slaughter field, although hidden from anyone who might approach it more directly than through the woodlands. Leonath is in the near distance, peering into the woodlands to see if our enemy comes from that direction.

I've allowed a fire because our foemen expect to find their allies here. They'll think it strange if there's no fire or the smell of cooking food drifting in the chill air.

'Is that nearly ready?' I eventually demand of Rudolf. He's been cooking and stirring for what feels like forever. I'm not starving, but I could certainly eat.

Rudolf looks at me as though from far away and then looks down at what he's doing.

'Bugger,' he exclaims, and I smell the sharp tang of the pottage catching on the pot as he swings it clear too hastily, slopping the mixture over the side, where it sizzles and smells even worse.

'Sorry,' he apologises.

'We've eaten far worse,' I assure him. Our foe has helpfully travelled with bowls and spoons, we've swilled them through at the nearby stream, and quite frankly, a bowl is a bloody bowl.

Hastily, the pottage is offered, and those surrounding the fire eat eagerly. It only tastes a little burnt, and no one thinks to complain to Rudolf. There's also some bread from Hereford, kept before we sent the horses home, and I tear into it. After I'm finished, I refill the bowl and take some to Leonath. It's almost too dark to see, but I find him by following the sound of his breathing. There's no other noise.

'Here, eat,' I push it into his hands and move aside to stand a watch while he eats. Again, I feel as though we're being watched. I scour the area close by, seeking out any tell-tale sign of flashing ironware.

'Where is that bastard?' I mutter to myself.

'No sign of him yet,' Leonath assures me between spoonfuls. 'He won't take on eight men? Alone?'

'No, you're probably right,' I confirm. And yet, I would, and Leonath knows it.

Leonath eats quickly, and I leave him with a hunk of bread to keep him going while the rest of us attempt to get some sleep. Come the morning; we have fucking Viking raiders to hunt down.

It feels strange to roll in my cloak without the usual nicker from Haden, and for a while, I can't sleep, thinking of how he fares and when he might return to me. The men of the camp are as slow to settle as I am, and no sooner have I fallen asleep than Icel wakes me for my turn on watch.

'Nothing,' he rumbles. He's taken the difficult watch, so he's had a broken night's sleep. I told him I'd do it, but Icel can be a law unto himself.

'My thanks,' I murmur, making way for him to settle in my warm patch close to the smouldering fire. I stride out into the woodlands. I consider how many times I've done this before. While men and women sleep, beasts as well, apart from night-time owls, I've been awake more often than not, watching, waiting, hand never far from my seax. It doesn't bear thinking about.

I listen carefully, the noise of our small camp obscured by distance. In the quiet time, I consider the demands of the archbishop of York. Is he right to approach me? Should the Saxon kingdoms devise a means of coming together to counter the Viking raiders? Is it the only way we'll prevail?

Or, as I believe, is it merely the desperate actions of men determined to force another to stand in the path between them and the Viking raiders? My experience of Wessex and Mercia working together against the Viking raiders has soured any enthusiasm for such a project. But perhaps I could look to the Welsh kingdoms. As this newest infiltration shows, the Viking raiders don't see boundaries. They only see possibilities.

I muse to myself, considering the advantages and disadvantages, aware that while I don't want to ally with the archbishop or King Alfred, there'll be others who think the same of the Welsh kingdoms. Still, I don't dismiss the thought, and as dawn begins to break, I return to my warriors, aware that today, we'll continue our adventure on foot. I wish I'd thought to wear a better pair of bloody boots.

The going is slow, as I knew it would be. My warriors, encumbered with their weapons and supplies, are surprisingly lacking in complaints. Leonath and Hemming walk as well, Petre and Perry taking some of the heavier goods, such as the food and our thick cloaks, which are little good to us even though it's cold, because we sweat from being the ones to forge paths through, over and under, the undergrowth of the woodland.

We could have taken the road, but no, I opted for this, even as slow going as it is.

It's easy to pick out the path our enemy took to their campsite, and so we follow it in reverse. I'm alert, eyes peering into the gloom when not focused on where I place my next foot. Rudolf scampers at the front, Hemming close to him. The two are light on their feet. I envy them with such grace as I once more trip on an unseen tree route.

'We should have brought the horses,' Edmund complains, not for the first time, at the noise.

'Shut the fuck up,' I bark. Icel turns to me, a smirk on his lips.

'In the reign of King Wiglaf, I had no horse,' he offers. 'I slipped through the woodlands like a wraith. No one could track my path.' I shake my head. Icel almost grins at the memory, only for his face to turn sullen once more. I thought the memory was a good one, but perhaps not.

'In the reign of King Coelwulf, second of his name, I stubbed my toe and fell on my arse,' Edmund counters. I shake my head. I should find myself some less foul-tempered warriors to escort me. But, where would the fun in that be?

The woodlands are alive with the sound of birds busy at their tasks, and more than once, a rustle in the undergrowth has me reaching for my seax, only for a hare or stout to appear, see me, and scamper away. I think I'm more scared of them than they are of me.

'How much further?' Lyfing complains as he hops on one foot. I'm pleased he's stubbed his toe and that I'm not the only one to struggle to stay on two feet.

'Fuck knows,' Edmund helpfully offers. I don't know either. I'd ask Pybba, but of course, he's not here anymore.

'I think it's thinning,' Rudolf calls back over his shoulders. I wince at the volume of his reply. It reverberates through the trees, startled birds taking flight. I'd tell Rudolf to hush, but the sound of iron being pulled from weapons belts is suddenly louder.

'My lord king,' Edmund offers me with no enthusiasm and a great deal of bile. 'I believe we've found your enemy.'

And we have.

'Rudolf, Hemming, get back here,' I shout the order, hand on my seax, pulling the shield from where I've been carrying it over my back. I don't know how many foemen there are, but I can feel their menace and detect flashes of bright eyes and iron weapons. Behind me, Perry and Petre stop, far out of reach. They've been picking their own path, and their reins are tied tightly to saddles. They'll run from here if they need to do so.

The youngsters come quickly, avoiding falling over felled branches and stones that jut from the packed earth floor.

'Who the fuck are you?' Icel calls, his words sending yet more creatures fleeing from the trees. In the far distance, a woodpecker falls silent. I'd not realised I was counting his loud knocks until they died away. Three hundred and sixty-two. He's evidently been my companion for some time.

There's no response from the enemy, and that's more telling than sound.

'We'll take them all,' I glower at my warriors, gaze settling on Hemming and the scar on his cheek from the last time we fought a contingent of our enemy a few months ago. What wounds will we gather this time?

'Aye,' Lyfing confirms. He stands to the end of our short line of warriors, his gaze half on any potential attack from behind. Hereman is doing the same from the other end of our short line. Beside me, Edmund and Icel are ready. We're few in number, but we'll prevail.

And then the extent of our enemy becomes apparent, and for a moment, I reconsider my optimism. There are more than double our number. They glimmer with iron and helms, and some even wear byrnies. I catch sight of Brimman to the rear, his gaze calling to me. He's laden with supplies, but no one rides him. I don't imagine he'd let anyone sit in his saddle. I'm surprised he carries as much as he does. Perry and Petre echo his neigh of welcome. The horses are pleased to see one another.

'Focus on the ones without byrnies,' I speak as an aside. I can't see that my men don't know how to fight superior numbers, but I need to say something.

But our enemy holds in position, unmoving. Are they waiting for someone else? Do they think the rest of the allies will appear from behind us?

I allow them a few moments, but I will not wait indefinitely.

'What the fuck are they doing?' Hereman growls. He's ready. I'm ready. We're all bloody ready. But still, the enemy stays away from us. Edmund mutters beneath his breath. I glance at him and note his usual pale visage. This is the worst part for Edmund. It always has been. Yesterday was the aberration when he was desperate to kill. Now his usual worries assail him.

I also squint at Icel. He holds his seax and shield in loose hands, his breathing even, preparing for what will come. Does he even worry anymore, or has he killed enough men that it doesn't matter?

It's one of the horses who give them away. I think it's Perry who squeals with fright, but I could be wrong. I turn, eyes narrowed, and see one of the bastards trying to take our remaining horses. Petre bucks, our enemy's hold on his rein slipping away. Petre's chestnut coat catches a stray burst of sunlight, and I see the man's smirking face, his thick black beard and meaty hands.

To finish the task, Petre rears, stamping down on our foeman's foot as he fumbles for the reins again. The man's howl of rage is all it takes. Icel leads the men onwards, Rudolf and Hemming rushing to protect the horses. There are three of our enemies trying to steal the horses. I want to help but with Petre and Perry to assist them; they outnumber the enemy.

I focus on the bastards before me.

They're still not moving to engage us, but Icel has decided for them. He thunders towards them, and the first man he encounters takes the full force of his fist. Our enemy shudders to the ground. Icel doesn't even stop to stab him, but Lyfing bends to do so behind him.

Hereman's ambling run seems to shake the forest floor. I scurry after them. We might be outnumbered, but that's an advantage. The Viking raiders, caught by surprise, despite everything, fumble to counter the attack. Icel kills another with a slash of his seax across an exposed throat. Hereman fights two men at once. The woodlands are alive with the attack. Overhead, what birds remained, take flight, and I focus on my first target.

He wears no byrnie but has an overly large shield held before him, a war axe in his hand. Above his hair, he wears a dented helm. His eyes menace from behind the bent nose guard. I notice his stance, the way he holds his weight on his back foot, not his front, and I plough into him using my shield and the heft of my shoulder.

His war axe hand flails feebly, and he hits the floor while my foot stays weighted on his front one. He hits the hard ground with a clatter of elbows, shield and war axe. I grin into his bleeding mouth where he's bitten his tongue. I slide my blade through his neck, turning aside so that I don't watch him choke on his own blood.

'Bastard,' I huff through tight lips.

I turn to face two men, one to the left and one to the right. Their eyes flicker from the dying man to me. I menace the man to my left, gritting my teeth and growling simultaneously. He takes a step back, face filled with fear, even as I turn too quickly, and slice my seax along the other man's byrnie. He thrusts his shield before him, but it's too late, and a line of blood erupts. With my seax hand raised, I use my elbow to knock the other man who's recovered his poise and now thinks to attack me from behind.

The crunch of the impact is satisfying. The dampness down my sleeve fucking isn't.

The rebound forces my seax against the second man's throat, and the blade just nicks it as his shield knocks my hand aside. I feel a blade coming too close to my back. I jump clear of them both, right over the dead man, and turn to face them. The broken-nosed man glowers at me from behind tear-filled eyes. He lifts his elbow, smears more blood over his face, and then spits it aside. The other man's teeth are gritted, but I eye the blood that's started to drip down his byrnie. He's far from dead, but first blood goes to me, for both of them.

Hands and elbows, feet and knees, who cares what does it? It's only a blade that forces blood to the surface.

The bleeding-nosed man threatens me. I offer him a raised eyebrow and take a step back. I don't want to fight over the dead man. The daft sods follow me, not even looking where they're going. The second man stumbles, falling over the slippery wetness of his fallen comrade. He drops to his knee, his shield hitting him in the nose, and now they both look like they've been in a fist fight with one another.

I shake my head at the sight of them and then rush into the first man, whose nose I broke with my elbow. His tear-filled eyes must block his vision, and it's too easy to raise my hand and stab into his chest. I don't think he even sees the movement. He sways from side to side, and I have the impression he believes he's moving toward me. He falls, landing on the first man to die, with a terrible wet sound, and now I only have one enemy. But he's pissed.

'Skiderik,' he calls to me.

'Aye, if you like,' I retort. With two dead men, well, one dead man and one who shudders in death, we really need to move aside from the slick floor. I take another step back and feel a blade at my back. I turn, dismissing the first man, and feel the sting of something slicing my byrnie. Other men might look and move their hands to feel for blood, but I swing my shield, knock the seax aside and grin at my new opponent.

He's a blond-haired brute, an almost white beard and moustache framing a thin face. He wears no helm, but his body is encased in a shimmering byrnie. I wince against its brightness, so used to the darkness beneath the trees. He carries a seax and a war axe but no shield. Looking behind him, I see movement amongst the trees and consider if there are even more of them than I first thought.

A horse neighs, and I hear hooves over the hard-packed earth. I know they're coming closer and closer, but I don't turn to look. If it's Rudolf or Hemming, then all will be well. If it's one of the enemies, then I might be well and truly fucked.

'Come on, you bastard,' I menace him with my seax. A grin touches his cheeks, only to drop away. I breathe deeply, listen with half an ear, and just as my enemy looks like he's about to rush away, I launch myself to the right, rolling, ensuring my hand stays out on the right side of my body, dropping my shield at the same time.

I scramble to my knees, hand reaching for my dropped shield, even as Perry crashes into the too-bright man, sending him to the ground where his head bounces up and down, impacting an upright tree root. I watch his eyes dim and grimace.

'Fucking bollocks,' I roar to Hemming even as I hear Hereman's laughter. Such a move is more like something that mad fucker would do. Hemming is bent low over Perry's shoulders, and I want to watch what he's doing, but now my initial enemy rears before me.

'Right, come on with you then,' I huff, staggering to my feet. The man's eyes flicker from side to side. He must see that his allies are dying and that his only chance of living is to escape, and yet he fights me. I admire his stones.

His seax wavers before him. His nose is a bloom of blood, and fluid drips from the thin cut I landed on his byrnie. He's far from dead.

Feeling unsteady on my feet after my roll, I take a moment, eyeing up my opponent. I want to dismiss him, but the fact that he still stands and faces me means that despite my derogatory thoughts about his skills, he is a man who knows that standing and fighting are what really matters.

Perhaps we'll slug it out between us. Maybe we'll take it in turns to slash one another.

Fuck that.

I rush him, dropping my shield to the floor and pushing him down with my bunched fist. I aim my blow to land on where he already bleeds, and I feel his heat and slickness. For a moment, I think he'll hold his posture. I kick him, aiming for his knee. He buckles, falling backwards, and as he tumbles to the ground, I follow him down, blade ready to slice his throat only, he too lands heavily, and one of his ally's seaxes erupts out of his eye, from where it's been abandoned in the ground by one of the dead.

I rear back, grimacing at the heat of another dead enemy. I stand and take in what's happening around me. We're doing well, but the battle isn't won yet. Hemming has Perry under his command and is heading back towards me, Brimman being led behind him. I don't catch sight of Petre, but I do see Rudolf repeatedly punching a prone figure on the ground. Rudolf's furious, and yet he fights with concise movements. I admire him for holding onto the threads of his anger.

Edmund faces four men, Icel battling his way to his side. At Edmund's back, there's a thick tree trunk, the branches of the tree only beginning far above his head. I consider going to help him, but if the two of them can't fight off four of the fuckers, then there's no hope for the rest of us.

My gaze is drawn to Leonath and Lyfing. They fight back-to-back. Both of them have an enemy trying to kill them. Yet, they fight with the easy confidence of trust in one another. I don't believe they need my help.

A rumble of outrage draws my eye, and I spy Hereman. He's surrounded, and I amble to a run, eager to help him. Why I consider the daft fucks have decided to fell the tallest man here, I've no idea. But five of them think Hereman an easy target.

'Rudolf.' He looks to me as his enemy drops to the ground and then to Hereman and jogs to meet me, casually bending to stab a man whose reaching hand thinks to trip him.

'I'll go this way.'

'Aye, my lord. You do that,' Rudolf's barely broken a sweat. I curse his youth as I slash into the back of one of Hereman's enemies.

'Five against one. That's not playing nice, is it?' I mutter, forging a line through his byrnie so that it slips open. He turns, mouth open, and I jab my seax into his teeth, wincing at the sound of teeth over the blade.

'Bastard,' I slide him from the blade and aim at the next man.

He's old and lined, grey-haired, and sprightly. He has more scars than skin, and I offer him a quirk of my eyebrow.

'Well met, fucker,' I continue. He carries a huge war axe and lifts it to counter the blow. I aim at him with my seax. My shield counters the war axe, but the judder through my arm makes it throb.

'How can you even lift that?' I ask him, noting the thick slab of muscle on his upper arms. He grins, showing me a mouth missing most of its teeth, a thin tongue poking through his gums.

'Well, it's not because you're pretty,' I confirm, trying again with my seax, but he skips out of my reach and, indeed, out of the circle. I see that Rudolf's engaged with one of the Viking raiders and that Hereman has finished off one of the others. The body lies still and bloody, pouring its last into the hard earth. The odds are more even now, but I've got the mean-looking fucker to contend with.

I follow him, keeping my shield before me. I don't want to be hit by that war axe. It's probably heavier than my ceremonial helm. It'll knock me to the ground, that's for sure. But it takes him both hands to get a grip on the weapon, and as he swings it one more time, he leaves the right side of his body exposed. Holding my shield to protect me as much as possible, I rush into him, slashing with my seax and raising a thick line of blood on his right arm. I follow up by stabbing beneath his arm pit, and still, the war axe hits my shield, knocking me aside so that I stumble into him, and we both fall to the floor.

I land atop him, wary of his war axe and my seax. I'd look a fucking idiot if I sliced myself with my blade. I'm taller than him, and yet my head only reaches his chin. I can feel his body beneath me, straining to roll me clear. I try to aim my knee at his stones, but I'm too low to do that. I want to stab him with my seax, but my arm thrums with the reverberation of the fall, making it difficult to clasp my blade. My opponent rocks from side to side, heels digging into the ground.

Increasing the grip on my seax, I lift it high, hopeful of hitting his neck, but he veers away from the attack, swinging his head aside, and it hits the ground with a dull twang.

'Fuck this,' I mutter, finding somewhere to place my hands on the ground and rear backwards, knees sliding to either side of my enemy. My seax snicks his byrnie but not enough to draw blood. I'm above him, and still, he bucks and twists, trying to dislodge me, and somehow, he manages to lift his war axe one-handed. I sense it behind me. I've trapped his legs, not his arms. If it hits me, I'll be dead or knocked unconscious.

I growl, lift my hand and again try and impale him. But this time, my blade bounces from his byrnie, the slickness of my hand compromising the grip.

'Are you going to fuck around like that all day?' Hereman's voice drifts to me. Wonderful. He's killed all his enemies, and I'm the one left to look like a bloody arse.

'Give me a few fucking moments,' I menace. I reach out with my left hand, aiming to knock aside the enemy war axe, but it's not enough. The man's grip is fierce on his weapon.

I'm aware of movement behind me, but trust Hereman to watch my back while I labour to kill the damn bastard. Once more, I try and pierce my enemy with my seax, and only then do I realise the fights left him. He no longer resists beneath me but rather lies quiet, silent. I glance at his face, unsure what I'll find and grimace at the seax sticking through his forehead, piercing him to the ground. Hereman's hand still holds the handle.

'There was no need to panic,' Hereman offers conversationally, offering me his hand so that I can stand. I pull on his arm, but he doesn't so much as skip forward. My weight is nothing to him.

'Good, good, fucking good,' I retort, turning as I stand. Rudolf has killed his enemy and now wipes his blade on the man's tunic. I circle, surveying what's happening, but, as I expected, my men have prevailed, as I knew they would. None of the enemy move, and my warriors bend and dip, checking they're all genuinely dead.

Hemming rides Perry towards me, a grin on his face to add to the slash of maroon that covers his chin and helm.

Rudolf shakes his head as he surveys the scene before him, and then he dips, rustles through the man he's just killed weapons belt and stands holding what looks to be a heavy purse containing coins or silver.

'Bastards,' he exclaims.

'Is everyone uninjured?' I demand. I'm breathing heavily. I can't say I'm impressed with my performance, but I can't be the one who always kills all the enemies.

'Aye.'

'Yes.'

'Are you?' The responses assure me that we're all well as I stride towards Brimman. The horse fixes me with a fiery glare. If I didn't know better, I'd take it as a complaint that we didn't come sooner. Hastily, I lift down the heavyweights on his back. One sack contains pungent cheeses; another contains a sack that rattles as though filled with gems and coins. I also notice a poorly healing scar down his rear right leg and that he seems to limp a little.

'Is he well?' I ask Rudolf. Rudolf's abandoned his perusal of the dead man's wealth and whispers to Brimman. I catch the eye of Edmund. He shows little sign of having been in a battle. His boots seem clear of blood, and his byrnie is spotless. Did he bloody kill anyone? It doesn't look like it.

'Is this all of them?' Leonath calls. He's moving amongst the dead, kicking them to check they're truly lifeless. 'I count nineteen of them,' he continues.

'And how many did we encounter the first-time round?'

'Twenty-three, well, twenty-four including the lady jarl.' Rudolf confirms. I might have known he'd have taken a full accounting.

'It sounds like a full ship of Viking raiders,' I suggest. I'm unsure how we'll know if we've killed them all. But I don't expect more to attack us, not now.

'So, we can return to Hereford?' Icel demands.

I want to say yes, I really do. It's no fun being on foot. Our progress is far too slow, and I need to contend with the problem of the archbishop of York and King Alfred. Or do I? Maybe we should stay here, just to be sure there are no more of our enemy.

'Maybe,' I attempt.

'It's a yes or a no,' Edmund's voice is petulant. 'If we've killed them all, there's no need to bloody linger.' I consider then that he knows why I don't want to return to Hereford and the problems facing Mercia's kingdom. It's far easier to hunt down our enemy and kill them than it is to make more far-reaching decisions.

'Aye, we return to bloody Hereford,' I concede. But I'm not happy about it. Not at all.

Chapter Eleven

T he going is tediously slow with only three horses between us. We've opted not to ride, and the horses easily keep pace with us.

Emerging from the tree cover, we face the aftermath of our encounter with the vengeance-seeking jarl's wife. The place is strewn with bodies, pale flesh on display, as well as the grey and almost brown colour of the long-since dried blood. I don't get close enough to look closely. It's evident that they've been set upon by the scavengers making this area their home, an abandoned arm in my path showing chew and bite marks before I kick it aside. The smell is becoming noxious.

All the same, I don't like leaving them there, but Edmund presses on. He doesn't even pause to look, unlike Rudolf and Icel, who detour to kick and glower at the bodies, just in case. Rudolf dips and grips something from one of the dead, but I don't ask him what. Icel, meanwhile, scowls down at the deceased. I think he's counting them, or perhaps, looking for faces he might recognise. The pair are forced to run to catch up when we don't stop our onwards journey, and Rudolf comes to my side to slip a coin into my hand. I turn it, glowering down at the image of bloody King Burgred.

Edmund is silent, an uneasy presence amongst our group. His shoulders are tense, his posture angry. Not for the first time, I wish he were an easier-going individual, more likely to laugh like Hereman or rumble his complaints, as Icel does. But no. Edmund is a moody sod.

Luckily, the weather stays cold enough to make the activity of walking almost pleasurable. But still, I wish we could ride. I don't want to return to Hereford and the problems there. But neither do I want the trip to drag out. I shake my head. I'm as fucking contrary as Edmund.

'Brimman will be well with some decent food and rest,' Rudolf assures me. He walks beside the older horse. Brimman has been badly treated. His coat has rubbed away in places where his saddle has been fitted too tightly, sacks and supplies added to it so that the Viking raiders had no need to carry anything. For now, he plods without saddle or reins, allowing his skin to breathe and begin the process of healing. I've not noticed, but someone has thought to dab some ointment on him. I don't think it was Rudolf, but I don't ask. I have my suspicions, and that's what they'll remain.

That first night, we shelter in a shepherd's hut, sturdier than the one close to the River Wye. We have a fire and even find something half decent to eat from the saddlebags we found, but Edmund paces outside the hut, his boots resounding through the thin walls. I'm not the only one to glare in his general direction with frustration.

'Get your arse in here,' Hereman eventually calls to his brother.

'Fuck off,' Edmund retorts.

I look to Hereman, but it's Rudolf who voices the questions on everyone's lips.

'What's eating him?'

'Why?' Hereman asks, a glint in his eyes. 'Is he behaving any differently from normal?' Hereman smirks as he speaks, and Rudolf chuckles softly. Edmund is more on edge than in the past, but he's never been an easy travelling companion.

We settle to sleep, wrapped in cloaks and close to the fire. Edmund takes the first watch, Icel the third, and I take the second. And so, the night passes fairly quickly, as does the next day. My feet ache from all the walking, but I keep my mouth shut. Edmund is doing enough bitching for all of us. Once more, we seek shelter in an abandoned shepherd's hut, but, in the morning, I hear the thunder of hooves coming ever closer as soon as we resume our journey back to Hereford.

'Bugger,' I exclaim, turning to ensure my men are ready. I'm not sending anyone to the front to scout, and no one protects the rear. There seems little point. Often, we can see a fair distance from the peaks we traverse in any direction, and where we can't, I don't believe having a few more moments to prepare will aid us. Not when we're on foot.

But the horses that pound towards us are recognisable, and I grin to see Haden tossing his head and generally being unmanageable as he tries to outpace the other horses. Wærwulf and Goda lead the return of our horses, but there are others as well. Gardulf and Cuthwalh have joined them, and I squint at the strange collection of warriors.

'My lord king.' Wærwulf speaks with relief, but his use of my title warns me I'm not going to like what he's about to say.

'Tell me, and do it quickly,' I order as Haden comes to my side, lowering his head and hitting my chest with his warm breath. The other horses eagerly welcome their riders, while Brimman is clearly pleased to be a part of his pack once more.

Wærwulf looks at me, but his glance settles on Edmund. I notice then that Gardulf is muttering urgently to his uncle, and my heart stills.

'Tell me, quickly,' but I'm standing beside Wærwulf, and he drops his voice. Rudolf, as always so alert to these things, begins a loud conversation with Cealwin about how Pybba fares, and I'm grateful to him when Wærwulf speaks.

'Lady Cyneswith has disappeared,' Wærwulf informs me hurriedly. 'There's a fear that she's been captured by the enemy.'

My mouth drops open in shock, my heart hammering in my chest. My aunt? Why would anyone want her? I turn to gaze at Edmund and notice that Hereman has taken it upon himself to inform his brother of what's happened. The weak man in me is pleased not to face Edmund's wrath.

'I sent her to Kingsholm,' I mutter, my voice urgent, as I make ready to mount Haden.

'Aye, my lord king, you did, but then there was a report from Northampton of some problems, so she set out for there but never arrived.'

'How many warriors did she have with her?' If she travelled alone, my anger will know no bounds. My warriors should have known not to let her go alone.

'Ten, my lord king. A suitable number,' Wærwulf confirms, as though already determined to counter my complaint against my men.

'And where are they?' I demand, even as Edmund lets forth a roar of pain and outrage combined.

'Stop fucking about,' Edmund bellows at the men, startling those who don't yet know the news. 'Get on your bloody horses, and ride.' He grips Jethson's reins and jumps into his saddle, his intentions clear, as he urges Jethson onwards.

'Edmund,' I use my loudest voice, the one I employ in battle, to ensure my orders are obeyed. 'Hold,' I urge him, but there's no chance he'll do as I say. Hereman meets my gaze as he struggles to mount, and Gardulf is already streaming after his father.

'Stay close to him. We'll follow,' I urge Hereman. He nods, settling himself and gently encouraging Billy.

I meet the shocked eyes of the rest of my warriors then.

'My aunt has disappeared,' I announce. 'Somewhere between Kingsholm and Northampton.'

Then I turn to Wærwulf.

'Tell me, where are my warriors?' And now Wærwulf hangs his head low.

'Hiltiberht managed to escape. He returned to Kingsholm, wounded but alive.'

'And.' I can tell I'm not going to like what he says next.

'Siric and Eadberht are dead.'

'Fuck,' I explode, grief shattering me. My warriors. Good men, both of them.

'Hiltiberht didn't stay to watch what happened. They sent him for reinforcements, but so far, the others haven't been found.'

'Bollocks,' I cry again, aware my cheeks are damp as I direct Haden to follow the path of Edmund. I've only been gone a few days. How can such a catastrophe have befallen my aunt and my warriors when Mercia's borders should have been secured?

I vow then to kill all the fuckers who've taken my aunt and killed my men.

All of them.

* * *

Haden thunders beneath me. The speed of his passage wipes the tears from my face as I consider my dead men. Death has ever stalked my warriors. The older men, who came with me when we rode into the borderlands last time, are the exception and not the norm. Men who live so long are lucky in battle or extremely skilled, knowing when to pick a fight and when to leave it well alone.

I don't think I'll have that ability should my aunt have been harmed.

I consider what might have befallen her. Have the Viking raiders taken her? Or is this some ploy by Alfred of Wessex to secure my assistance? Or perhaps, even something that the bloody Archbishop of York has arranged? It must certainly have been planned. They've considered all of this. How could they have known that I was seeking Pybba? How could they have known it would be my aunt who went to fulfil whatever was needed in Northampton? Unless, of course, they didn't, and this was actually an attempt to apprehend me? Are there still Viking raiders in Mercia who think to kill me as the jarls of Repton commanded only last year? Fuck. It boils me.

It's a relief to see Hereford come into focus ahead, the haze of smoke assuring me that the settlement is continuing its activities despite what's happened to my aunt.

I don't want to stop, but it's been a long day, and the horses need the rest. We clatter over the bridge, and I dismount to be immediately greeted by Bishop Deorlaf, who's arrived back at his bishopric in my absence. His face is etched with worry. Behind him, I notice that Archbishop Wulfhere has joined him and now smirks. Has the fool thought to chase me down? I can't see why else he'd be here. How I want to wipe that smug smile from Wulfhere's face. But there's an argument already brewing, and I shake my head, holding out my hand to stay Bishop Deorlaf's words.

'Give me the fastest fucking horse you have.' Of course, it's Edmund who argues with the stablemaster. Hereman watches on, even as he tends to his mount. Gardulf, his lips a thin line of displeasure, dusts down his trews. I can well imagine why he has hay and straw stuck to his legs and a fat lip brewing. It would take a braver man than me to get between Edmund and the fastest horse in the stables at the moment.

'You need to rest,' I hurry to get myself between the man and Edmund. 'You can't go haring off into the countryside alone.'

Edmund turns to face me so quickly that I'm surprised his eye can focus on me. It blazes with fire, fury and desperation. I can't see he'll heed my words. I consider my best option. I can refuse to let Edmund leave, but he'll go anyway. I can give him my blessing and send him with some of my men so I can follow on later. I can't see they'll get far before Edmund needs to sleep, but equally, he can force himself past all endurance, and maybe it's what needs to be done.

I turn to the stablemaster. He's a tall man, arms as powerful as though he's the blacksmith. He knows his stuff. He meets my eyes evenly, and I dip my chin quickly so that he knows he has my respect.

'Is there another horse?' Jethson whinnies indignantly at my words, but his coat is sweat-lathered, and he needs to rest, even if he doesn't realise it.

'Aye, my lord king. We have five fast beasts.' The man's words are assured, my title falling easily from his lips. He knows the worth of those animals, and he's not afraid to vouch for them.

'Have them made ready,' I confirm. Edmund's eye gleams at my words.

I look to Hereman. He nods. I know he wants to go with his brother. Next, I look to Gardulf. He's furious. It might not be good to send him with his seething father. Equally, if I order him to remain, he'll go anyway. The lot of them are bloody bastards.

'You take Hereman and Gardulf with you. Gyrth and Cuthwalh as well. We'll leave at first light and catch you, no doubt sleeping somewhere.' Edmund growls at me, taking one step closer to me, fist pulled tight, and I glower at him.

'Really? Would it make you feel better to fucking hit me?' I demand. The tension in the small courtyard is heavy. I'm aware of everyone breathing, of the rustle of a mouse, somewhere hiding beneath the straw. Time seems to slow as I meet Edmund's incandescent gaze. I grin at him, daring him to do it, but after what feels like a long time, he shakes his head.

'My thanks,' he confirms, reaching for Jethson to relieve him of his saddle.

'We'll do it. Get what you need, and leave while there's still some light to see.'

I'm aware that the stableman has moved away, that he shouts instructions to the two stableboys who scamper to do his bidding. Gyrth has also stalked away to retrieve his possessions, while Pybba has belatedly joined the gathering. He looks hollow and weak, and I know he won't be going anywhere for some time.

Fuck. I don't like my men splitting up like this, and I hate not knowing what's happened to the men who escorted my aunt. Just from a brief look, I can see who's missing, as those who brought the news to Hereford mingle with those who escorted me into the border-lands. I note Ordlaf and Osbert, Ælfgar, Eadulf, Eahric, Ordheah, and Wulfstan. I mourn Siric and Eadberht, who I know to be dead, but what of Beornstan, Ingwald, Eadfrith, Cealwin, Wulfred, Osmod and Oda? Where are they, and how do they fare?

'The same for Billy and your horses, Gardulf and Gyrth. We'll tend to them and bring them on afterwards. Head towards Northampton. We'll find you along the way, and if we don't, then stay in Northampton until we catch up with you. I don't want anyone riding off any further than that alone.' I infuse my voice with as much threat as possible, but I don't see that Edmund will do as I demand. By the time I arrive at Northampton, he'll be long gone.

And then Archbishop Wulfhere bloody speaks.

'It'll be the Viking raiders? Stealing your aunt away to hold you to ransom. This is why you must ally with me and assist me in returning the Northumbrian kingdom to its rightful king.' I round on him then, his strident words echoing in the busy courtyard. All activity comes to an abrupt halt, even those men and women who labour to bring forth a ditch and wall to protect the settlement, as arranged at the witan.

'You sound like you know something about this?' I seethe, turning to face him.

I expect to see denial in his eyes, but instead, there's only defiance.

'My lord king,' he bows his head just enough for me to see the hair on the back of his neck, curling beneath his rich tunic. 'How could I know anything about Viking raider activity?' I can hear my breathing and that of the mouse, which has also ceased its scamper-ing. I glower at him, meeting the eyes of Bishop Deorlaf over the bowed head. Bishop Deorlaf shakes his head, just a small movement, and I don't know what it means.

'Rise,' I mutter, turning aside to tend to Haden. I don't have time for such politicking. I have little intention of helping the archbishop, and now I have even less. If he knows anything about what's happened to my aunt, I'll be hard pressed to stop Edmund from severing that neck he so eagerly shows me.

'I have much to discuss with my men.' I mutter to both church-men. 'I'll join you in the hall momentarily.' With that, I expect the discussion to be at an end. I move to relieve Haden of his saddle, aware that most of my men do the same, apart from Hereman, Cuth-walh, Edmund, Gyrth and Gardulf, who prepare to leave once more. Jethson eyes me with a tired expression. I'm unsurprised. Edmund has ridden him hard to get here, and what has he accomplished? Little more than the rest of us.

'My lord king.' It appears Archbishop Wulfhere doesn't under-stand my words.

'I'll speak with you when I've dispatched my men,' I throw over my shoulder, trying not to stiffen at his words.

'It would do you well to listen to me now. Your aunt is in danger. My men could aid yours.'

'What men?' I round on him then, shrugging my shoulders and looking around as though mounted warriors might appear from behind me or even above me. 'You have no men, archbishop. If you had men, then by rights, they should be in York, with you.'

A mutinous expression touches Archbishop Wulfhere's lips.

'What? You have more warriors?' I demand. I want to speak with Edmund before he leaves, and this fucking bag of wind is slowing me down.

'My lord king.' There's outrage in his voice this time.

'So, you do have more warriors?' The archbishop's failure to respond is all I need to hear. I turn aside once more, stride to Edmund, and grab hold of the reins of the sorrel mount he's been given. The animal has a cream stocking on its front leg, but other than that looks like the edge of a blade after a battle. I envision the animal as fierce. I pretend not to hear the footsteps of the bishop and arch-bishop moving back inside the hall.

'Get the fuck off,' Edmund growls at me, but I don't, even when he puts his hand over mine and tries to lever it from the reins. Only when he subsides, do I relinquish my grip and begin to speak.

'She's my aunt, no matter what she is to you. Don't imperil her further, and don't do anything anymore fucking stupid than you already have. And remember. We don't know who the enemy is, and I'll follow you tomorrow. Don't engage with whoever has her.'

Edmund's eye bores into mine.

'I love her,' the words are an anguished cry.

'As do we all, in different ways. Do what you must and what you can, but don't fuck it up.' As I speak, I fix him with my gaze, ensuring he knows the weight behind my words.

'I'll find you, and we'll find her together, and together, if anyone has harmed her, we'll wipe them from the face of this earth.'

'Aye, Coelwulf. I know.' The words are spoken on an exhalation, and I nod, relieved to see him listening and understanding what I'm saying for now. I doubt the same will be true once he finds the tracks of whatever's befallen, my aunt. 'And tell that whinging fart of an archbishop that I'll personally geld him if he had anything to do with this.'

I nod, a tight smirk on my lips, and then the five men lead their horses from the stables and through the gateway. The thundering of hooves can be heard for a long time; throughout that time, no one speaks or returns to their labours. Edmund's words could have been spoken by anyone there, and no one would have taken umbrage.

Chapter Twelve

I stride into the hall, fury guiding my steps. Pybba has returned to his family, and they're settled around one of the tables. I raise my eyes to smile at them, but then the scowl immediately returns. I catch sight of Bishop Deorlaf, eating beside the archbishop, and I swerve to avoid them both. I can tell, or interpret from Deorlaf's martyred expression, that he's enjoying Wulfhere's presence as little as I am.

Damn the man. Why did he have to come here?

'My lord king,' Archbishop Wulfhere's words cut through my strident steps. I breathe in deeply. I must speak with him, so it seems.

'Bishop Deorlaf, Archbishop Wulfhere.' I think my voice is almost pleasant, but Deorlaf's wince assures me that it isn't. I glimpse the thinning of his lips. I'm unsure if it's directed at me or the pestilent bastard that won't stay his flapping tongue.

'I would speak with you, my lord king, once more about the events in Northumbria.'

I eye the seating arrangement and realise I have no choice but to perch between the two men. Fucking wonderful.

I sit with ill-grace, aware I stink of blood, sweat and horse shit, my thoughts turning to what my aunt would think of that, only for the memory of her on previous occasions to remind me of what's happened to her. The archbishop would do well not to speak to me now, but he's too desperate. I wish I'd gone with Edmund. I'd sooner face our enemy than bloody Archbishop Wulfhere.

'You've had some time to consider my suggestion?' Archbishop Wulfhere begins before I even manage a mouthful of the succulent breaded fish laid out before me. My belly growls with hunger. I chew, taking my time, not wanting to respond just yet. I merely want to eat, find a bucket of water to pour over my head, and sleep. I don't want to discuss the archbishop's requirements.

'I've not. I've been seeking one of my lost men, killing the bastard enemy, and getting back here as soon as possible. At first light, I'll leave again.'

'But time is of utmost importance,' Archbishop Wulfhere persists, wincing at my sharp tone. I confess it brings me pleasure to shock him with my coarse words. And that surprises me. He's used to dealing with the Viking raiders. I can't imagine that they're aware of his sensitivities.

'I'm sure Jarl Halfdan will face a struggle against the Picts. I can't see that he'll be returning anytime soon.' But that's not really my answer. I sigh and turn to face him. 'Archbishop Wulfhere. I understand your wish to reclaim the kingdom from Jarl Halfdan. I would only wish that Mercia had the warriors to assist you with such a desire. As you must be aware, from your brief time here, Mercia is threatened from all sides. There are enemies everywhere, thanks to King Burgred's weak stance against the Viking raiders. They still think of claiming the kingdom for themselves. They held Repton for some time, as you must know, and Torksey, and an attempt on Gainsborough.'

'The Grantabridge jarls have passed a quiet winter. I know that won't last. I only fought against Jarl Halfdan recently in the north, just to the south of the River Humber. It's my deepest regret that he didn't fall beneath my blade. I had believed him dead, and then all this would be over. But, for now, my focus must remain on Mercia and not Northumbria.'

'But, my lord king, Mercia has always been an ally to Northumbria.' I shake my head and reach for more fish. Once more, I take my time chewing and considering my answer.

'Mercia has not long been an ally to Northumbria. For centuries, Northumbria and Mercia have tried to best each other, killing men, women and children in the process and murdering one another's royal family members. I accept that we now face a common enemy, but Northumbria has even fewer warriors than Mercia. Should Jarl Halfdan be killed fighting against the Picts, would your king have enough support? Would your king be able to hold any of the royal sites? Even the mighty fortress of Bamburgh?'

'With a strong ally, yes, we could.' The archbishop refuses to see the reasoning behind my answer. I admire him then, even as I curse my reputation for accomplishing the impossible.

'I am not that strong ally. Not at this time. If we manage to dislodge the Grantabridge jarls and tame an unruly London, then yes, perhaps we could be, but at the moment, those things aren't going to happen.'

'You can't allow your concern for one woman to allow two kingdoms to fall.' I wince at Archbishop Wulfhere's tone, even as Bishop Deorlaf inhales sharply, nostrils flaring.

I stop eating and turn to face Archbishop Wulfhere.

'If not for my aunt, I wouldn't be Mercia's king, and then Mercia would be as broken as Northumbria. My aunt has done all she can to ensure Mercia remains whole. Other than fighting beside me in the shield wall, there's nothing she won't do for Mercia, and I can assure you, she'd do that if she bloody could. I must rescue her, no matter what, and if she's dead, then Mercia will suffer. And if she's dead, then I won't give a shit about the kingdom of Northumbria. On that, you have my oath.'

Only when I come to a halting stop do I realise that everyone in the hall is listening to me. I turn slowly, meeting the shocked and saddened eyes of those who acknowledge me as their king. Many carry compassionate looks, many more fury, but overwhelmingly, I see understanding and acceptance in those looks. None of us here are blind enough not to see just what my aunt has done for Mercia.

And still, Archbishop Wulfhere opens his mouth to speak.

'I think you've said more than enough.' It's Icel who arrests Wulfhere's complaints. He's standing close to the hearth, watching the archbishop with a knowing look in his eyes. He doesn't look wild, furious or even resigned. He does look determined. I nod to thank him for his words and reach for yet more fish. Archbishop Wulfhere says nothing further, but I hear his huff of frustration as I turn to Bishop Deorlaf.

'Tell me, when did everyone leave the witan?'

'The same day as you, my lord king. No one lingered once the witan had come to an end.'

This is what I expected to hear from the bishop, but it sets my mind tumbling down all sorts of paths. I don't yet know who has my aunt. I have a few thoughts in mind, but who, I consider, would be foolish enough to do something such as this? Is it truly the work of the Grantabridge jarls, or is it something to do with Bishop Smithwulf and that man's fixation that Mercia must unite with Wessex? Does he know that my aunt is one of many who will not ally with Wessex?

These holy men are as much of a scrouge on the kingdom of Mercia as the bloody Viking raiders. What I know for sure is that whoever has done this, won't live long to enjoy whatever chaos they hoped to cause.

* * *

It's raining when we leave. Dawn is still a long way off, the clouds hanging low in the dark sky, but it doesn't matter. My men are ready and alert, the horses rested, and no matter what Pybba says, I've ordered him to remain behind. His daughter's grateful for my intervention, as she is for my command that Bishop Deorlaf sends his warriors to seek out her missing daughter and husband. I've alighted on something else as well.

Æthelred, the young lad I found in the stables at Worcester, has attached himself to my men. Somehow, in all the coming and going since Worcester, he's arrived in Hereford. He should have been with my aunt, but it's a blessing he wasn't with her after all. I can't take Æthelred with me now that we ride to an uncertain destination, but Pybba can take command of him.

'Here, Æthelred, come to me,' I'd said the night before. The lad, looking better now with a week of good food in his belly, had come willingly enough.

'This is Pybba.' Æthelred had met the eyes of Pybba with only a slight wince for the welter of bruises on the older man's face. 'He's remaining in Hereford. You're to tend to him, and his horse like you're one of my squires. Pybba will tell you what needs to be done, and you must ask him if you're unsure of anything.' I'd watched Pybba, waiting for him to argue with me, but the other man had simply pursed his lips and nodded unhappily. That solved the problem of the pair of them. For the time being.

'Fucking weather,' Sæbald complains. None of my men is in a good mood, and the weather isn't helping. To know that Siric and Eadberht are both dead is like a dagger to our hearts. And, as is so often the case, we don't even have time to mourn them properly. Our enemy is relentless.

'It's not as though it's not fucking wet enough as it is,' Sæbald continues. I smirk behind the hood of my cloak.

Unsurprisingly, we encounter no one as we begin our journey. I made sure we left while the bishop and archbishop were engaged in the church, the words of their prayers tumbling from behind the walls of the building. I'm sure that when all this is over, I'll have to face Archbishop Wulfhere again, but by then, I'll have killed some more of our fucking enemy. I might just be able to stomach speaking with him about Northumbria and his dreams for dispensing with Jarl Halfdan once that's happened. If Archbishop Wulfhere only knew how much I hungered for that bastard's death, he'd probably dispense with badgering me.

We reach Worcester long before our horses, including the five left behind by Edmund, and my men are exhausted, but still, I call a halt for the night. I'm keen to see what Bishop Wærferth has to say and to know if Edmund came this way. It's still raining. I'm sodden, and so too is Haden. I don't throw off my cloak until I'm in Wærferth's hall. I remove my boots as well, the rich mud turning them the same colour as the horse that Edmund borrowed, which I note is now in the stables at Worcester. But, seeking out Edmund in the hall is a worth-less exercise. He'll be long gone.

'My lord king.' It's evident that Bishop Wærferth has been expecting me, and quickly, my drenched men and I are served with warm food, and our cloaks are taken away to be hung above the fires in the kitchen.

'There's no news,' Bishop Wærferth quickly tells me. 'My men have been scouring the roads, and your men, led by Edmund, left here at first light, having rested for no more than a third of the night.'

'You provided them with fresh horses and food, my thanks.'

'It's the least I could do.' Bishop Wærferth is agitated as I sit beside him. He keeps rubbing one hand inside the other. 'I told her not to go. I was concerned. It seemed too happenstance, but she was adamant.'

'What exactly was the message?'

'The jarls of Grantabridge were threatening to besiege Northampton once more.'

'And what, she went with only ten men?'

'Yes, my lord king. She wouldn't take more than that with her. I should have sent some of my warriors with them.'

'Perhaps, but then we'd be missing them, as well as my aunt. And we'd have more than two dead Mercians. Tell me, where were the bodies found?'

'On Watling Street. Almost in sight of Northampton.'

'So, the attack was brazened and clearly well-planned?'

'It would seem so, yes.'

'And your men have had no success in finding her?'

'I fear my men will only just have reached the site of the attack. Everything happened very quickly. But we sent word to you as soon as possible, and Ealdorman Ælhun is aware. Tell me, did you find your missing man?'

'Yes, and we killed more bastard Viking raiders as well. It was a Viking raider woman who led them, seeking revenge for the death of her husband.' I shake my head as I speak. If not for that damn bitch, my aunt wouldn't have been forced to travel to Northampton. I would have gone in her stead.

'They breed them fiercely in the north,' the bishop muses, not without some appreciation for the jarl's wife's actions.

'They do, yes.'

'Your aunt is a strong and fierce woman as well. She won't give in to anything they demand from her.'

'No, she won't. Have we heard why they've taken her?'

'No. And the lad, Hiltiberht, he was sent on his way before the battle was truly lost so he knows little as well.' I startle, realising that Hiltiberht has joined the rest of my warriors. He stands and talks to them now, and I can see that Icel is clearly questioning him intently.

'It's a bloody mess,' I muse, running my hand through my damp hair, and grimacing at the unpleasant sensation.

'She'll prevail,' Wærferth murmurs, and I do appreciate his trust in my aunt. I want to think the same, but these Viking raiders are bastards, one and all. They sent three hundred warriors to kill me. It was never going to be enough. But to take my aunt? That seems to have been far too easy.

'Do you believe it's the Viking raiders then or something that Bishop Smithwulf or Archbishop Wulfhere have set in motion?'

Bishop Wærferth rears at my words as though I've punched him. I think he'll deny them, but then his lips twist in thought.

'I don't know, my lord king. I didn't consider that possibility. I wouldn't like to think it of them, but the bishop and Archbishop

Wulfhere do seem particularly determined to bend you to their will. I imagine that anything is possible.'

'And so, events in Northampton could have been a bloody ruse?'

'Yes, and one they knew would force your aunt's hand.'

I nod. I'm not happy to have the bishop considering my other scenario. It would be better if it was the bastard Viking raiders. If it's Bishop Smithwulf, then he and I will have a real problem. If it's Archbishop Wulfhere, then he should probably have remained in Northumbria and taken his chances with fucking Jarl Halfdan.

Chapter Thirteen

'Tell me?' I demand from Hiltiberht. He looks from me to Icel, swallows heavily, and then meets my gaze. He's pale beneath his cloak, almost blue, and I don't think it's just with the cold.

'My lord king,' he begins, his voice cracking only a little. 'We rode from here in all haste, but with adequate precautions. The Lady Cyneswith was not remiss in ensuring she was well protected, nor was Ingwald, who led the expedition.'

I nod. I want to tell him to hurry, but I appreciate that this is hard for him. I'm also not about to assign blame to anyone but the fuckers who've taken my aunt.

'All went well for the first day. We travelled quickly, but not too quickly, the roads being poor after the winter.' I nod again. I can sense my impatience for the story to be completed, but I bite down on my tongue, grip one hand inside the other, and stay silent.

'All was well. Lady Cyneswith went ahead, with Siric and Eadberht as her constant companions. Only then one of the hounds, Wiglaf, dashed into the woodlands, and she followed. Siric and Eadberht hurried to catch her, and I called her name, asking her to wait, but then the cries of the hound became fevered, and she ignored us all.'

I close my eyes at this. I can imagine only too well what happened. Whoever attacked my aunt knew of her love for her hound, the dog that once belonged to my brother. No one had told me of the dog's death, but I know that he must be. No one has mentioned the other hound. Where is the animal? I feel my fist clench even tighter.

'Go on,' I urge, my voice hoarse and tight with my fury.

'Beornstan and Ingwald were even quicker to follow, but I was bidden to rush for assistance by Oda. We weren't that far from Warwick, and I dashed away. Only when I returned with half of Ealdorman Ælhun's men, under Wulfsige's command, did I truly know all that happened. The bodies of Siric and Eadberht were badly used.' Hiltiberht's voice quivers at this, and I reach over and grip his shoulder with my hand. I can feel his entire body trembling and tears sheet his face. It's one thing to know that men fall in battle, and quite another to see it laid bare before you. I meet his eyes, but his lip quivers and I swallow against my sorrow.

Siric was a good man. A loyal man. I'll miss him. He shouldn't have died in such a way. Already, he'd dodged death on more than one occasion, my aunt ensuring he lived. I know, oh how I know, that he'd have wanted to give his life to protect her. And Eadberht.

'And Wiglaf. The poor hound was all but slashed in two.' Those words silence me. I find it strange that I can grieve for a dog just as much as I can my lost warriors, and yet, Wiglaf was much more than just a hound to me, and to my aunt.

'And the rest of the men?'

'They were nowhere to be found, my lord king. Even Oda was gone.' Once more, it's hard for Hiltiberht to speak, and I squeeze his shoulder once more.

'And the other hound?'

'Missing, my lord.' His words are edged in guilt and pain.

'Can you take us to the location?' I demand, not wanting him to dwell on it anymore. Now is the time for action.

'Aye, my lord, I can. Ealdorman Ælhun has his men searching already.'

I nod and release my grip on him, the world suddenly rushing back on me. I can see the shocked faces of Icel and Rudolf, Goda and Wærwulf.

'We'll travel at first light. We'll go quickly now. It's been too long already, and we must catch Edmund, Hereman, Gyrth, Cuthwalh and Gardulf as soon as possible.'

Not one of my men argues with me, and that troubles me. I'm not used to their fucking silence.

Ealdorman Ælhun rides with me from Warwick, alongside Wulfsige, the commander of his warriors. Ealdorman Ælhun's face is a mask of tightly suppressed fury. Whatever our differences in the past, he's unhappy about all of this. Deeply unhappy. The words we've shared have been short and sharp, but I'm not about to bring him to task. Worry shrouds him like the dead.

Ahead, the daylight is fading rapidly, but I'm not about to bring a halt to our headlong dash. I trust the horses, and those who race ahead along the roadway to ensure that we avoid all pitfalls. It won't be long until we meet Watling Street, and from there, it won't be far to Northampton, to where my aunt was taken from me and my men murdered.

'I've had scouts prowling the area, and the men and women of Northampton have also been doing all they can. I feel we've left no stone unturned.' Ealdorman Ælhun's voice is rigid with rage as Wulfsige nods along in corroboration. What we're leaving unsaid is what we both know. There's the River Nene close by. If it was the Viking raiders who took her, or even someone acting on Bishop Smithwulf or Archbishop Wulfhere's orders, it would have been too easy to stow her aboard a vessel and take her to wherever they deemed would do me the most damage.

'And Edmund?' I query.

'He rode past with barely a hello, very early this morning or late last night. I've lost track. They changed horses and went on their way. He,' the ealdorman hesitates.

'Is furious,' I conclude. Now isn't the time to discuss Edmund's fury. All that needs to be known is that Edmund is seeking my aunt and the bastards who killed my men and took others elsewhere if they're not dead as well.

'Aye, my lord king,' Ealdorman Ælhun's sudden formality assures me he won't question further. After all, he must know. He spent enough time with my aunt at Northampton when Edmund was in residence to appreciate there's more to them than might first appear acceptable for a lady of her birth, and a man who's merely a member of his lord's household troop.

'Halt,' from in front, where Icel and Goda ride, the cries ripple back through the fifteen men accompanying Ealdorman Ælhun and my own collection of warriors.

'What is it?' I ride onwards, fear making my heart beat more loudly than Haden's hooves. I know my voice wavers.

'It's bloody me,' Edmund calls from out of the growing gloom. I can hear the frustration in his voice, and smell the smoke from a fire, belatedly. 'We've been resting. I intended to resume my search during the night.' Edmund sounds ancient, his voice cracked from lack of use, and as he leers at me from the shadows of the fire, I startle, and so does Haden. My horse nays unhappily, rearing on his back legs so that I'm forced to struggle to reassert my control.

'My apologies,' Edmund murmurs, but Haden recovers quickly enough, and settles easily.

'What have you found?' I demand, dismounting and rushing to Edmund. I fear to ask, and yet I must, all the same. If he sounded ancient, then his appearance is even more shocking. He's weighed down by more than just exhaustion.

'Little and nothing. There are people everywhere searching for your aunt and my lost comrades. There are so many of us that we've been tripping over one another.'

'Then why are you here?' Ealdorman Ælhun demands. 'She was taken much closer to Northampton.'

'She was, yes, but there's a trail, leading this way. I determined we should follow it. I wouldn't put it past those bastards to hide her in plain sight, in the heart of Mercia.'

I shake my head. I can't see it, and yet Edmund sounds desperate, and I know better than to dismiss his suggestion outright.

'You should rest for the entirety of the night,' I order Edmund. 'We're here now, with Ealdorman Ælhun's men. In the morning, I'll visit the place of the attack, and from there, we can determine where we think she's been taken.'

'It'll do you no bloody good,' Edmund complains moodily. 'It's been trampled and disturbed by all those who came since. It's impossible to tell who left what footprints in the mud, and so we have no idea where she's been taken.' His voice is bereft, his shoulders slumped, and his sense of loss is palpable. I could slap the bastard for giving up.

'All the same. It's what we'll do.' I turn then to the rest of my men. 'Goda, Icel, you'll take first watch. Rudolf and Hemming the second, Lyfing and Leonath, the third.' They don't grumble, and neither does Ealdorman Ælhun or Wulfsige show any unease that I don't commission their men to the posts.

Edmund marches from my presence, his shoulders hunched, and from the gloom, Hereman appears. He looks exhausted, his shoulders rounded, while Gardulf merely murmurs in his sleep, and is entirely oblivious to the arrival of so many men, with all the noise that entails. I'd berate him for being a terrible warrior, but I imagine he's had no sleep in the last few days. He must be exhausted. Gyrth appears from where he must have been keeping watch towards the south, whereas Cuthwalh leads back two of the borrowed horses they must have used to get here so quickly. Even the horses exude exhaustion. Cuthwalh grins at me, no doubt relieved to see me. Gyrth tumbles to the ground and is asleep before I can so much as say hello.

'I'll organise the other men,' the ealdorman informs me, dismounting, and barking instructions to his men. I'm grateful for his tact as Wulfstan takes control of the tired horses. Cuthwalh and he murmurs softly to one another.

'He's not slept,' Hereman mumbles, pitching his voice low so that only I can hear. Hereman's tact astounds me. I feel my mouth dropping, and he finds a tired smirk on his lips. 'I'm not that much of an arse. All the time,' he counters quickly. 'And I think he's wrong. I believe Lady Cyneswith has been taken by the Viking raiders, not by Bishop Smithwulf. I can't see that your warriors would be overpowered by their fellow countrymen, and certainly not the weaklings of Wessex. We should go east, not west.'

I nod. I can't help but agree, but my decision is purely based on my gut reaction. I'm not above admitting it might be wrong.

'We'll view the site of the ambush, and then I'll decide,' I repeat and Hereman nods, his eyes lingering on mine.

'He loves her, in his own way,' Hereman confirms. 'He's about as loyal as a dog in heat, but somehow, she overlooks it, and he pretends not to see it. If something's happened to her, it'll kill him. He'll be a man changed.' Hereman pauses then. I don't look away, and he coughs.

'He thinks I don't know, but Gardulf's mother was murdered by the bastard Welsh. If the Viking raiders take Lady Cyneswith, I don't know what he'll do.' And so spoken, Hereman takes himself back to the fire and wraps himself in his cloak. I swear the bastard snores before his eyes are even shut. I know sleep won't find me as quickly. And it doesn't.

Ultimately, I don't allow Hemming to be woken but take his watch. Rudolf, quite wisely, stays away from me, as he watches Watling Street from the north of our campsite. I can hear men tossing uneasily as they try and sleep. The position Edmund settled on for his sleep was on enough of a slant that most of the summit was dry, but at the bottom of the slope, the ground is boggy and fetid. I wouldn't have chosen this location.

I stand on the slope, peering into the south. My thoughts are busy and unpleasant, now that I can spend some time with them. Astride Haden all day, my mind only on getting to Northampton as quickly as possible, I've tried not to consider what might have happened to my aunt. But now, those thoughts consume me, and I feel myself growing as mad with rage as Edmund. Should anyone swerve out of the darkness at me now, I'll kill them before I ask them for a bloody name.

I pace the top of the summit, aware I might disturb my tired warriors, but unable to stop myself. At any moment, I expect Icel to bellow for me to be still, for Hereman to announce he'll spear my bloody feet to the floor if I take another step, but neither of those things happen. And the mass of sleeping men is hardly still. I can tell, from the way men breathe, that they don't sleep, or at least, they don't sleep well. That applies to everyone apart from Gardulf, Hereman, Cuthwalh and Gyrth, who are oblivious, catching up on lost sleep.

What will I do if something has befallen my aunt? I've never thought of myself as particularly beholden to my family. My brother and I were far from allies. I didn't know my mother, and I hardly recall my father in a favourable light. But my aunt? Well, my aunt has been all those things to me that I never had from any other. She's supported me, no matter what I've done. Even when I left Kingsholm and refused to serve my brother, she had half an eye on me. Not that I knew that at the time.

My aunt has always had mine and Mercia's best interests at heart. Without her, what will I be fighting for, if I continue to fight? It is her dream of Mercia that has made me become her king. And I'm not foolish enough that I don't realise that others sense this as well. Is that why they've taken her? Do they mean to make me less of a man? Do they mean to take from me all that emboldens me to be Mercia's king?

On and on I pace, not even turning to my bed when Rudolf calls that our watch is at an end. I allow Leonath his rest as well, and as the sun finally begins to rise, in little more than a thin slit of pink on the far distant horizon, I have no answers and only more questions, but Edmund is in no mood for my disorientated state.

Where he's been all night, I don't know, but I can well imagine, as he moves to saddle Jethson whom he's been reunited with and lead Ealdorman Ælhun and me onwards. I try and speak to him, but he cuts me off.

'There'll be time for bloody conversation when the men are found.' Although he doesn't name my aunt, I know she's foremost in his mind.

'Fine,' I grouch, Haden side-stepping as a response to the snarl in Edmund's voice. 'Lead on,' I order him, and he knees Jethson harshly, and follows up the movement with a sharper kick.

'If you treat your horse like that,' I bellow, losing my patience with him, 'I'll have you run alongside the rest of us.'

Edmund glares at me, his eye bloodshot, his head unsteady on his shoulders.

'The damn brute is useless.'

'A bad rider blames the horse,' Icel calls, his words drowning out all the activity in the camp, as my men hurry to be ready, and Gardulf douses the embers of the fire.

'A bad horse is a bloody bad horse,' Edmund roars, all trace of his wits deserting him. I never thought to hear him speak of Jethson in such a way. I can tell, as well, that Jethson's stubborn streak is making itself known now.

I pause, take a breath, and then another one. There's no one in the camp looking at Edmund. Even Hereman and Gardulf are conspicuous in not looking at their brother or father.

'No, Edmund, a bad rider is a bad rider,' I offer calmly, keeping hold of my temper. I understand his distress. I just wish he bloody did.

'Fuck all of you,' Edmund exclaims, jumping down from Jethson, and hurrying to a run. I roll my eyes at such folly and turn to

Hereman to order him to follow his brother, but Icel shakes his head.

'Leave the daft bastard alone. It'll do him some good.' Icel speaks so decisively that I snap my mouth shut on my next shouted command.

'Gardulf, take Jethson, will you?' I ask instead. This is something Gardulf rushes to do, his shoulders relaxing. I can't see that the lad has been able to breathe deeply since we parted ways at Hereford. That'll teach him that loyalty is not a cloak to be worn easily.

'Lead on,' I instruct Hiltiberht instead. The lad nods, but I see him swallow heavily. He doesn't want to be here; that much is obvious. I think back to young Penda, and not for the first time, or the last, I realise that boys who dream of being warriors can't always fulfil those dreams when faced with the harsh realities of what it entails.

Quickly, Haden overtakes Edmund, where he runs along Watling Street. I'd call to him, tell him to mount up and be done with it, but he looks fit to punch me, and so I leave him, urging Haden onwards. If Edmund arrives just as we're ready to leave, it might make him hold his tongue in place.

'It's not far from here,' Hiltiberht confirms when I join him at the front of the line of men. Ealdorman Ælhun has sent two of his men forwards with Wulfsige, and along with Icel and Goda, the men form an honour guard for the remainder of us. I'm alert in the saddle, but I don't feel as though I'm being watched. The day continues to dawn, cool but bright, a real promise of the summer to come. I could half pray I won't spend my summer fighting, as I did last year, but that would be a waste of my words. War will come to Mercia once more, and I must just hope that when it comes, my aunt is safely restored to Kingsholm. If not, I fear what will happen. I truly fucking do.

Chapter Fourteen

'Here, my lord,' Hiltiberht beckons me beneath the boughs of overhanging trees. I squint along Watling Street, trying to determine just how close we might be to Northampton. I don't think it's far away, but it's far enough that any attack wouldn't have been seen, thanks to the thick forest. If the attackers were stealthy, no one need have seen them, especially if they used the river to escape; even now, a faint rustle to the rear of the woodlands.

Hastily dismounting, I glance down at the mud-churned ground, and realise, not that I doubted him, that Edmund is correct. Too many people have stepped this way to make it possible to determine where the bastard attackers took my aunt.

'The dead were taken to Northampton,' Ealdorman Ælhun confirms, his head bowed as he contemplates the churned mess. This isn't the first time he's seen it, but all the same, his face is pale, and he stands beside me quietly, his expression blank.

'They ambushed the men when Lady Cyneswith went after her hounds,' Hiltiberht reiterates, his voice desolate. I know that Wiglaf is dead, but where's the other one?

I can't deny that they chose a good place. It's not far from

Watling Street, and yet there's more than enough tree cover to mask their actions from the roadway. Even if the ambush was poorly timed, it's unlikely anyone would have seen anything beneath the dense foliage. I know the truth of that only too well. It can't be far from here that we hid beneath the trees to evade the Viking raiders who'd taken control of Northampton last year.

'And were they buried there?' I question. It pains me to speak of Siric and Eadberht, even of Wiglaf. Leonath stills at the conversation. It must pain him to hear his comrade spoken about in such a way. I try to catch sight of his brown eyes, but his gaze is firmly averted, as he stands beside the ambush site. It's too easy to see what happened here. The muddy ground is disturbed, the marks where dying men dug their heels in, too easy to see. I swallow down my grief. When this is done, I'll have yet more men to grieve, and that's never easy.

'Yes, my lord king. They were buried in the church grounds there. A good Christian burial for men who served their kingdom, and defended it with their life.' Ealdorman Ælhun's tone is strangely hollow. We've all known too many good men who've met their death in battle.

'Then you have my thanks for arranging that.'

'It was not me, my lord king, but the men and women of Northampton who recognised them. They were determined to honour the lost men.' I bow my head, suddenly remembering that Tatberht might have been amongst that number. He was left at Northampton months ago and has been there ever since. Is it Tatberht who's arranged the burial of his comrades?

'And the hound?' I ask instead, and the ealdorman looks pained, and I turn aside. I would have wanted something better for the beast. He was a friend to me, as he had been to my brother. In the end, it was Wiglaf who bridged the gap between the two of us, merely by outliving his master.

'He was buried here,' the ealdorman offers. I round on him, testing the truth of those words. I don't want to know that he's just telling me what I want to hear.

'Aye, my lord king. I knew to whom the beast belonged. Come, I'll show you. I didn't think the monks would respond well to a hound in consecrated ground. I wouldn't allow him to be left for the carrion crows.'

The ealdorman leads me back towards the road but at an angle. I stay close to him, but I'm not in any danger. There are more than enough of my men to ensure my safety. I can hear my warriors from the roadway and others crashing through the undergrowth. And, I'm armed, as always, my weapons belt glistening with the means to kill any who try and kill me. My hands itch to touch all the blades, to slice them through the necks of the men who took my aunt. Once more, I understand what drives Edmund.

In the sight of the road, the ealdorman pauses and indicates the disturbed ground with his outstretched arm. Here, there's a single tree, a mighty oak, branches spreading outwards, so that much of the area is shadowed. It's a pleasant spot.

I walk forwards and squat down, hand outstretched, as though to greet the black and white muzzled dog. I close my eyes, and can just about feel his breath on my fingers, and his fur beneath my hand. I feel my throat close, and hope I'm not about to cry over a bloody hound.

Opening my eyes, I smile, for on top of the earth, Wiglaf's collar has been placed around a small stone, devoid of any carving but still, a testament to a dog who died defending his owner.

I go to stand, only to notice something else. No one mentioned poor Beornwulf, my aunt's other dog. I've feared the animal dead as well, but instead, fierce eyes glower at me from the far side of the tree trunk, a soft rumble of a growl emanating from the hound.

'Come here, boy,' I call. 'Beornwulf, come here, to me.' I think the dog will stay away, but then he moves towards me, and I see how he limps, his rear right leg unable to take any weight.

'Come on, here boy,' and Beornwulf hangs his head low as he noses the stone and the collar that encircled Wiglaf's neck.

'I'm sorry, boy,' I murmur, as he moves under my outstretched hand. His coat is ragged, and a nasty slice mars the top of his leg. For a moment, I know fury. Why has no one thought to seek out the other dog, but I subside before I attack anyone? They must have assumed the other hound was dead as well, but his body lost to them.

'Come on,' and I scoop the animal into my arms, and then stand. I need to get the hound to Northampton and hope someone there can tend to his wound.

Ealdorman Ælhun watches me, and I think he'll call for one of my warriors, but he snaps his mouth firmly shut. Instead, I resume my questioning, as I walk free from the trees, encumbered with the weight of the hound.

'And the path to the river has been scouted?' I query. It would be easy to rush to London along Watling Street, but I just can't see that happening. It would have been too great a risk. Northampton isn't without its men and women determined to defend it with their lives. They would have chased any Viking raiders away. But the river is an entirely different problem. Although, I reconsider.

'Which way does the river flow from here? Towards Northampton?'

'No, my lord king,' the ealdorman advises.

'Although, they could perhaps more easily have crossed the river, and headed east.'

I shake my head at these words, muttered by Icel with his usual directness. He notes the hound in my arms and reaches out to rub his hand over the beast's nose.

'Give him to me,' Icel offers, but I refuse.

'We'll take him to Northampton,' I say instead.

'Aye, well, I'll take him then?' His words are soft, but still, I don't want to relinquish my hold on the surviving animal. But, I do, and Beornwulf goes easily enough, the fight gone from him, which worries me more than if he'd bitten my hand.

'Come on, lad,' Icel offers in a soft tone, and I consider whether Icel knew King Beornwulf of Mercia, the hound's namesake? I'm sure he must have done. Perhaps, I think, he also knew King Wiglaf. That brings a wry smile to my lips. After all those years, what did Icel the warrior think of my aunt and my brother naming hounds after Mercia's enfeebled kings?

'And where would they have gone from there?' I persist, trying to drag my thoughts away from Mercia's weak kings. But I know I'm asking all the wrong questions. What I really need to know, is where my aunt has been taken, but no one has an answer for me.

'And no one else has been found?' I wince to say those words, thinking of my lost men.

'No, my lord king, no one.' That both cheers and fills me with foreboding.

'I think we need to follow the river,' I confirm.

'We have been, my lord king.' Ealdorman Ælhun is repetitive in his answers, and yet, I have some pity for him. Faced with my wrath, what more can he do but be honest and concise.

'Along the River Nene, and over the Nene?' I ask, just to be sure.

'And north, as well, to both sides of the river. Everyone has been looking for her. So far, there has been no sign.'

'Well, people can't just bloody disappear out of thin air,' I glower. 'They're not wraiths or spirits.'

'No, my lord king,' the ealdorman confirms once more. I find a tight grin on my lips. It's either that or I, too will lash out, as Edmund has done.

'And no one has sent word, or claimed responsibility?' I manage to utter through my gritted teeth.

'No, my lord king.'

'As I thought. Then, from here, we'll split the force, half along the Nene, and half to the far side of the Nene. We'll ride to Northampton, and split the force there.' It'll mean a cold dip in the Nene for some of my horses and warriors, but I can't help that.

'No,' Edmund huffs the word, coming into view beneath the low-hanging trees. His face runs with sweat, but I'm impressed he's managed to keep such a good pace with the horses. Not that I pushed them hard. While I've been desperate to reach this place, suddenly, I've not wanted to. I didn't want the words I've been told over and over again to actually be true.

'No?' I menace.

'No,' Edmund huffs, hands on his knees as he regains his breath. 'Listen to them,' he points. I meet the frantic eyes of three men and four women, seven children scattered around their legs. In the distance, I hear an oxen bellow and the strange he-hore of a donkey.

'Tell him what you told me,' Edmund gasps. I'm unsure why he's out of breath while the people he's discovered are merely scared. Then I remember he's been running, foregoing his horse rather than his evil temper.

'My, my lord king,' it's one of the women who speak. She steps forward from the rest of the group, unravelling the reaching hands of one of the children that grip her simultaneously. 'I've come from Icknield Way, our intention to travel to London, but what we saw, made us hasten this way.' I nod encouragingly. What is it that these people have seen?

'Mercian warriors, my lord king, and a fine lady amongst them, all being taken to Grantabridge, bound atop their horses by the Viking raiders.'

'Along Icknield Way?' I gasp. Such an affront puts thunder into my words. I was convinced they'd not have been so bold as to travel along Watling Street, but it's evident they've not only done so, they've also journeyed along Icknield Way. The woman, older than the other men and women, juts out her chin and stands firm. She's the matriarch of this group, and her stance so reminds me of my aunt that I too want to tangle my arms in her skirts and hear the words that 'everything will be all right,' trip from her tongue with all the sympathy of a cold bath.

'Aye, my lord king. We hid from the devils, but we heard them well enough. They spoke in the tongue of the Norse, and I know, for as a trader, I must speak the language or risk being duped by them, and losing my profit.'

'And what did they say?' My tongue tastes like ash in my mouth.

'They said Mercia's king would have no choice but to bow down to their demands now. They said they would gain half of Mercia in exchange for the woman.' My blood thrums through my body, my head pounding, as Edmund shrieks his outrage. I look to Ealdorman Ælhun, desolate, unable to make sense of what has befallen me, because, damn the fuckers, I'll give them all of Mercia if only my aunt is returned to me, safe and well. And they know it. I have failed Mercia.

I'm greeted on arrival at Northampton by Tatberht, his face grave. I dismount quickly and make my way to him. Damn, it's good to see the old goat, and I grip him tightly in an embrace. He's weak beneath me, somewhat shrunken in on himself, and yet hale, for all I wouldn't trust him to lift a seax and shield, let alone fight with either. His single blue eye peers at me from behind his heavily furrowed eyebrows as though reading my thoughts. But, when he speaks the words he uses aren't about himself.

'She'll be well,' he assures me, his voice cracking. All the same, I take too much comfort from them. Tatberht has known my aunt for a very long time.

'Ah, you found the other hound,' Tatberht acknowledges, as soon as I release him. He casts an eye over Icel as he and Rudolf work to lower the dog to the ground, and then take him towards the hall. Beornwulf remains happy to be carried, and that's not at all the dog I know.

'It'll be good to have a friend here,' Tatberht confirms. I force my gaze away from him, to look at Northampton itself. The high walls remain in place, and I can see where those people not involved in welcoming the king and his entourage, scramble over them to ensure they remain in good condition.

'I've left you for too long,' I confirm, pleased to have the conversation focus on him.

'No, my lord king. I've stayed here through choice, but after this, I'll return to Kingsholm. But first, I'll lead you to the graves.'

It seems I'm not to be allowed to forget my true purpose. I nod.

'Go on, then. I need to say my goodbyes.'

'Aye, my lord king. You're a good man to offer prayers for them.' I swallow again, a throb of grief in my throat.

'Tomorrow, we'll resume our journey to Grantabridge.'

'I've heard the intelligence that she's there. It pains me to know she was so close but slipped through our fingers.'

'So, you didn't send word for her to come here then?'

'No, my lord king. I bloody didn't, and neither did anyone else. If we'd had need of assistance, I assure you, I would have first sought out Ealdorman Ælhun. He's closer.'

Together, we skirt around the mass of horses and warriors, squires and young girls running to tend to the horses that need housing for the night, and then we're walking down the central street. I remain silent, my thoughts frustrated. My aunt should have realised all wasn't as she thought, but then, it would have depended on just how convincing the messenger was.

'In here,' and Tatberht indicates the wicker fence that encloses the church and its grounds. I look upwards, noting the wooden tower that crowns the building. I see my aunt's hand at work here, in the evident extension to the building, or rather, the addition of the tall tower that crowns the church. That wasn't here before. I consider whether it's being built to remind the inhabitants that they're Christian, and not pagan worshippers, like the Viking raiders.

But, the settlement is still contained within its walls, as far as I can tell, and that pleases me. That's something I'll need to ensure happens at Hereford and Worcester as well. The people of Mercia need to have all they require behind their defensible walls, should the Viking raider bastards think to attack again. Anywhere with a river close by is at risk. I've seen that too many times of late.

I can see that the burial ground has been used for some time, but there's a place where the earth has been disturbed, and it's to that I walk. My steps feel heavy and leaden; my head bowed low.

I think of Eadberht. He was a fine warrior, most of the time. His death will leave a hole amongst my warriors, and more than just the physical gap in my shield wall. And Siric? Well, Siric has survived death many times already. I knew, of course, that one day, his luck would run out, but to know it came inside Mercia's borders, defending my aunt, who above all else, should have been safe on Watling Street, infuriates me.

Tatberht doesn't accompany me but instead stays away, and eventually, my thoughts clear, and I'm aware of young Wulfhere and his grandfather talking. That brings a smile to my lips to see the pair reunited. I breathe deeply and redouble my resolve. I must find my aunt, and then, like Tatberht and Wulfhere, we'll be reunited as well, and between us, we'll wreak bloody havoc over all of Mercia's fucking enemies.

Chapter Fifteen

Since our last visit, Grantabridge has changed a great deal. I eye it now, from my vantage point to the western side of the river, feeling my heart thudding in my ears.

How the fuck are we going to make it across the boundary of the river, and into their stronghold, rescue my aunt, and leave again, without being bloody seen?

I turn to Edmund. His expression is easy to read in the dulling light of the day. It's hopeless. There are Viking raiders everywhere, including on this side of the river, watching the bridge to ensure that no one can get past their guard. Beyond them, are more and more people. The Viking raiders haven't come alone. They're brought their children, their wives, their slaves and even their pets. From here, I can hear dogs barking. The bastards mean to stay in Grantabridge, and they mean to do that by holding my aunt as their captive. They've learned valuable lessons since trying to hold Repton after they ejected King Burgred. They've determined that if they can't kill me, then there's something better that they can do.

Around their settlement is a deep ditch, as well as a rampart. The trees which once hid Edmund and I have been felled, and now there's a huge space close to the bridge. It's evident they don't mean to be caught off guard again.

And inside there, as far as we can tell, is my aunt. I suppose I should be grateful that my aunt wasn't taken by Bishop Smithwulf, but at least if it had been him, I might have stood half a chance of using diplomacy to win her back. Bishop Smithwulf, a man of God, even with his ungodly attempts to ally with Wessex, would have seen reason. The Viking raiders bloody won't.

'We'll have to swim the river,' Icel murmurs. There's no inflexion to his words. I can't tell whether the thought pleases him or fills him with foreboding. We swam the Nene to get here. I think we've just about dried since yesterday morning.

'What of the ditch and rampart?' Hereman queries.

'We'll have to get through it, somehow.'

'So, what? We swim the bloody river and then work out what we do next?' Edmund's voice is filled with disgust for Icel's half-thought-out plan.

'Then what would you do?' Icel queries. Again, there's no anger there. I think we're all just trying to work out what we can, and can't do when faced with such an insurmountable obstacle.

'I wouldn't swim the bloody river without some sort of fucking plan,' Edmund huffs angrily, running his hand through his long hair. He needs to shave. We all need to shave.

I look back to face my warriors. There are just more than twenty of us now. It's not enough to take on the might of the Grantabridge jarls, but I don't think it needs to be. As much as it pains me, we don't need to kill every one of the bastards. We just need to make sure we retrieve my aunt and escape with our lives. If the Viking raiders still hold Grantabridge, then that will be a battle for another day. For once, this isn't about stopping the Viking raiders. Our objective is very different. It has to be.

But how to do it? When the Viking raiders took Northampton, we managed to sneak inside on the farmer's carts. I'm sure they'll be wise to that tactic now. So, we need something else? But what? The thought keeps circling through my mind. How can we get to my aunt?

And then I feel the air leave my body, and it's an effort to remember to breathe. I can see her. I reach out and grip Edmund's arm, Hereman to his other side, holding him down so that he can't give away our presence.

'Silence,' I growl, the words an exhalation. On the far side of the river, my aunt is being led through the mud and wooden rampart, and over the ditch via a plank of wood that makes her footsteps echo loudly, assuring me that there's a chasm beneath her. She walks proudly, head held high, although her hands are bound together in front of her. I can't see all the details. I can just tell from the way that she walks that she doesn't have free movement. I would like to know if she seems hale. If she's wounded in any way. But that would involve asking Edmund those questions. I decide not to, unless he speaks himself.

'Where are they fucking taking her?' Edmund whispers, his words cracked with the effort of not rushing to her aid. Beneath my hand, his body shakes. I imagine it must be with relief. We know she lives, and that, in and of itself, is reassuring.

'If you watch, we might bloody know,' Icel retorts. I'm glad he speaks and saves me the trouble of trying to find a means of speaking when I'm so angry; I might be the one that needs restraining and not Edmund.

My eyes are fixed on the far side of the river, and a ship oared close to the river bank, catching my attention. I watch as figures move quickly to secure the boat, making it ready for people to board. The craft is long, and the wood gleams, even in the dim light.

'Where are they bloody taking her?' It's apparent that she's being taken somewhere. Why perplexes me just as much as the where.

'Shit.' We've tracked her this far, and now they mean to move her. I look along the course of the river. There is some tree covering, and of course, we're on the far side of the river, but how easy will it be to follow without being seen?

Yet, as we watch, I quickly realise that my aunt isn't being taken to the ship to board it. Rather, there's someone there who's being brought to visit her.

'Who's that?' I demand to know, hissing at my men and pointing towards the ship. It's Rudolf who first scrutinises the figure. It's hard for me to see much. It's just too far away for clear sight. I'll have to rely on one of the others telling me what's happening.

'They're bloody wearing a cloak,' Rudolf complains, as though that's the worst of our problems. I might not be able to see all the details, but I can certainly see the spears and shields of warriors as they stand ready either on the ship or on the well-churned earth beside the river bank.

'I have a fucking bad feeling about this,' I mutter, trying not to think what I'm thinking, but of course, as soon as I've thought it, it's all I can think about.

Is it? Could it truly be? I'm sure I was told he was fighting the kingdom of the Picts. If it is Jarl Halfdan, I'll be letting go of Edmund because I'll be charging down the slope, keen to kill the bastard once and for all.

'The shields carry the emblem of the wolf,' Edmund growls.

'Fuck,' I turn to the rest of my men, meeting the eyes of Hereman, Icel, Rudolf and Goda. Goda's eyes are narrowed, glaring at what's happening before us.

'If he's here, then we fucking should have helped the sodding archbishop,' I growl. I can see all my careful reasoning becoming nothing. Damn the bastard jarl. He has my aunt, and she can't fight like my warriors can. Well, she probably can, with half a chance, but I doubt Jarl Halfdan will give her the opportunity.

'Why the fuck are they working with Jarl Halfdan?' I ask the question of no one. Bad enough that I have the Grantabridge jarls on Mercia's borders, but at least they'd cast Jarl Halfdan to one side. It seems that's not the case anymore.

'That's not Jarl Halfdan,' Rudolf announces slowly, as though not quite believing his words. 'That's not him. He's not tall enough.' I peer at the figure, making his way from the ship towards my aunt and the warriors who guard her, but I just can't see well enough. I wait, hoping Edmund might be able to tell me more.

But the silence stretches between us as we watch a conversation taking place. I can't tell what's being said. There's no indication in the gesticulating of the people involved. My fear is that they'll take my aunt from this place. The river that flows beside Grantabridge could take her to The Wash and the coastline, and from there, they could take her anywhere. Why, for the time being, perplexes me, but it's a real fear. And then, the cloaked figure turns back towards the ship, and I hear Rudolf inhale in shock. I turn to him, but in front of me, I'm aware of Edmund rushing to his feet, and it takes all of my skill to redouble my grip on him before anyone can see him. The enemy mustn't know that we're here, and ready to rescue my aunt.

'Bishop Smithwulf,' Rudolf states, and I turn frantic eyes on him.

'Bishop Smithwulf?' I can hardly believe what he's saying.

'Aye, my lord. That bastard has allied with the Viking raiders.'

'Or has he gone to rescue the lady?' Icel counters, his forehead furrowed. I'm surprised he's the one to think well of the London bishop with his Wessex leanings. I know what Icel thinks of all things related to Wessex.

I'm already shaking my head.

'No, he's in on this. The fucker. He means to tie my hands so that I'm forced to do what he wants.'

'Perhaps,' Icel muses. Beneath my grip, Edmund is unruly. Without Hereman's aid, Edmund would be off down the slope and haring across the open expanse of land that separates us from the river.

'Calm the fuck down,' I breathe into Edmund's ears. I'm trying to do too much at once. I want to watch the bishop, my aunt, the Grantabridge jarls and it's impossible with Edmund bucking like a fish caught on dry land.

'Hold him,' I urge Hereman and Goda, but it's still not enough.

'She's watching you,' Icel rumbles, and this stills Edmund like nothing else.

I turn to Icel, and he inclines his head, even as I focus once more on my aunt. I can't say that she watches us. Certainly, she's facing us, and I'm grateful for Icel's quick thinking.

Edmund finally stills, allowing all of us to watch events unfolding on the far side of the Granta.

Bishop Smithwulf might have faced us for a short amount of time, but now he has his back to us again, and there's a renewal of the conversation taking place.

'Why the fuck is he here?' I muse out loud. 'This smacks of politics, and I fucking hate politics,' I continue to growl. I can't work out all the parts of this treachery in any sort of order.

It seems the Grantabridge jarls took my aunt captive, but that now Bishop Smithwulf is involved, and also, so it seems, Jarl Halfdan, for Rudolf told me the shields carried that bastard's sigil, and so the men who hold those shields, must be oath sworn to him.

'What are they hoping to do?'

'Divide Mercia between them all,' Icel is the only one to answer my question, and his words fall, doom-laden, into our uneasy silence.

'What?' I gasp, turning to face him, even though I don't want to. His words astound me. Mercia is Mercia. It is a whole. A kingdom. It can't be divided.

'Bishop Smithwulf works for King Alfred. The Grantabridge jarls want Mercia, as does Jarl Halfdan. By taking your aunt, they mean to force you to accept their rule, as you never did at Repton, much to their disgust.' Icel's words are calm, spoken with sound reasoning, and still, I want to fucking punch him. 'They had King Burgred where they wanted him, but you, you wouldn't allow it. They meant to kill you, but you countered their every attempt, and then you kicked them out of Repton.'

'No,' I shriek, and then stuff my hand in my mouth to cut short the cry.

'Aye, my lord. We're really fucked this time,' Icel confirms in his expressionless voice. Icel, who never answers a question directly, has pronounced on what's happening here, and it all makes horrible sense.

I shake my head, trying to deny the words, but there's an element of truth in them. I know there is. Mercia has too many enemies. I've been trying to fight them off, one bastard at a time, but it seems they've finally realised Mercia's true weakness. If they all work together, they can overthrow my kingship and take Mercia for themselves.

I won't have it. I won't fucking have it.

* * *

'We need to think about this calmly,' I try to force the words past my tight throat and dry tongue. We've moved away from our vantage point, well, most of us have, Goda has remained to watch what's happening. Not that anything is happening at the moment. My aunt has been returned behind Grantabridge's defences and Bishop Smithwulf has joined her and the rest of the Viking raiders.

I don't know what they plan to do next, but I can make a reasoned guess.

'We need to gather your allies,' Icel urges me. 'Get Ealdormen Ælhun, Beornheard and Aldred. Have them come here with all their men and we'll make war on the Grantabridge jarls.' But I'm shaking my head.

'There's no time. Even Ealdorman Ælhun is too far away in Northampton. If we're going to stop this from meaning the end of Mercia, then we need to strike now, while no one knows we're here apart from the people at Northampton, and Bishop Wærferth. We might win with the element of surprise.'

Edmund paces through our group. He's furious, so much so, that he's not stopped shaking ever since we found my aunt. If we don't keep a careful eye on him, any chance of a surprise attack will be entirely lost. He's just about crazy enough to run at the enemy and think he can hack them down, one at a time, and rescue her. I wish it were that easy.

'Did you see any of our missing men?' We've found no sign of them, yet. That worries me. We found the site of the battle easy enough. But not my missing warriors. If I knew they were inside Grantabridge that might aid me but more than anything, I should like to know that Cealwin, Wulfred, Oda, Ingwald, Eadfrith, Beornstan and Osmod are alive. I know two of my warriors are dead. I can't lose more of them.

'No,' Rudolf confirms, just loud enough that I can hear over Edmund's stamping steps.

'You can't trust them to be inside,' Icel warns me. I round on him. He's being altogether too accepting of what's happening here, and yet, as he meets my eyes, I sense something deep inside him. He's trying to hold on to his reason. I nod my head, prepared to admit his determination. And yet, how much easier would it be if they were inside.

'We can get at them from the other side of the river.' It's Lyfing who speaks. I feel my forehead furrow as he nods in confirmation of his suggestion, as though he spoke the words, and now needs to reassure himself of their truth. 'From here, we'll be seen. We need to find another entrance. This river entrance won't be our ally.'

'But we don't know the scale of their defences over there.'

'And, it'll cost us only time to find out.' Lyfing's idea isn't without merit. As much as I'd like to smash my way across the bridge and reach my aunt, it's the surest way of being defeated. That's what they'll be expecting.

'We don't have fucking time,' Edmund seethes. 'Who knows what the bastards are doing to her inside there.'

I turn to Rudolf. His lips are twisted in thought.

'Did she seem harmed?' I ask. I've not been able to bring myself to voice the question. She must be. I can't see how else they'd have managed to grab her and bring her here.

'She has a bruised face, but much of her was covered,' Rudolf offers hesitantly. This time his words are even softer, no doubt trying to ensure Edmund doesn't hear them.

'We can't wait. We need to get fucking in there now,' Edmund stamps to a stop in front of me, and I look up and up, remembering how tall and fierce he is. Edmund is a warrior of Mercia, and he's been wounded, in the worst possible way.

'We fucking have to,' I grudgingly admit. 'Lyfing's suggestion has merit. We need to sneak into their defences, and this time, we can't do it with two oxen and a hay cart. I really wish we bloody could, but that's the problem in showing our hand in the past. That's what they'll be expecting now. Just as at Repton, when they took us to be their own men, and you were bringing me in as a prisoner. We've revealed our deviousness. They'll be alert to something similar.'

Edmund shakes his head, incandescent with rage. I feel his pain. I really do.

'Then we need to move, sooner rather than later,' Icel confirms, already standing, and turning to slide back through the trees to where we left our horses.

'Aye, we do,' I confirm, but although my warriors all make a move, Edmund doesn't, and of course, Goda still watches what's happening. I pause then, surveying the men I have. We are few in number, but that's never fucking stopped us before.

'Edmund, you can remain here, if you wish, watch what's happening, and if you suspect something, you can make an attempt to save her yourself. I'll leave two others with you.'

'No,' he shakes his head. 'No. I'll stay here, but the rest of you must remain as one unit. I'll watch, I assure you. I won't do anything stupid.' I hold his gaze. I notice how he meets my eyes, and yet, I detect the lie in his words. He'll do something bloody stupid. I know it. He knows it. Can I leave him here? Would it be torture to tear him away? I walk towards him, grip both of his wrists in my hands, and make him meet my gaze.

'Whatever fucking stupid thing you do, don't let it be the last fucking stupid thing you do.' And then I turn aside, not waiting for his answer. I know him far too well.

'Send Goda back this way,' I order as a parting shot and make my way to Haden. My heart feels heavy. If I lose my aunt and Edmund, I'm really going to have to kill every fucking Viking raider that thought to make Mercia their home.

Chapter Sixteen

My warriors are as sullen as I am as we ride into the growing darkness. I'm not a fool. I anticipated what might have befallen my aunt, but it's one thing to contemplate it, and something else entirely to see it.

I knew Mercia was alone and with too many enemies. I didn't consider, not for one moment, that those enemies might decide to unite to splinter the kingdom. All these years of trying to keep Mercia whole, chiding our weak king, accepting the grudging support of Wessex, and now this?

The path is easy enough to follow. I've made a very similar journey in the past when Edmund and I needed to return to Northampton from Grantabridge. Yet, it all feels very different to me now. I've always believed there would be a way to keep Mercia united. I never doubted my abilities. I'm not saying I believed myself invincible, far from it, but I thought Mercia strong enough to hold against all comers.

'How will we sneak into Grantabridge?' Rudolf breaks the silence, riding close to me. I believe he's the only one brave enough to do so. I lead the trail of horses, of my men, and for all the noise of hooves over the floor of the woodlands, I would wish I led an army of ten thousand warriors to finally chisel out the Viking raiders from their stronghold in Grantabridge.

'I don't know. Not yet, but there'll be a way.'

'Will there?' I turn to scrutinise Rudolf. He sits upright in his saddle, Dever keeping a leisurely pace beneath him. Dever has found fitness in recent weeks. He's no longer the slowest of the horses. That worries me more than it should. I don't want him to have finally reached the end of his days and be enjoying a reminder of his youthful days when he was my brother's horse. I've already lost the hound, Wiglaf, once beloved by my brother. I don't want to lose his horse as well.

'There has to be,' I growl, but I appreciate the caution all the same 'Icel.'

'My lord,' he brings Samson to my side.

'I think you're right. We need to summon all the ealdormen.' Icel nods slowly, his grey hair seeming black beneath the gloom of night, although his beard shimmers darkly.

'Who'll do that for you?' he queries, making a good point. I don't truly wish to send him away. I have few enough men as it is. I consider those riding with me. I have some younger warriors, and some older ones as well. I nod.

'Ælfgar,' I call the hoary warrior to my side. He comes immediately, Poppy quick to obey his commands. I think he knows my intention.

'And where do you want 'em to meet you?' Ælfgar demands to know. I smirk, pleased not to have to give the command.

'They must amass on Grantabridge, but from the western side of the Granta. They might be lucky and find Edmund if he's still there.'

'Aye, my lord. I'll do my best. And my lord,' I meet his eyes, and they show too much sympathy and understanding. 'All will be well, and your aunt will eat those bastard's stones for breakfast,' and with that, he shouts his farewells, and bends low over Poppy, guiding her back the way we've come so that he can reach

Northampton quickly. From there, others will summon the ealdormen. Of them all, only Ealdorman Ælhun will be close enough to come quickly.

I can't help wishing that we'd known all this before I convened the witan. It would have been quicker to bring my sworn men and their warriors to my side then. But the orderliness of the witan, with its rules and prescriptions on who can speak and when, seems as though it belongs to another lifetime. So much has changed since then.

I'm grateful for the sliver of moonlight that lights our path, but even I have to admit defeat eventually. Before we emerge from the covering of trees close to Icknield Way, I call to my men.

'We rest here, for the rest of the night. Ensure the horses have all they need. Once we're on Icknield Way tomorrow, we run the chance of meeting warriors under the command of Bishop Smithwulf or even the Viking raiders.'

I slide from Haden's back, showing my men that I mean it, and although there's a murmur of unease from them, they follow my commands. I don't allow a fire, and quickly, my warriors roll in their cloaks and find sleep. I take the first watch, aware my mind is too filled with fears and worries for my aunt and for Mercia to sleep.

I'm unsurprised when Icel joins me.

'Can't sleep?' I ask him, over the sound of horses and men, snoring and farting in their sleep.

'There'll be time for sleep one day,' Icel murmurs. He settles beside me, where I've found a mat of dry leaves to sit upon. I'm amazed they're dry after all the rain we've endured of late.

Silence falls between us. I look upwards, but the branches of the trees blot out the light from the moon, and so I have little to actually look at.

'She wouldn't want you to give up Mercia for her,' Icel finally murmurs. I can't say his words surprise me. I know that. He knows that. Fuck, even Edmund knows that although he won't want to give voice to it.

'She has no choice, and it's not her fault that our enemies conspire against us.'

'She'll appreciate that, but all the same, she's spent her life fighting for Mercia, just as you have yours. And she's been doing it for much longer than you.' I turn to Icel then. He's not looking at me.

'How bloody old are you?' I demand to know. He's never told me, not in all the years I've known him.

'Old enough to have known your aunt for a very long time,' he confirms. 'Old enough to remember, just, when Mercia had peace and wasn't surrounded by enemies.'

'Fucking hell. You're bastard old then.' I huff. Icel surprises me by chuckling.

'Aye, lad. I am. I was there when you came into the world as a screaming little bastard, and I'll probably be here when you leave it, in much the same fettle.'

'And still, you fight?'

'And still, I fight. And so does your aunt. Mercia has been beleaguered and served by ineffective kings, but your family have suffered more than most.'

I shake my head. I can't see that, but Icel nods slowly, assuring me of his words.

'If we're to retrieve your aunt, we'll need to do it by stealth and with some luck. And then, what will you do? Mercia is too weak to survive as she is.'

Icel's words are terrifying to hear because they're so, so true.

'Who would you have her ally with then?'

'The lesser of all evils.'

'But that's no one. Wessex is an evil. The Welsh are a scrouge on Mercia, and I can't make an alliance with the Viking raiders, or Northumbria, which is mainly filled with bastard Viking raiders anyway.' I shrug my shoulders. It all feels so helpless.

'There will be a way,' Icel offers, without elucidating. 'And you'll find it,' he advises me. Fuck. Icel has more faith in me than I have in myself. 'Now, get some bloody sleep. You won't be able to think yourself out of this shit storm without a good night's sleep.' I open my mouth to argue with him, but instead, I yawn, and then I smirk.

'Fuck, Icel. You're a mean bastard,' I mutter, getting to my feet.

'Being nice never got me anything I wanted,' he murmurs, and I'm not really sure whether I was meant to hear those words, or not.

* * *

I sleep, surprising myself, but I urge my men onwards as soon as it's light enough to see. The night has been surprisingly cold, and now the horses move through leaves shimmering with the remnants of a frost before emerging close to Icknield Way.

Goda leads, with Lyfing, and the pair of them beckon us onwards, as soon as they're sure it's safe to be seen. I've been in two minds about using the road, but there's little choice. I don't know the way to the other entrance to Grantabridge, but Icknield Way will take us close to it. I'd sooner get there quickly and risk being seen, than not make it at all.

Still, I'm wary as are all of my warriors. Icel and Rudolf take themselves to the rear of my small warrior band, whereas Hereman rides with Gardulf in front. I can't see that any of us are happy. Even Haden must detect the unease. He's unbiddable, stepping from side to side, and shying at the smallest of things. I slide my hand along his shoulder and urge him to speed and calm, but I can't feel it doing any good.

'How long will it take us?' Gardulf asks the question of his uncle.

'Fuck knows. It's not like we travel these parts. We're asking for trouble.' Hereman's response is far from reassuring. I bite down my acerbic reply. We're all feeling the strain of being so close to the Viking raider stronghold. We've seen how many warriors are inside it. We know that we run too great a risk being here, but there's no choice, not if we're to rescue my aunt.

The day becomes almost warm before the temperature quickly falls away once more, but by now, we can smell the smoke of hearth fires drifting on the gentle wind. We turn our horses away from Icknield Way. Somewhere ahead lies another entrance to Grantabridge, and my warriors and I, who number only twenty, are prepared to take on the might of those bastards if we can.

* * *

'It's impossible,' Goda's voice is filled with frustration. 'There are too many of the bastards, and they never let their guard down. It's not like when we encountered Jarl Halfdan's warriors at Torksey.'

I shake my head, not dismissing his words, but in annoyance. We've spent the night and most of the day scouting out Grantabridge. It's proving impossible, just as Goda says. The Viking raiders here are alert to everything. The Granta encircles much of the settlement, and so there's another bridge not far from where we shelter, but it's heavily guarded, just as the one to the west of the settlement is. I can't help feeling we've wasted our time in journeying here. We should have stayed with Edmund, and hoped that the ealdormen and their household troops made it to our side quickly. Ealdorman Ælhun may even be there by now, and that would have doubled our force. And no doubt, those who can fight would have come from Northampton as well. There's been enough time for Ælfgar to reach Northampton.

'We need a ship.' It's not the first time Hereman has offered the ridiculous suggestion.

'Where the fuck will we get a ship from?' Goda queries, his voice filled with irritation. I'm almost excluded from the argument taking place between my warriors. Most of us are hidden in trees just off the Icknield Way, but Icel and Rudolf are on scouting duty. Goda's just returned from doing the same.

'Even if we get over the river, how do we get through the bloody walls?'

I hadn't realised, and now feel stupid for not thinking of this, but Grantabridge might be a new settlement for the Viking raiders, but it's being constructed on top of an older one. The hint of ancient walls and ditches, makes it seem even more impossible to gain entry. I had assumed, wrongly it seems, that they wouldn't have had the time to build walls to encircle the settlement, but they had the remnants of walls, to begin with and have merely extended them.

'We can't burrow beneath the sodding walls,' Goda complains, slumping to the ground, as though all the life has left his body. I nod. I understand his anger. I've rapidly reached the same decision, but I'm not prepared to give up. Not yet.

'We need a bloody ship,' Hereman reiterates calmly. I lift my head and glower at him, surprised to see him smirking.

'What the fuck do we need a ship for?' I'm stung into demanding.

'To get over the river and to pretend that we're good Viking raiders, come to join them.'

'We've done that before. It worked, but there was an army at our back.'

'Aye, my lord, and this time we don't have that, but I've seen some of our men. They're inside Grantabridge, along with Lady Cyneswith. If we get inside, there'll be more than twenty of us to fight the fuckers. And hopefully, by then, we'll have the ealdormen to assist us as well. We can open the other gate by Edmund and entirely overwhelm the fuckers.'

'But how do we get inside the walls?' I growl. He's speaking in riddles.

'With a bloody ship,' Hereman continues to crow. I feel my eyes narrow at his words.

'What do we need the ship for?' I try again.

'To get over the river,' Hereman offers, eyebrows high, amusement on his broad face.

'And then how do we get through the guards?' I feel that we're talking in bloody circles.

'We kill the fuckers,' he exclaims, as though I'm the fool for not thinking of this.

'What? All of them?' Goda's perked up and is listening along with me. Many of the others are still busy with other tasks, tending to the horses, and keeping a guard. It would be bloody typical if we came all this way only to be apprehended by our enemy now.

'Yes, all of them. It's not like we don't need to kill 'em anyway.'

'And then how do we get through the bloody gate?'

'There'll be a fucking way,' Hereman confirms with confidence. I turn to Gardulf, but he looks as confused as I am.

'We need to know what that bloody way is,' I urge Hereman slowly.

'Do we?' Hereman demands. 'Or do we just need to find our stones and do what we always do, which is think on our feet and win all the same?'

'It's not the same, Hereman, not this time.' Hereman has long been a lucky bastard, but I think he's pushing it now.

'It doesn't have to be any bloody different,' he smirks, not to be dissuaded. 'We just have to think about it in the same way that we normally do. We make it across the river, in a boat because we can't capture the bridge, and then we kill all the fuckers, and rescue Lady Cyneswith. It's easy.'

'I only wish it bloody was,' I confirm in a rush of words. I don't have the answer, and that boils me. If I had a means of moving forward, of containing the problem, then I'd be able to think more clearly, I'm sure of it.

Hereman lifts his chin and glowers at me, his eyes fierce in the gloom. He twists his beard between his fingers, and I'm reminded of just how like Edmund he is. Only, without the predictability. Hereman might well be thinking of doing something irrational. With Edmund, it's just about certain that he'll be doing something stupid. With Hereman, there's always the possibility that he might be.

'You don't move without all of us,' I urge him.

'No, my lord king, you don't move without me,' and so speaking, he stands and threads his way through the trees.

'Come back here, you daft fucker,' I'm on my feet immediately, desperate to chase him down, but with only ten steps, I've lost sight of him through the dense undergrowth and low hanging branches. I can't even hear him moving through the trees.

'Don't get lost,' Rudolf cautions me, returning from his scouting mission, eyes down. 'We all know you're not very good in the woods, alone.' I glower at him, and he finds a smirk for his face, even though I can tell it pains him.

'Where's he gone?'

'You saw Hereman?'

'I heard him. He moves like a flock of sheep, and so do you,' Rudolf's words aren't reassuring.

'He's got some mad idea about needing a boat, and I fear he's gone to find one.'

'I wish him luck with that. The warriors of Grantabridge don't let anyone disembark until they know who you are. I imagine you've quite the reputation, my lord, and Hereman as well.'

'Did you discover anything?' I face Rudolf, admitting that I've lost Hereman for the time being. Together we walk back to the small clearing where the rest of my men and horses are waiting for a decision to be made.

'Not really, no. Icel thinks he might be on to something, so he'll be back later. I'm bloody starving,' Rudolf mutters to explain his early return.

'Eat what you can. I'm going to find Icel.'

'Alone?' Rudolf demands, turning shocked eyes my way.

'Yes, alone. I'll be bloody fine.' I don't wait for his answer before directing myself towards a glow in the sky coming from the fires inside Grantabridge. 'I'm not that bloody crap at getting myself lost,' I mutter as I walk. Every single one of my men seems determined to remind me of my mistakes. Without thought, my hand lifts to run over the scar of my neck wound. It's far from smooth and is a constant reminder of just how close I came to dying. But, in all the mad and stupid ideas I've enacted in my time as an ealdorman and now a king, I'm hardly surprised I've gained some wounds that have left scars.

All of my warriors have. Some have been physical, some to the heart, and yet others to their confidence. Young Penda, even now, remains at Kingsholm. He'll never become a warrior. Not now. Well, only if there are truly desperate times and there's no other option. It pains me to understand that he might not have the life of a scribe that so suits him if I can't keep a firm grip on Mercia.

I stop then. I've been crashing through the undergrowth. I need to take my time and recover my poise. Whatever Hereman's up to, he has the stones to see it through, and I'll just have to be happy with that. In all our years, and despite all his strange actions, he's not managed to kill us. Yet.

'Anything?' I whisper to Icel, when I join him, looking out over the broad river towards the bridge and settlement behind it. From here, and in the flickering lights of the brazier the guards are using, I can just make out the ancient walls that have been incorporated into a new system of defence.

'Not yet, my lord. But there'll be something. The enemy never considers everything. Behind those walls and that ditch, they'll feel safe unless an unknown ship appears around the bend in the river.' I wince at the reminder of Hereman's determination but hold my tongue. Not even Hereman would be that stupid. Would he?

I settle to watch beside Icel. I'd sooner be doing that than doing nothing but worrying.

'Any sign of Edmund or the ealdormen breaking through from the other side?'

'No, not yet.'

'Fuck,' I murmur. I would sooner have everything in place and be ready for my aunt's escape.

'What's Hereman up to?' Icel queries.

'Why, have you seen him?'

'No, but I could tell he had something on his mind.'

'He's gone to find a bloody boat,' I murmur. Icel's huff of annoyance reassures me that I'm not the only one to think the idea ridiculous.

'We've tried boats, dressing as our enemy, and carts and oxen,'

Icel murmurs. 'This time, we need to attempt something else. But it'll be bloody risky.'

'Like what? And what isn't risky?'

'Fire.'

'Fire?'

'Yes, if we burn the place down, there'll have no means of protecting themselves. Those stone walls are barely above shoulder height. It'll be easy enough to get over them once the rest of the wooden defences have been burned away.'

'It'll take a while to do that,' I argue.

'It will, yes, and that's if one of us can even throw a firebrand over the river, which I doubt, but it's a good option to have. No man can stand and fight in the face of fire.'

'But again, we have the problem of how to set the place aflame, and if we do manage it, there's no assurance my aunt won't be stolen away by the Viking raiders in their boats.'

'Then, my lord king, what do you want us to do? We can't just ask them to return Lady Cyneswith to us without giving them something in return. If that were going to work, they wouldn't have taken her in the first place.' Icel's words are surprisingly reasoned.

'How do we set the fire?' I ask him, curious to see how much thought he's given to the idea.

'Someone will have to swim the river and start the fire.' Icel confirms, assuring me that he has given the matter more thought than I have.

'And who would that someone be?'

'Well, we know Rudolf's good in the water,' Icel offers. I can just see his grey eyebrows rising on his face. Once more, I consider just how old he is. I have men amongst my warriors who are perhaps older, but they no longer ride at my side unless pressed into service because I'm low on numbers. Icel has never faltered. He's right. He's been a stalwart at my side, just as my aunt has been.

'We do, yes. But it's risky.'

'Then we'll use Hereman's boat, should he find one.'

'But it'll be seen?' I immediately counter.

Icel turns to face me then. 'My lord king, there's no easy solution to any of this. If there were, then the Viking raiders wouldn't have bothered taking your aunt. They'd have done something else. This way, they think they've got you by the stones, and it's not like you to veer away from the impossible. So, find your stones, and let's get fucking on with it.'

Chapter Seventeen

Hereman finds a boat, if you can call it a bloody boat.

'What the fuck is that?' Rudolf demands, casting his eyes over it in disgust.

'A bloody raft,' Hereman grins as he speaks. It's been a long night, but I've managed to get some sleep. Icel's words, while far from reassuring, have proven to me that I'm spending too much time worrying, and not enough time actually doing something. That's not like me. For a moment, I consider that my aunt might be pleased with me for such actions, but quickly realise that if there's one occasion when she wouldn't be, it's now. It's all well and good her demanding that I think before I act, but I doubt she'll appreciate it where her safety is concerned.

'It's either that or swimming?' I face Rudolf. The three roped-together pieces of wooden posts look about as sturdy as a dandelion flower shuddering in the wind, trying to hold on to its thin white petals. It'll only take someone being slightly off-balance, and the whole bloody thing will sink.

'Swimming?' Rudolf counters, a squeak in his voice, and then his eyes narrow. 'So, you think I'm bloody getting on that, do you?' he demands to know.

'Aye, lad, it's you or me, so take your pick.'

Rudolf shakes his head, lips pursed, and then he glowers at me.

'I nearly drowned in the bloody River Trent and now you mean for me to try my luck with the bloody River Granta, as well? My thanks, my lord.' He sweeps a bow and behind me, I hear Icel chuckle, the sound dark and filled with malice.

'Don't wear your byrnie,' Hereman offers conversationally. He's still grinning. Mad bastard. He thinks to have accomplished some great task by bringing the pieces of wood to me. Quite frankly, we could have picked up thicker trunks from the floor of the woodlands, and lashed them together with pieces of hemp rope. 'You'll drown if you do,' Hereman warns, as though we didn't realise what he meant.

I shake my head. Breathe deeply, and look from the barely afloat raft to the far side of the Granta River. I think it might just be safer to swim, but there's a current here, and if Rudolf's caught by the current, he'll be helpless as the river takes him closer and closer to the Viking raider settlement. Mind, the raft might do the same.

'Fuck. This is such a shit idea,' I complain.

'What exactly is the bloody idea?' Rudolf asks petulantly, glowering at Hereman.

'To fire the place,' Icel rumbles. 'One of us goes over on the raft and sets fire to it, and then we get inside when their defences are destroyed.'

'And how will the rest of you get over the river?' Rudolf queries. 'If I take the raft, will you all swim? Wearing your byrnies?' This is directed to Hereman, who smirks at the quickly rebounded comment.

The river is wide in places, and deep. It would be folly to risk my aunt's safety on a swim. What if we all drown? What if we all get caught?

'The horses will take us across,' Icel announces quickly. 'That's why you need a raft. You can't take Dever with you when you set the fires.'

'Oh, so now it's more than a fire. It's bloody fires, is it?' Rudolf shakes his head, eyes unhappy. Even Rudolf's lost his customary daredevil approach to life. I'm not the only one; that's some consolation.

Icel shrugs his massive shoulders, and Hereman continues to grin.

'We do what needs to be done. It's always been the same,' Icel offers, no hint of apology. I shake my head at Icel's words. Is this how I normally think? Is it just the fact the bastards have my aunt that's filled me with trepidation?

'So, when are we doing this bloody thing?' Rudolf queries. Daylight floods the woodlands. It would be folly to go now, surely?

'At dusk,' Icel confirms, Hereman nodding along, and I consider, when did I let my warriors start to dictate what and when we do things? And then I reconsider. Did I ever really truly lead my warriors, or did they always lead me?

* * *

The day is long and dreary. I send Goda and Lyfing off in opposite directions to scout and keep an eye on events taking place inside Grantabridge. I don't want my aunt to be taken from the place without us knowing, so that we waste time, effort and possibly lives, on trying to reach her when she's not there anymore.

Icel spends the day sleeping. I glower at him repeatedly as his snores fill the small camping site. Bastard. I wish I could sleep, but I'm too jumpy. Every snap and crack of a branch has my hand reaching for my seax. Even Rudolf shakes his head at me and meanders away to tend to Dever. I look at Haden, and he won't meet my eyes. It seems I'm pissing off everybody.

Moodily, I stamp my way to where I spoke to Icel during the night. From here, it's possible to see the Viking raider settlement. I glower at it, thinking Icel and Hereman's plan impossible to accomplish. How, I think, will we burn so much wood? There's stone in places to just above knee height. On top of that, the Viking raiders, or perhaps Mercians who once lived there, placed planks of wood, extending the protection to the height of two men.

There's a gateway cut into the stone. It consists of only one, huge door, that can be pulled inwards, not outwards. I imagine that behind it, there are guards aplenty. They must, surely, expect some retaliation for what they've done. I can't see the Grantabridge jarls letting any old Olaf, Halfdan or Sigrid stand a watch after what happened in Repton. If anything, I expect one of the three jarls to be there, personally directing their men to ensure everyone's safety. But of course, there's nothing of the sort.

Indeed, I don't even see any Viking raiders. They're staying firmly behind their walls. From here, I can't even hear anything, not over the rushing of the water and the general noise of the woodlands.

I stare, and I lour, and I peer to the left, to where I anticipate Edmund must be, far in the distance, but of course, I don't see him. If I could see him, then why would we have needed to take such a long diversion to get here?

'Do you see it?' It's Rudolf who joins me. The poor lad has undoubtedly drawn the luckless task of speaking to me. I can just imagine the argument that must have entailed.

'See what?' I mutter. 'The fucking great big gate or the even taller walls. Or, the bloody wide river that stands between us and those sodding big gates.'

I sense Rudolf's scrutiny and turn to scowl at him as well. He's changed in the last year. When we first encountered the Viking raiders seeking my death, he was a mouthy and cocky little shit, more likely to run around than stand and talk. Now he seems far more settled, and much easier with himself. He might still be tall and lanky, and his elbows and knees might not be under his complete control, but he holds himself as a warrior, hands resting easily on his weapons belt. I've made him a warrior, or rather, circumstances have. I'm not sure how pleased about that I am.

'No, not those, although it's good that you do note them.' When

Rudolf offers nothing else, I turn my gaze back towards the gate and the walls and allow my eyes to track it. In places, the walls are perilously close to the river bank. I can't see that the river was always so close to the walls. Has the river altered its course, or is this a result of the floods earlier in the year? And then, a smile plays around my lips, and I turn to meet Rudolf's eyes.

'Aye, lad, I see it.' And he nods, as though pleased with me, and then speaks again.

'It took you bloody long enough, Coelwulf. I think you've got fucking old,' and with that, he leaves me to ponder what Hereman, Icel and even Rudolf saw long before I did.

'Fuck,' I muse. I need to be more alert. I'm missing things that are more obvious than the nose on the front of my face.

Chapter Eighteen

At dusk, I gather my warriors together. Icel has deigned to wake up. Hereman, however, has to be nudged to full wakefulness.

'Right,' I begin. 'Rudolf will use the raft, and we'll take half of the horses. No more. They should be able to take the weight of two of us when we're in the water. Hemming and Wulfhere, you take your mounts and stay on this side of the river. Your task is to fish our horses out of the river further downstream. Don't lose any of them or let them go too far past the bend. Agreed?' I fix the two youngsters with my stare, and they nod, although Hemming is unhappy about it. I should probably take the pair with me, but I need seasoned warriors for this.

'Osbert and Eadulf, you stay here with the rest of the horses, and just in case some of the beasts come back this way, and not towards Hemming and Wulfhere.'

'That leaves sixteen of us, or rather, fifteen, as Rudolf must start the fires.'

My warriors are stony-faced in the gloom. Rudolf has removed his byrnie and wears only his tunic, trews, and boots. The rest of us remain garbed for battle. That's because we have the horses to assist us across the watery expanse and not a flimsy piece of fucking wood.

'We make it inside when all is confusion because of the fires, and we find my aunt and the rest of my warriors. Understood?' Again, my warriors nod, all apart from Hereman, who grins as though this is the most fun and excitement he's ever fucking had.

'We fight as one,' I urge them. 'No fucking about and running off. If we become separated, then we're even more in the shit than we are at the moment.'

'Aye, my lord.' Icel's the only one to speak, whereas the rest merely nod, grunt, or generally reassure me that while they hear my words, they're not actually listening to them.

'Do you have everything you need?' I direct to Rudolf.

'Yes. I have a basket of twigs and the means to strike a flame,' he confirms, although his voice lacks its usual confidence. 'Provided I don't get fucking wet.' Rudolf is the unhappiest of all my warriors. It doesn't surprise me. I'd sooner go in his place, but apparently, according to bloody Icel, Hereman and Wærwulf, that's not going to fucking happen. Not this time. I'd argue with them about it, but they might be right to be low on trust. I might just be the one to go off on my own and cause all sorts of problems – the biggest one being I could be caught, and for real this time. I have so few warriors with me that it's best not to tempt fate.

And I can even hear my aunt's voice in my head, telling me not to be so damn pig-headed about the whole thing. Pig-headed and damn would be the strongest words she might use, even on this occasion. The reminder of why we're doing this makes me eager to be gone and also hesitant. What if we're too late and my aunt's stubbornness has betrayed her? I try not to consider that possibility.

'Then we might as well get this shit show underway,' I inform my men. I look at each of them, holding their eyes for a few moments. There are so few of us. Eahric will never be pretty again because his nose will never be straight. Goda carries his scars as well, although the loss of a finger never seems to concern him. He can fight as well as any man with four fingers and a thumb on each hand. Ordheah and Wulfstan stand side by side, as so often is the case. They should both be sitting before a warm hearth fire, not here, preparing an attack on a Viking raider stronghold.

Wærwulf grins at me as though determining my thoughts. Rudolf looks defiant. Icel is calm, merely waiting for what must be done next. Leonath offers me a toothless grin. Sæbald's bearded chin shows his most recent scar in the way the hair refuses to grow over the barely healed cut. At least he doesn't need to shave there.

Ordlaf's square face watches me evenly, whereas if I focus on Lyfing for too long, I'll see only the trail of the wound that almost sliced his nose from his face. Hereman grins at me, the big bastard that he is. Gardulf licks his lips nervously, and I'm reminded that it wasn't long ago that I thought he might die from his wounds and that it took all of my aunt's skill to ensure he lived. Cuthwalh looks resigned to what must happen, whereas Gyrth seems determined. These men are all my warriors, and carry the scars to show it. Not for the first time, I wish they didn't.

'Remember,' I growl, turning back to face those who'll escort me and also those with other tasks, 'stay the fuck alive, or I'll kill you myself.' Hemming swallows heavily at my ferocious words, but Wulfhere grins. At that moment, he reminds me of his grandfather. It was good to see Tatberht at Northampton, but I fear he might never return to my side after the terrible wounds he took in the forest close to London.

I take Haden to our chosen location on the riverbank. Icel also brings Samson, and Wærwulf leads Cinder. Dever has been left behind, and I think Rudolf's pleased about that. The other horses we've decided upon are Billy, Berg, Aart, Kermit and Petre. These are the biggest horses. Hopefully, they'll easily take the weight of two of us and still be able to swim across the expanse of the river and, more importantly, back again. We've removed their saddles, and all they have is their reins, tied up tightly behind them. I fear it means they'll become entangled or trapped either around their legs or in submerged obstacles in the river, but equally, we need something with which to grab them should it be needed.

Rudolf walks beside me, carrying his bundle of combustibles in one hand and holding onto Haden with the other. He's silent, no doubt thinking about the upcoming task.

'Do you think Pybba is well?' Rudolf surprises me by asking.

'Aye, lad. He's survived worse injuries than his current one.'

'But the illness?'

'He'd have died from it long before we found him if it was going to take him.'

My surety reassures him.

'He won't be pleased to have missed all this,' Rudolf continues, finding some cheer to lighten his tone.

'You can tell him all about it when you see him again,' I inform him over the top of Haden's shoulder.

'I don't know. I think he'll be pissed with you for putting me in such a position again. I think I might keep my mouth shut,' Rudolf chuckles darkly, and I shake my head to hear it. But then what would I prefer, that he was too bloody scared to take advantage of our only chance?

Hereman strides along with the pathetic raft he's found held close to his body. It's rank with the smell of the river and the tangled weeds that have become trapped between the flimsy pieces of wood. I think it's more likely this was once someone's fence than it was actually intended as a boat, but Hereman has proved it'll float, the daft grin on his face showing his pride.

At the edge of the tree line, we all pause, peering towards the settlement of Grantabridge. We're downstream of it, but its edges are clearly defined against the shadows of the coming night as I look to my right. The gate remains shut. There's been no sight of anyone all day.

'Let me through,' Hereman forges a path behind Haden and then lowers his stinking raft to the grassy bank. The river is about an arm's length lower than the bank. But I hold him back. I want to be sure before we do this.

'It's not too late to change your mind,' I caution Rudolf. His white teeth grinning at me from his slim face, he speaks. 'I didn't realise I even had a bloody choice,' he mutters, turning as though he'll walk away, back towards our campsite, but he quickly turns back.

'It's not a problem. For Lady Cyneswith, I'd do bloody anything, no matter how reckless, as would the rest of your men. I'm just lucky that I'm the one that gets to say they saved her before all the others so much as bloody tried.' I shake my head at his puffed-out chest and bragging tone. It masks his worries, and I allow it. I need him to do this. I can't see another way of getting inside Grantabridge unseen.

'Well, I think there's no better time than now,' I confirm. I release Hereman to lower the raft into the river, which he does so, lying almost flat on his belly. He's tied a hemp rope around the raft, just in case the current takes it, and the plan is that we'll keep a hold of it until we know Rudolf has safely crossed the river.

Just before Rudolf shuffles forward to slide onto the raft, I reach out and grip his forearm.

'If this is a fuck up, run as fast as you can, and for as long as you, and then make it back to this side of the River Granta.'

'I know how to hide and fight, my lord,' Rudolf's serious now. 'I don't need telling how to stay alive.'

'Fair enough,' I mutter, allowing him to slide onto the raft, where it bobs uncertainty. Hereman is having to work harder than he'd like to admit to keep the raft steady. When Rudolf is precariously balanced, I reach over and hand him the bundle of combustibles tied up inside one of the treated cloaks we'd wear if it were raining. I doubt anything inside it will remain dry for long.

Rudolf grips it tightly and slides it over his left hand using the rope tying it together.

'Let me go,' he calls over his shoulder, and Hereman begins to release the rope. The craft lurches out into the river, and I rush to add my weight to it before the entire thing spools out of Hereman's hands.

Rudolf's suppressed shriek reaches me as the contraption bobs on the water, and then he's on his way over the width of the river, having found his balance. I watch in the gloom as the raft moves with the water, first fast, then slow, and realise there's something we've not considered. Just how is Rudolf to direct the raft to where he wants to go? The raft is content enough where the water flows, at the centre of the river, but Rudolf needs to get to the far side.

'Bugger,' I exclaim, still holding the rope, watching helplessly as Rudolf fails to move to the opposite river bank. I want to warn him not to get off the raft, but he does so before I can even shout the words, having realised the predicament. Trying to keep his bundle above his head, Rudolf splashes into the cold water, flailing for the opposite bank, even as Hereman and I work to gather the raft back to this side. We can't allow it to continue around the curve in the river. I might think it looks like little more than a pile of twigs, but to the Viking raiders, I'm sure they'll see a ship worthy of crossing the wide Whale Road should it wash up closer to the entrance that Edmund guards.

Just as we pull the raft back, I realise that Rudolf has completed his journey and is kicking himself free from the fast-flowing river to lie drenched on the far bank. I imagine I can hear his teeth chattering from here.

'Bollocks,' I exclaim, hoping he can still light his fire and that not all of him is drenched. The journey has exhausted him. He lies for some time without moving. I'm tempted to shout to him, but that would give him away. He's still just about out of sight of the gateway, on a very slim strip of the bank between the walls and the river, but if we make too much noise, the Viking raiders must surely come to investigate what's happening.

Eventually, when Haden has grown tired of waiting and has begun to drowse on his feet, Rudolf stands and lifts one arm to show he's well, Icel informing me of this because I can't see well enough now that full night has fallen. I watch a Rudolf-sized shape duck beneath a strand of low-lying bushes that almost masks his approach to the gateway. I've still not seen the gate open, not even a little bit, not one piece of light from the fires inside those walls has shown itself outside them. I consider whether the Viking raiders use the gate or prefer everyone to arrive at the river gate, where Edmund waits. Perhaps this entrance is only used for goods travelling over land or to gain access to London.

'We just need to wait now,' I murmur, as though I was the one outside the Viking raider walls, even though everyone knows the plan.

I can no longer see even a shadow of Rudolf, nor can I smell smoke. Haden isn't the only one drowsing now. Hereman has moved the raft out of the water, and it rests against a tree trunk, should it be needed again.

And so, we wait.

'What's he bloody doing?' Goda mutters when it feels like we've been immobile for far too long. I've heard little from the far side of the riverbank, but then, the woodlands are abuzz with activity. I fear mounted warriors could have ridden up to the gate, and we wouldn't know with the blackness of night. The wind is gentle, a soft shush of leaves, but the temperature drops with every breath I take.

'There.' A spark of light on the opposite bank finally appears.

'Get ready for it,' I murmur, running my hand along Haden's face to ensure he's awake. I won't be going into the water first. Instead, Samson will lead the way, with Icel and Sæbald to either side of him. If Haden still doesn't get into the water, Billy will take Hereman and Gyrth and so on until my bloody horse does as he's told.

The small fire that Rudolf starts just outside the closed gate of Grantabridge suddenly blazes brightly in the darkness of the night. There's little light leaching out from inside the settlement, although I'm sure there are hearth fires as the smell of food being cooked reaches us every so often. It reminds me that I'm hungry and could do with something good to eat.

I don't move my eyes away from the flicker of flames, where first one blaze begins and then another, getting ever closer to the gate, and then across it, and around the side of the walls, where they almost spill into the river.

The flames leap merrily, fiercely. Despite all the rain of recent weeks, the wood has dried quickly. Now I can hear the roar of the fire as it dances from one place to another, merging to form one massive conflagration. And that's when all fucking hell breaks loose.

Chapter Nineteen

'Now,' I order Icel, but he's already leading his mount to the water's edge, Sæbald to the other side of Samson.

'It's bastard cold,' Icel rumbles. I can feel the cold from where I stand. Samson doesn't seem to mind the coolness as he slips into the water with his cargo to either side. The flames are now leaping upwards on the far side of the river. Any moment, I expect the Viking raiders to run to the river and begin bailing water to quench the flames, and that's why we're slightly upriver, away from where their eyes might think to look when they do approach the river.

As if I've conjured them with thought, a loud roar erupts from behind the walls of Grantabridge. The flaming gateway bursts open as shapes rush outward while others thrust their way through them to reach the water's edge.

I can hear them calling one to another, and one voice rises above them all, but I don't understand the words that rumble forth. I can easily imagine what they might be. I spare a thought for Rudolf, hoping he's made his way to safety, and then I watch as Billy begins his swim, Hereman and Gyrth to either side of him. I try to spot Samson further out in the river, but the three of them have moved out of my line of sight, and with the flames at the corner of my vision, the darkness is even blacker.

Haden nudges me then, and I smirk. The damn beast isn't happy at not being led into the water first, although he'd never have gone first, and he bloody knows it. Lyfing's eyes meet mine over the back of Haden's shoulders. Haden dips his hoof low, and I slither to my arse and then into the water, Lyfing doing the same to the other side.

'Fuck.' The water is even colder than I thought it would be. I grit my teeth and turn to reach for Haden. He's slowly sliding into the water, allowing his right front leg to lead him. And then panic takes him, and he rears backwards as though refusing the offer of a cold swim. I grab his reins, pulling him to my side.

'Come on. I'm all bloody wet now, so get on with it.' His white eyes meet mine, and for a moment, I think he'll refuse, his warm breath blowing into my face. Only then he's entirely in the water. I aim him towards where I want to go, and he begins to move away from the bank of the river, obeying me for once in his long life.

The flow of the water is both fierce and bloody cold. I hold onto Haden's shoulder, legs floating behind me, almost horizontal, so that I can kick against the current. I can feel Haden's powerful legs trying to do the same, but I also realise we're being pushed by the current, and if we're not careful, we won't be where the rest of the men are.

'Pull him towards you,' I urge Lyfing. Behind us, I hear another horse entering the water, and the flames are dancing around the gateway of Grantabridge. I can see shadows against the flames. A train of men and women is starting to bring water from the river to quench the fire, their loud cries covering any sound we might make, but I think it'll all be too late. And quite frankly, I don't really care if it burns or is saved. By then, we should be inside Grantabridge.

I catch sight of movement up ahead and appreciate that one of the horses is still struggling with the crossing. I'm pleased then that we chose the largest and strongest horses. Dever wouldn't have been able to hold his own in the deep water, no matter his recent return to form.

I lower my head to the side of Haden's head and finally see what I'm looking for. Ahead, two figures crouch low on the thin lip of the river's edge. And while they do that, another horse is making his way toward Hemming and Wulfhere. I hope they manage to retrieve him from the river. The current pulling us northwards is stronger than I expected. It's worrying to realise that there's so little between me and a very wet death beneath the vast expanse of the almost black sky.

Ahead, I hear some murmurs and a shriek of outrage and startle. What's happened? I wish I could see more. And then, a slight ripple over the top of the water alerts me that something's happening. I don't know if it means Hereman and Gyrth have made it to the far side or if something's befallen Billy, and then I need to focus on Haden. He falters, his head almost going beneath the water. I release my hold on him. We're too heavy for him, despite everything I said. I'm not sure if Lyfing does the same, but I float free and feel the pull of the water around my legs.

'Bugger.' Between one breath and the next, I'm too far away from Haden as he regains his rhythm and continues on his way, Lyfing's eyes glaring at me over the top of my horse.

'Shit.' I kick with my legs, feeling the weight of my warrior's belt dragging at me, with all the weapons I refused to leave behind, even as the water tries to tumble me down the river.

I kick again, gritting my teeth against the cold, but I can make no progress. Haden is almost at the river bank where Icel and Hereman are alert to what's happening, but I'm being forced away, back into the centre of the river, and no matter what I do or how much I fight the current, it has a firm grip on me.

And then a rope slaps me in the face, and I just stop myself from shrieking. I reach for it, lifting first one arm and then another until I'm sure I have a hold on it. I wrap my arms around it, and even with it, and even though I'm still kicking, I feel the current trying to force me away from my destination.

'Fuck this,' I growl through tight lips, the taste of the water on my tongue. It's not got a bad taste, but I don't want to drink horse and mud.

Finally, I start to make progress towards the river bank, only as I do, Haden, eyes wide and perplexed, makes his way past me in the opposite direction. I reach out to encourage him, only for him to stop, trying to aid me.

'Bloody get on with you,' I urge my horse. He's already blowing heavily, and he still needs to make it to Hemming and Wulfhere. 'I'll be well.' I think Haden will continue to fight the current, only for my warriors to really get a good hold on the rope, and abruptly, I can reach out and touch the bank as I'm pulled through the water. I kick quickly, arms on the river bank, and haul myself upwards with the aid of Icel and Hereman. I'm gasping, my teeth chattering. I'm drenched, but my concern is for Haden.

'Has Haden gone?' I'm turning as I speak in a harsh whisper, even though there's no room on the river bank. I don't know how Icel and Hereman managed to help me. If they so much as bend over, their arses will be touching the low stone wall and that'll send them into the water. I didn't even know they'd taken a rope with them.

'Aye, he's on his way,' Lyfing assures me, just as softly. He's puffing through cheeks so white, I can clearly see them despite the darkness. He has his hands rammed into his armpits in an effort to get warm.

I'm aware of noise coming from beyond the walls. Men and women snapping commands in the Viking raiders tongue and I breathe in, trying to quell the thudding of my heart and the shivering of my body. I could do with Wærwulf, to tell me what the Viking raiders say, but he and Cinder have yet to make the crossing alongside Leonath. Or so I assume, as I see Berg making his way to the river bank, head slick with water, with Wulfstan and Ordheah on the other side of him. It's cramped on the shard of riverbank, but I don't want to make our move until we have as many men as possible ready for the attack.

Certainly, the hubbub of voices from inside the wall, makes me appreciate all over again, just how small my force is against so many others. They once sent three hundred men to kill me, and it was never going to be enough, but there are only seventeen of us, provided Rudolf makes it to our side. That can't be enough to take on the might of Grantabridge.

Although, well, is that really the fucking plan? Perhaps not.

I bend and assist Wulfstan to stand beside me. He's breathing heavily, and shivering at the same time. Berg, eyes wide, but steady, seems majestic as he pushes off in the direction of Hemming and Wulfhere. Wulfstan wobbles on the edge of the bank.

'It's fucking narrow,' I confirm. By now, I'm confident that all of my men will make the crossing. I thought it impossible, and yet, here we are. Aart has managed to convey Cuthwalh, the horse only responsible for one man. Petre has brought Eahric and Goda, Kermit has aided Gardulf and Ordlaf.

Now it comes to the more difficult part, and it'll be difficult. I turn and face the stone wall and additions of wooden slats running atop the stone part of the wall, that the Viking raiders thinks protects them. And yet, somewhere along the way, they've grown too confident and assured of their safety here. I mean to take advantage of that.

'This way,' I urge Wærwulf in a whisper, now he too is on the river bank.

'Aye, my lord, I'm coming.' His lips are compressed into a thin line, the cold piercing him as well, his teeth set in a grimace. I wish we hadn't needed to get so bloody wet to make our way here.

'What are they saying?' I once more whisper to Wærwulf. He shakes his head,.

'Just the usual bitching about why this sort of shit only ever happens when most of the people are halfway to pissed, and it's time for sleep.' He grimaces, his foot slipping out behind him, and I grab his shoulder to steady him.

'My thanks,' Wærwulf confirms, eyes wide once more.

'It's not much further.' The way is perilous. Not for the first time,

I think what we're doing is fucking ridiculous. It's bound to fail. And yet, it can't and I know that. Nothing we do ever fails.

I try to rear back and look upwards, but my foot slips as well, and I'm gripping for anything I can hold on the wooden wall that separates us from the Viking raiders inside. My finger manages to hook on a bole hole and I can pull myself upright, breathing heavily. Behind me, the roar of the river is loud. Fuck, I hope the horses have survived their swim.

'Steady,' Wærwulf offers, countering my words to him only moments ago. I swallow heavily, and move once more. It really can't be much further. I cast my eyes along the edge, and see that my warriors mirror my steps. We're all as fucking reckless as one another.

'This is it,' Wærwulf informs me. He's managed to hook his hands in such a way that he can lean back and get a good view of the wall that towers over our heads.

I nod, grateful to at least have made it this far. I reach upwards, running my hands over the wooden slats and hoping that we'll find what we need. If not, we will struggle, but it's not impossible.

I run my hands higher, and the right one catches on a hook, and I test it. It might do. I reach above my head and find another, but that's it, and there's nothing for my left hand. Not at all. I grimace. We need something for both sides of my body, even if the wall here is the good height of a horse lower than elsewhere on this one stretch of the defences. Perhaps they meant to build a lookout here, or maybe they simply ran out of wood, or maybe there are a hundred warriors behind it, just waiting for their enemy to make a mistake, but I don't think that's right.

'Do we have the hammer?' I whisper to Wærwulf.

He turns to the next man, and the next and while I eavesdrop on what's happening beyond the wall, the hammer makes it into my hands, along with a wedge of wood. Wærwulf's listening carefully to what's happening beyond the wall, and I wait for him to nod to show it's safe to start my work. We brought just enough with us to enable us to climb the lowest wall. Now we just need to do that.

Hereman has fashioned the piece of wood from a stray piece of a thick branch. He's honed it with his knife so that it has a point to it, and also a flatter edge to stand on, or grip with my hands. Of course, I've not considered how to actually get enough of a swing to force it into the wooden slats.

'Do it,' Wærwulf insists, and I bite my lip and lift both arms hoping there'll just be enough room to swing the hammer into the wood as I hold the wedge close to the lower handhold I found. It's fucking awkward. Just holding the wood before me, forces my body outwards, my toes desperately gripping inside my boots, as though they're what hold me on the river bank, and not my boots.

I swing my right arm but immediately feel my balance faltering, and I sag against the wall, reaching for the right-hand hold to steady myself, even with the hammer in my hand still.

'Fuck,' I huff. This isn't going to be easy.

'Can you do it?' Wærwulf demands from me.

'I think so,' I retort, but I'm really not sure. My heart's hammering so loudly, it's as though it makes my chest vibrate like a drum, hitting the wooden wall and alerting the Viking raiders to my presence. But I need to do this. I steady myself, move the wooden block in front of my eyes once more, and consider what I need to do. I'm not a wood-crafts person. I'm sure there's a particular way to hit the wood and to ensure the wedge goes in correctly, but I don't fucking know what it is.

'Don't,' Wærwulf's hand on my right arm, just stops me from striking the wedge on my next attempt. I'm frustrated now. I had the angle right. I'd worked out how to do what needed to be done, but he shakes his head. From beyond the wall, I can hear voices. I strain to hear what they say, but of course, they speak in their tongue and it's impossible. And yet, I recognise the voices, all the same.

'Jarl Guthrum,' Wærwulf mouths to me, and I nod, thwarted all over again that I don't understand his words. I catch sight of wide, white eyes, and I'm not the only one to look up, as though expecting the Viking raiders to appear over the wooden wall at any moment. Do they know we're here? Do they suspect that we might try and rescue my aunt? Have they realised that the fires Rudolf set and which still cast the area far to my right in dancing flames are merely some means of distracting them?

And then I have my answer.

'He's telling them to double the guard on your aunt. She must be just behind here,' Wærwulf whispers, and my resolve redoubles. We must get here, although she's not going to think kindly of us if she has to swim across the bloody river. Or maybe she won't care, as long as she's free.

The conversation rumbles on a little longer. I can hear the chink of metal on metal, and some running steps, and then Jarl Guthrum must move away because the conversation ceases.

'Now?' I whisper to Wærwulf, but he winces and shakes his head still.

Fuck, I'm cold. I can't feel my feet and my hands are shaking from my swim. If this goes on for much longer, I'm not going to be able to hit anything with a hammer. Even the hammer is weighing down my arm. I should have had Hereman do this. Or perhaps, I should have merely tried to climb on someone's shoulders to gain entry. But, there really isn't the room, and I know it.

'Now,' Wærwulf urges me, and this time, I take careful aim. I hold my left hand as still as I can, and swing my right arm wide enough that there'll be some force to it when it eventually connects. And it does connect, but the damn wedge doesn't slide into the wooden wall but rather glances of it, to tumble down at my feet.

'Fuck.' It lands on my right foot, sending stabbing pains along its length. Wærwulf bends quickly and retrieves the lost wedge, a look of concern on his face. The pain, as trifling as it should be, is immense and I really want to fucking get this over and done with.

'Give it here,' I urge him quietly, and he hands it to me. Once more, I settle myself, my left hand holding the wedge in place, at just about chest height, while my right hand swings to the side. This time, I'm greeted with a satisfying crunching sound as the wedge finally bites deep. I follow up the movement with two and then another two strikes, just to be sure the wedge is in place.

I test it with the weight of my hand, pressing down on it, and the bloody thing doesn't even so much as slip.

'Thank fuck for that,' I murmur, and then Wærwulf has the next wedge passed to him, and if I thought the first wedge was a bastard to get into place, this is going to be even more difficult. I shake my head.

'When I'm ready,' I whisper to him, and now I lift my left foot high, banging my knee against the wood in the process so that it bloody hurts as well. With my one hand holding the higher-up wedge, I force myself up by counting to three under my breath, and then I'm higher than Wærwulf and the rest of my men, but still the top of the wall is out of reach.

'Now,' I hold my hand out and Wærwulf passes me the wedge and I remove the hammer from where I'd hooked it on my weapons belt. I need to be even more careful this time. If I lose my balance, I'm really going to hurt something on my way to landing in the surging river.

I eye the one hook in the wall and move the wedge into place. There's still too little room to move in, but I'm sure that this time I know what I'm about. Only then I pause, consider what I'm doing, and instead of hammering the wedge into place, I hand it back to Wærwulf and remove my seax from my weapons belt. I hollow out a small gap in the wooden slat that makes up the wall, and only then hold the retrieved wedge to it. This time, it slips straight into the wood.

'I should have fucking done that last time,' I mutter to myself. I test it, and the wedge and the other handhold, seem safe enough.

'Here goes fucking nothing,' I order myself. I boost myself upwards, and then immediately lower my head. This is it. I can see into the enemy encampment, and it's well-lit with the fire which still burns and the lights pouring from open doors. The sudden brightness blinds me, and so I close my eyes, curse my stupidity and then boost myself upwards again. This time, I slowly open my eyes, holding my head just level with the top of the wooden wall so that I can make out more and more.

There are dwellings here, buildings made of wood and wattle and daub. They all have turfed roofs and look sturdy enough, laid out in seemingly neat rows with wooden drains lining the backs of the buildings. I shake my head, dismayed by the orderliness of it all. This isn't some temporary camp. No, while I've been pleased that the Viking raiders have left Northampton alone throughout the winter months, the bastards have been making themselves at home in Grantabridge.

'Fuck,' I mutter under my breath, trying to seek out the place where my aunt must be being held. I dare not stand fully upright for fear of being seen, but my thighs are starting to twinge. I'm cold, wet, miserable and aching and yet, I have to get over the wooden wall and rescue my aunt.

I peer all around. There's one building with two men standing close to a brazier. Neither of them seems keen on their task, and they're peering towards the gateway where the fire still blazes. They think the danger is coming from there, and that plays into my hands, provided I can make it over the wall.

A hand on my foot, and I duck down and meet Wærwulf's eyes.

'Can we do it?' he demands to know. I also see the heads of my warriors, waiting patiently, clinging to the wooden wall as best they can.

'Yes, but we'll have to jump down inside,' I caution. This was always going to be the problem. Easy enough, well, almost easy enough, to get into this position, but now we need to get inside the walls and rescue my aunt without fucking getting caught, or killed.

Chapter Twenty

I heave myself over the side of the wooden wall, no matter Wærwulf's frantic entreaties that he should go first. I don't fucking think so.

I've checked the guards aren't looking my way, and that no one is watching the wall. I force myself over the top, dangling precariously on the thin slats of wood at the top, my eyes catching sight of so much more now that I'm that little bit higher. Towards the burning gate, many people have congregated, attempting to dampen the flames which lick along their constructed wooden-topped wall. I smirk at the sight of the devastation, and then pull my legs over the top, and hang as far down as possible, my arms extended.

My feet kick out, but there's nothing there, so I let go and drop, feeling the swish of cool air over my face, landing awkwardly, and with a loud thud of weight and jangle of weapons inside Grantabridge.

Immediately, I grab my seax and stare into the darker corners of the space. The smell here is ripe with dampness; no doubt the water from the river and something else, less pleasant. Perhaps it's here that they cure skins to make leather, because it sure as shit smells like piss.

My arrival doesn't arouse any suspicion, and I peer upwards and meet the flaring eyes of Wærwulf. I beckon him to follow me, and he forces his legs over the wall and then lowers his body as well. I offer my shoulders for his boots, and so he walks his way down the wall, using his hands until I can bend, and he can almost step off me and onto the slippery mud of the ground.

'Urgh,' Wærwulf comments softly, wafting his hand in front of his nose, and reaching for a seax with his other hand.

'Fragrant,' I offer and he nods, but quickly turns away to scout out the darkness that engulfs us. The rest of my warriors begin to follow on, one at a time. It's painfully slow. I help Gardulf down, in the same way I did Wærwulf, and Leonath and then Hereman, but with a wince of pain. Hereman takes my place, and Icel joins us, Goda and Eahric, Cuthwalh making the climb look easy, which impresses me because he's as bloody old, if not older than Icel. We move our way along the wall, then, clinging to it, as we did on the outside, only without the river at our backs.

They spread out to ensure that we're not seen, and the rest of my warriors descend without any problems, Ordheah, Sæbald, Ordlaf, Lyfing, Gyrth and Wulfstan. Some of them are noisy, and others quiet, but telling them to shut the fuck up would make more noise either way. Wulfstan huffs with the effort, and I spare him a thought. So, few of my men are young these days, and those that are, I've left elsewhere, or given even more difficult tasks. It fills me with pride to appreciate that my men have lived through so much already. I just hope they continue to do so.

When we're all over the wall, I turn and look at them, a smirk on my face for what we've accomplished.

'Fucking easy,' I mutter, feeling my confidence returning. Icel shakes his head at my summation, but Hereman grins, his pleasure that his idea has worked, evident to see.

'There are some barrels over there,' Hereman points into the settlement. 'If we get them, we can climb out the way we came in and it'll be a fuck sight easier.' I nod in agreement. I can see my men in the dashing shadows and flames of the fire. It seems Rudolf's fire is working in ways to aid that I hadn't foreseen.

'Get them then, while Wærwulf, Icel, Gyrth, Leonath and Sæbald retrieve my aunt. She's in that building, there,' and I point, hoping they can see where I'm looking.

'We'll go in the front. Cuthwalh, Wulfstan, Ordlaf, Lyfing, Eahric and Gardulf, you go around the back.

'Goda, Ordheah and then Hereman, when you return, you keep our exit path clear.'

My men nod to show they understand, and I scamper through the collection of buildings, trying not to breathe too deeply of the sharp stink of piss. It really catches the back of the throat, and I don't want to cough. It's bad enough that I stink of the river anyway, and swirling smoke is just beginning to work its way into the settlement as well.

There are three buildings, and all of them are built of wood and wattle and daub. There's no stone in their construction. I hold my ear to them but I can determine no sound from inside. If we're lucky, everyone has gone to help quench the flames. And then, at the last of the buildings, I pause and listen. This time, I can hear sound from inside, and I swallow down my frustration. I thought Jarl Guthrum had gone away, but it seems he's inside the building. I can detect the murmur of his voice, and I turn to Wærwulf, who shadows me so closely, I can hear his fucking heartbeat.

'He's trying to talk to your aunt,' Wærwulf confirms. 'He has someone in there who can speak our tongue, and he's having his questions translated for her. Your aunt isn't speaking.' This doesn't surprise me. She's a woman of few words anyway, and she won't want to tell Jarl Guthrum anything. 'But he speaks our tongue anyway,' Wærwulf looks perplexed as he remembers this.

'Fuck.' I can't imagine that Jarl Guthrum is in there alone. I think he must have warriors to assist him, and that means that if we attack now, the fighting's going to start a lot sooner than I want it to. I need to have at least extracted my aunt from the building before the slaughter begins.

'Fuck, fuck, fuck,' I murmur, looking all around me. Darkness still coats the land, but it's taken us a long time to cross the river and get inside Grantabridge. I don't know how long, not really, not between the shivering and the throbbing of my foot. My plan was to be gone from here long before the sun rose. If we're found, as we are, we'll have to fight our way through fuck knows how many of the bastards, and we'll still have the obstacle of the river to contend with, and we have no horses.

Yet, if we attack Jarl Guthrum now, he'll raise the alarm, and we won't be any better off.

'We need to wait,' I caution, and Wærwulf nods along with me. I indicate we should get back to where we entered the settlement, but then I have another idea. I shuffle forward, hardly daring to move for fear my weapons belt will clink and give me away, but I need to see.

A smile plays around my lips as I get a closer look at the two guards. One of them could be the very double of Wærwulf. I move backwards and turn to whisper in his ear. He shakes his head to deny my intention, but I don't give him the chance to refuse further. I'm already moving through the shadows, skipping from one to the next. I hear a soft murmur from inside the building where my aunt must be, followed by a bark of pain, and my blood boils.

My seax sinks into the first guard's underarm without sound. He sags against me, and Wærwulf is there, to offer the same death to the other guard, who turns from examining the fire fighting efforts at the gate, in shock at the gasp from his ally. Before he can raise his voice, Wærwulf has one hand over his mouth, and his seax hand jutting into his armpit as well.

I drag the dead man away, wishing he didn't leave trails where his boots dug into the ground, but unable to do anything about it right now. Gyrth hastens to take the guard's place, bending to rip the helm from the man's head, and ram it onto his own. Immediately, Wærwulf does the same, as soon as the body of his dead Viking raider is out of sight of the front of the dwelling. I shake my head.

'Bloody Gyrth,' I berate myself. I wanted that task, not him.

'Help me,' I urge my remaining warriors. Sæbald bends and takes the dead man's feet and together, we take him to the wall, and lie him out of sight, just below the eaves of a low-hanging turf roof that almost meets the wall. The other body is placed there as well. I look up and realise we could have used the roof to aid our entry, but then, we would have risked falling through it, or being heard.

Hereman has managed to roll one cask over to the wall, and he eyes the dead men with a grin on his face.

'Just the first of many,' he crows. I peer into the distance. There's no need to wait closer to the building until Jarl Guthrum leaves, and yet, I'm sure I heard my aunt cry out once more, and I want nothing more than to go to her. Icel's hand on my arm stops me as I take my first step.

'It's a good plan. Wait. He won't kill her. If he does, then what was the point in taking her in the first place?'

Icel's repetition of these words might be logical, but they burn all the same.

'What is he asking her?' I ask instead, eager to be distracted.

'He asks the usual questions, about number of warriors, and where you mean to make your next alliance. They are all questions we would ask, if we ever let our captors live.' I swallow against that realisation. Icel is correct. We kill our enemies, well, all but one of them usually. One must always live to tell of the events that have befallen their comrades.

'What you should be asking, is where the rest of our men are?' Icel prompts me. 'We can hear your aunt. But what of the rest of our comrades?' I feel shame then. I should have considered this. We're all stood there, trying not to be seen in the darkness, when we could be looking for my lost warriors. I know they still live, because they have been sighted, but their whereabouts is unknown.

I look to Wærwulf and Gyrth. Both have adopted the stance, and helms of the fallen guards. They don't exactly look like Viking raiders, but neither would a casual glance show them to be Mercians.

'We need to kill a few others,' I murmur. 'We can take their helms and weapons, and move more freely amongst the buildings then.' Icel nods, but his lips are twisted in thought.

'The fire,' we say at the same time, as it suddenly flares higher. I haven't considered where Rudolf is, but if he's still somehow responsible for the ongoing distraction, then he's continuing to assist our course. 'We can pretend to help and maybe find out where our men are in that way,' I confirm, and Icel grunts his agreement again.

'We should both go,' I confirm, but Icel shakes his head.

'No. We're both far too recognisable. We should send others, Gardulf and Cuthwalh. Neither of those two have fought as many battles as the rest of the men, especially Cuthwalh. Not in recent years.'

I shake my head. I don't like this, and yet there's some logic to it.

I turn and meet Gardulf's gaze. He's assisted Hereman in bringing another barrel to the side of the wall. With those in place, it means we beat a hasty retreat if we need to.

'Fine, I'll fucking send them,' I confirm grudgingly. 'Perhaps they'll find Rudolf as well.' I doubt Rudolf will have attempted an escape back over the river, even though Osbert and Eadulf are waiting at our camp. I know him too well. He'll be trying to find my aunt, and my men, and if not, he'll be ensuring the fires continue to bedevil our enemy.

I walk to Gardulf and beckon Cuthwalh to my side at the same time.

'Go and mingle with the men and women trying to put out the fires. See if you can find out where the rest of our men are.' Cuthwalh nods at the fresh challenge, but Gardulf's mouth drops open in shock. I think he'll argue with me, but then he nods with resolve.

'Here, take these,' and I hand the pair of them the weapons belts the two dead Viking raiders wore. Icel has retrieved them from the dead men. In the darkness, I can't tell if they're that different from our own, but as Gardulf and Cuthwalh exchange the blades for ones they're more comfortable with, sliding them onto the Viking raider weapons belts, I think it's a good idea to do as little as possible to draw attention to ourselves.

'Remember, say as little as possible,' I urge them. 'And if you find Rudolf, then so much the better. We'll remain here. Should we find my aunt, or the other men, four of us will remain here to help you escape. If it's impossible, swim back across the river.' Cuthwahl grimaces at my whispered instructions. I'm not surprised. The river current is strong, but it'll take them away from the enemy, if they're bloody lucky.

'Aye, my lord,' Gardulf confirms and I watch the pair of them dash from shadow to light in the lieu of the buildings, until they can easily merge with those using buckets to quench the flames.

Once more, I eye the rest of my warriors. I'm sure there must be something else that we can do to find the rest of my stolen men. Only then I hear a door opening, and my heart seems to pound in my throat.

Harsh voices ripple into the street as a splash of light from the open doorway casts Wærwulf into brightness. I watch, wishing I could merge more fully into the stone wall at my back, as Jarl Guthrum storms from the building, a string of angry words accompanying him. Two other men rush to join him, and he bellows something at Wærwulf and Gyrth. I have no idea what he says, but Wærwulf must understand him, and his reply is just as guttural, and ends on a growl.

I look to Icel, but Icel shakes his head. None of us knows what's being said, other than Wærwulf, and he can hardly shout and tell us.

My hand slips to my seax, just waiting for Wærwulf to indicate that we're about to be plunged into a fight, only for Jarl Guthrum to shout something else. His attention is on the fire, as it once more burns brightly, leaping from one roof to another. If we're not careful, the whole place will burn to nothing more than blackened ashes. That wasn't my intention. A swirl of wind, and a choking hot cloud, comes our way.

'Bugger,' I exclaim, blinking ash from my eyes, and trying to see.

Another gust of wind, and the hot cloud moves away once more, and now I can see Wærwulf more easily and he and Gyrth are beckoning me on.

I hurry forwards, the door into the building inside which my aunt is being kept a prisoner, still open.

There's a foul stench emanating from the open doorway, and I must imagine this is the tannery. I glimpse five men, their backs to me, a united front to block any passage, and behind them, bound and gagged, and tied to a chair, is my aunt. And she doesn't even look fucking terrified.

Chapter Twenty-One

A gruff voice calls out in their tongue, and Wærwulf responds, his urgings ever more insistent.

Icel is beside me, and Hereman to the other side, and my eyes are all over the place, trying to decide what's the best thing to do.

Another strident call from the same man, and I just glimpse his head starting to turn. There's fuck all for it.

With quick steps, I'm inside the doorway, trusting my warriors to follow me. My seax is in my hand, on nimble feet, I have my seax at his throat, and slice through it, while my aunt watches on, wide-eyed, but calm.

Behind us, the door finally closes, but not before one of the Viking raiders has sliced his neck clean through on Icel's seax, just with the motion of trying to find out why the door remained open. I take the third man as Hereman takes another. Icel the fourth. Wærwulf and Gyrth have remained outside, guarding the entrance, as though nothing happens inside, and somehow, the rest of my men have been too slow to follow the three of us.

The final man, jumps to his feet, grabbing for a seax, and in the process tangling his legs in the stool he's been sitting on. I know the bastard's intent is to reach my aunt, but he hobbles himself with the stool. I leap over the twitching body of my kill, and plunge my bloodied blade through the man's heart. His mouth opens to emit a cry of panic, but only a wet gurgle makes itself heard.

I rush to my aunt, slipping in the spreading pool of blood in my haste, and land heavily, just having the forethought to release my seax so that I don't cut my own throat as I tumble to the ground.

Ultimately, Icel beats me to her side, slashing through the straps that tie her hands to the chair, so that she can remove the gag herself. Her eyes are shadowed, and I want to say she looks relieved to see me, but her first words are hardly those of a captive in distress.

'You'd do well to take a little more care, nephew,' she urges, standing, brushing down her dress and then stretching, as Icel also frees her legs. I roll myself to my feet and take in the sight of her. It's good to see her. I can't deny it even if she speaks to me as though I were a child at her knee to be berated for grazing their elbows in a game of chase.

'I take it you're responsible for the fire?' she murmurs softly, her eyes on Hereman. Does she look for Edmund? I imagine she does.

'Yes, Rudolf. Where are the rest of the men?' I urge her. If I thought she was going to fall into my arms, all overcome with what's befallen her, then I was very much mistaken. Bruises mar her face, and I can see where a cut has begun to heal close to her collar bone. She's dirty and yet, her bearing is regal. I almost bow to her.

'You left Rudolf to start a fire?' she shakes her head, lips pursed unhappily.

'I sent Rudolf to start a fire,' I correct. 'Where are the rest of my men?' A flicker of sorrow now, and I know she must think of Siric and Eadberht.

'Wiglaf is dead,' she announces instead, and for a moment, I can't remember, and then I do. Her hound, the only thing that remained of my brother.

'Yes, he is. My condolences,' I offer, wishing she would show me the same for Siric and Eadberht, but she doesn't. I try and be charitable and think she doesn't know that men died trying to protect her.

'Well, are we going to stand here, or do you have a means of escaping?' she queries, her tone acerbic, as she helps herself to a beaker of something the guards were drinking, only to spit it onto the floor.

'They wouldn't know a good mead if a swarm of bees stung them on their behinds,' she exclaims softly, disgust in her words.

'My men, aunt? Where are they?' She finally meets my gaze, and I realise she's more shaken than it appears.

'I don't know. We were separated. Where?' but I cut her off.

'Edmund isn't far,' I promise her. 'But we need to get you out of here.' I'm worried we've been inside for too long. The door remains shut. What if something has happened to Wærwulf and Gyrth. It's possible that Jarl Guthrum might have returned and killed my men, or that Gardulf and Cuthwalh might have been discovered.

Hereman flashes a smile to my aunt, and strides to the door, Icel close to him. He opens it at a slant and then beckons us onwards. It's not a moment too soon, for the flames that Rudolf fanned into an inferno, have been buoyed by the wind, jumping from roof to roof, and the smell of damp straw is suddenly rife in my nostrils. I glance upwards, and there, in the corner of this stinking barn, the reddened embers of flames can be seen.

'Shit,' I exclaim, hurrying to encourage my aunt to leave. I don't want to be trapped by a distraction of my own devising.

'Ah, another one of your fine ideas?' my aunt taunts me, but as I encourage her out through the door, she grips my arm, and holds it firmly, even though I can feel her trembling.

'Thank you, nephew. Thank you. Even if this fails, you have my humble thanks for trying to rescue me. Jarl Guthrum is a man with huge ambition. Quite frankly, he terrifies me.' I nod, throat tight once more.

'You're not rescued yet,' I mutter. 'Now, do as I say, and stay close.'

Once more, Wærwulf beckons us furiously onwards, and it's not a moment too soon, for as we escape from the burning building, I hear a roar of outrage, and footsteps rush our way.

'Bastard,' I exclaim. The glow from the fire lights up my line of men as though they were candles at a mass, the two barrels easy to see, and it quickly becomes apparent, that we won't be escaping the same way we came in. The risk is suddenly too great. My aunt falters beside me, and if it weren't for Icel's quick reflexes, she'd fall to the ground. I reach out and grab her, even as Wærwulf rushes up behind me, Gyrth and Hereman to either side of him.

'Keep going,' I urge my aunt, as we hasten to where Lyfing and Wulfstan are the last of my men still visible against the lowest part of the wall, the rest having sensed the danger and slunk away from our means of escape.

'Fuck,' I mutter under my breath, gripping my aunt tightly. 'How the hell are we going to get out of here now?' I exclaim as we rush to the shadows offered by the next series of buildings, close to the wooden wall, which stretches up taller than three men standing one atop the other. Jarl Guthrum's harsh instructions can be heard once more over the raging fire and the thunder of my heart.

He's going to know my aunt has been rescued any moment now, and suddenly, we have no fucking means of escape.

Chapter Twenty-Two

With my aunt held tightly between me and Icel, we press tightly to the wall, traipsing through the stink of piss and rancid water that seems to be everywhere. The smoke from the fire is drifting our way, and it's getting harder and harder to see, and more and more difficult to breathe.

'Rudolf did a fine job,' Icel murmurs, his words just audible, and I'd glower at him for reminding me that this is all my own fault. But my thoughts turn to Rudolf. Where is he? Has he managed to escape, or is he too caught up in all this? And where too are Gardulf and Cuthwalh? Edmund will kill me if I manage to rescue my aunt, but in doing so, lose his son.

'Fuck, fuck, fuck,' I mutter under my breath, trying not to breathe too deeply, even while I rush away from the fire, along the wall. With each step we take, we'll be getting closer and closer to the river entrance to Grantabridge, closer to Edmund, but further away from my missing men, my horse and all of the horses.

'Shit,' I conclude, as ahead, my line of warriors' concertinas together, and I only just don't collide with the broad back of Hereman. He turns and sees my aunt.

'My lady,' he inclines his head, and a faint smile touches my aunt's pale, bruised cheeks.

'It's good to see you,' she replies, her words barely above a whisper.

'What are we to do?' Icel queries. What's caused our problem is that ahead, there's a building that meets the ancient wall, and there's no way through it. The Viking raiders have used the remnants of the stone wall, and the newer, wooden palisade as the wall for a building. It stretches forwards, into the heaving mass of the settlement. The cries and screams, and commands of more braying voices, fill the place, as does the crackle of burning thatch and wood. Fire is an enemy that no one can master. The irony isn't lost on me, that if it weren't for their walls, then they'd have ready access to all the water they might need to quench the flames. The poor design structure reminds me of the ancient walls surrounding parts of London, which prevents ready access to the River Thames.

'I wish I bloody knew,' I huff. Behind us, the skyline is a mass of dancing, flickering red and yellow flames. The veil of smoke from the fire lifts high, into the sky, and if it weren't bad enough that the fire is making everything so much more visible, there's the hint of the coming dawn in the greying of the horizon. We're well and truly tramped. And then Wærwulf rushes to my side.

'Jarl Guthrum has discovered Lady Cyneswith's missing, and his men dead.'

'Fuck, just something else to add to this bloody calamity.' I complain. My aunt is standing on her own feet now, and she looks imperial, even with the grime of her captivity etched onto her severe face.

'Come on nephew. Think your way out of this one,' she urges gently, but with iron in her voice. She's trusted me on so many occasions before, but I just can't think. I know too little.

'I found Gardulf,' Wærwulf continues. And the youngster dips his head to my aunt, a smile playing around his tight lips.

'Cuthwalh?' I query. Gardulf shrugs his shoulders.

'I lost him in the melee,' he confirms.

'Did you see Rudolf?'

''No, I just ran for it when I saw what was happening. I don't know where the rest of my comrades are either.'

'Fuck,' I glower. This really is a shit storm.

I look upwards, eyeing the roof of the building before me. It's high, and the wooden wall is higher, and yet, if we can just get over it, then we can drop down into the river. Even if we're swept away by the current, we'd still be free from the threat of leaving this place crispier than pork scratchings.

It seems that Hereman has had the same idea. Even now, he's encouraging Sæbald to mount his back to see if he can grip the thatch roof. But, it's just out of reach. It's unlike other buildings in the settlement, where the roofs dip almost to ground level. I can appreciate that whoever ordered the buildings construction, gave more thought to it than I might have done.

While the men and women of Grantabridge dash towards the engulfing flames, we're stuck here.

'Can we go through it?' I query, hoping the walls might be little more than woven willow branches stuffed with wattle and daub.

'No, it's built with wooden planks,' Lyfing informs me.

'Fuck.' I gaze forward to the thoroughfare where men and women run towards the flames clutching anything they have to hand with which they can throw water over the flames or dash the other way, clasping items in their hands that they hope to rescue from the path of the blaze.

'We go round,' I announce. If we stand here for any longer, we'll be found. I'm not going to die from indecision.

'Hereman and Goda, you go first, ensure the way is clear for us.' I'd go myself, but I'm not going to leave my aunt. Gardulf has the same idea as me, and he hovers close to her, his face soot-stained from the fires. His eyes peak from a pale face, his head turning at every little sound. And there are many sounds and cries. I wish I understood more of what the Viking raiders were saying. I keep Wærwulf close to me. I need to know, as soon as he knows, if we've been spotted.

I watch as Hereman and Goda creep forwards along the building wall, and then, just as they're about to enter the main thoroughfare, stand tall, strolling as though they belong, even though they're going against the flow of almost everyone else.

'We need to hurry,' Wærwulf dips low to my ear. 'Jarl Guthrum is quite determined to find your aunt.' I nod and then send another five of my men to follow Hereman and Goda, and then, when I hear no sound of a commotion, turn to my aunt.

'Keep your head down, and stay between Icel and me.'

She dips her chin in understanding, and we're moving. I'm worried someone will notice her skirts, and wonder why there's one woman amongst so many warriors. Surely, they'll put two and two together and determine it's their captive and her rescuers.

But, there's nothing else for it. We creep along the side of the building, my hand never straying from my seax, as I try and determine just what's happening. I don't look behind me, but I can feel the flames chasing me, even as I realise we've had a stroke of luck. More and more people have started to turn away from the rampaging fire. There are just as many people trying to retreat as there are those still determined to save their settlement.

Staying close to the side of the building, we circumnavigate it, Icel supporting my aunt, while I prowl behind them, eyes trying to look everywhere, even as the acrid smoke stings them. In front, Gardulf is just as alert, while behind me, Wærwulf is keeping pace with me. The remainder of my men are there as well. I can't imagine we look nondescript, bristling with weapons and not a bucket or bowl of water to be seen between us, but in the smoke-filled haze, I hope we'll make our way around the building, and back to the relative safety of the walled edges of the settlement without being seen.

The building is narrower here, the hall running at an angle to the wall. There's no door for people to emerge from at the end of the building. I finally release my held breath as we once more round the corner, and hasten to join the remainder of my men, who are again able to hide in the lieu of the towering walls.

Ahead, Icel and my aunt walk quickly, but not too quickly. I risk turning to look back at the way we've come. The flames remain visible, but only just. The roof of the wooden building does much to block them out. And that's why I don't see the bastard Viking raider until we collide.

A clang of iron, and I'm struggling to stay upright, while a string of foul vitriol emerges from the man's mouth. Turned around in the collision, I see Wærwulf's mouth opening in shock. Before he can translate the words for me, my enemy is back on his feet, seax already in hand. I don't think he knows I'm not one of his countrymen, but that doesn't seem to matter in his pissed state.

My foe stinks of ale and mead, and wine, but for all that, he's quick as lightning, and before I can protect myself, his seax is jabbing towards me.

'Fuck,' I complain, bending low to the ground to avoid his attack. I need to shut him up and quickly, but he's not the only one. From inside the building, I can hear the grunts of those enjoying themselves even as their settlement threatens to burn to the ground. My enemy raises his voice to shout an alarm, bringing such activity to an immediate end.

'Fuck,' I mutter again, bracing my legs, and erupting from the ground, shoulder out, eager to tumble him to the ground. But the man falls before I get to him, and I veer away from his sightless eyes, the end of a blade emerging through his neck, down which blood drips.

I catch sight of a grinning Hereman and swallow away my fears. The mad bastard could have too easily hit me. And then there are more Viking raider men. The first to appear is still fastening his weapons belt, and his eyes flicker from me to his dead comrade. He growls angrily, before launching himself at me, mirroring my intentions from moments ago.

Behind him, more and more of our enemy emerge. I'm grateful to have Gardulf and Wærwulf at my back. I skip clear of the charging man, but he twists quickly on his feet, and immediately comes at me again. I shake my head at him. There's a fucking massive fire, and still, these cocks want to kill us. They don't even know that we're Mercians. The Viking raiders are a feckless bunch.

Hereman hurries back from his place close to the wall, bringing Sæbald with him. I glimpse the two disappear inside the building, as I face my enemy. This time, I manage to evade his charge as well and even manage to raise a welter of blood along his arm, for he wears no byrnie, having been caught, as it were, in the act.

Words tumble from his mouth. '*Skiderik*,' I recognise; the others, not so much.

'Fucker,' I mumble beneath my breath, not wanting to give away the fact that I'm a Mercian before I can silence him. Should Jarl Guthrum realise he has not only the king of Mercia's aunt, but also the bloody king of Mercia in his midst, our situation will become even bleaker.

My foeman turns again, his jaw a grimace of pain. I rush at him, slicing with my seax as I go. We have no shields to protect us. We could never have swum the River Granta with them, and so although I have my byrnie, I wasn't leaving that behind, I'm almost as exposed as he is.

I spy two more of my warriors rush into the building. I have no idea how many men are inside it. Once more, blood plumes along my enemy's arm, but he's too quick, and still lives.

I really need to kill him, and quickly. Behind me, I can determine that Wærwulf and Gardulf are having more success. I can hear fighting from inside the hall as well, punctuated by the screams of women. One darts past me, running, a blanket all that covers her, right through the battle taking place between me and my opponent.

I startle back, not wanting to slash the woman, and my enemy is on me immediately. His seax flashes quickly before me, left to right, right to left, and it's all I can do to counter the flurry of blows as I feel a slash on my left arm. Frustrated, rage boiling, I curl my fist, and the next time the fucker comes at me, I stay where I am, parry the seax strikes with my weapon, only to jab out with my fist and punch into the man's nose. The crack of the impact brings a smirk to my face, and as his head snaps backwards with the force of the blow, my seax slices through his neck. His mouth opens and closes, and I think he'll still manage to give a warning to his allies, only all that emerges is a gargle of blood.

I retract my seax, and as I do so, he slides to the floor, while I bend and catch my breath.

'Hurry the fuck up,' Wærwulf grumbles at me, and I appreciate I'm the last one to make a kill. Hereman rushes from the building, followed by Sæbald, who limps, as well as Goda and Ordheah. I run my eyes over them, but other than the limp, which could have simply come from stubbing his toe, my men seem hale.

I dash to the relative safety of the wall.

'Took your fucking time,' Hereman muses. If he's waiting for me to thank him for what he did, then he'll be waiting a while yet. The mad bastard.

'Can we get over the wall?' I query, stepping back to try and determine its height. I know, from the time spent watching the settlement, that there was only one place where the wall hadn't been built as high as elsewhere. Everywhere else, it's too damn high to risk jumping from on the other side.

'We should just aim for the other gate now,' Icel murmurs, and I see that others agree with him. I can hear the rustle of nods, even if I can't see all my men.

'It's too far,' my aunt urges. 'This place is much bigger than you think.'

'But we can't climb the walls,' Sæbald confirms quickly. 'They're too high.'

'Then how did you get in?' my aunt turns a puzzled look my way.

'Part of the wall wasn't complete. We used it as well as some wooden prongs and climbed in, having swum the river, with the horses.' Her mouth falls open, just a little, at this news. 'It was the only bloody way,' I confirm. Now isn't the time to be berated for foolish risks. The smoke continues to build, but here, in sight of the dead men from the brothel, if that's what it was, we're in danger.

'We need to hurry,' Wærwulf urges me, as though I needed reminding, and I nod.

'Fine, we head for the other gate and the bridge. Edmund is there, and perhaps some of the ealdormen and their household warriors as well. We hunt for the rest of our men along the way.'

I meet the eyes of my warriors. This is all going to shit, but they don't seem unduly worried by that.

'If there's any way we can escape along the way, then we do so,' I urge them. 'Ensure you always keep two of your comrades in sight. We're not leaving anyone behind.' At those words, I think of Cuthwalh and Rudolf. Rudolf, I'm sure, will find a way to escape. He's just cocky enough not to consider the terrible danger he might be in. Cuthwalh, I'm not so sure about.

'Hereman, you lead the way.' With my aunt in front of me and Icel in front of her, we resume our progress along the settlement's walls. I can only see so far in front of me now. The light from the flames, largely blocked out by the towering roof of the building we were forced to run around, isn't enough to get a truly good look at what we're doing.

I rely on Hereman, and his damn luck, to plot our course, my warriors surrounding my aunt so that they'll face our enemy first, should we be discovered. Wærwulf stays behind me. Every so often, he speaks, translating the words he's managed to pick out from the calls of those who must search for my aunt. With the smoke seeping along every nook and cranny, the sound is distorted, and I can't always tell where the voices come from. But it's evident that they're looking for us.

Another five or six buildings are passed before we once more come to a dead end. Here, there's no building using the exterior wall of the settlement in its construction. But it's almost worse.

'Shit, a bloody pond.' The words are passed back to me when I almost collide with my aunt, who's stopped in front of me.

196

'What?' I exclaim. So far, we've seen no one else, but I know even Hereman's luck can't last.

'There's a bloody great big pond,' Hereman whispers to me, as I rush forward to determine why we've stopped. I look down and catch sight of the murky depths.

'Go through it,' I urge him. If we can swim through the river, we can manage a bloody pond.

'And where would you have us go?' He points, and now I realise it's not just the pond. If anything, the pond has probably saved us.

We've scampered through Grantabridge, and now we've reached a pond, no doubt used to keep a stock of fish from the river, but beyond that is a vast open expanse before we reach yet more buildings.

'What the fuck?' I glower. 'Why have they done that?' I demand to know, but I don't really want to know why they've done it; I want to know how to get through it without being seen.

'They've found the dead men at the brothel,' Wærwulf unhelpfully informs me, as I look back the way we've come and onwards. The cloud of smoke is even thicker, and I think that something must be burning that's not wood, for the stink is growing increasingly noxious.

'Furs, or something,' Icel murmurs, reading my thoughts. We stand, huddled together, as I gaze outwards. More and more people seem to be retreating, and there's a growing and haphazard pile of household furniture in the open expanse. There are sobbing women and wailing children, and men limping or crying from burns they've earned battling the fire, but whatever we do, as soon as we emerge from the relative safety provided by the all but abandoned pond, we'll be seen.

'Fuck,' I mutter once more. It's not helping me, but I need to say something.

'We'll have to split up and pretend we're running from the fire,' I urge my men, thinking quickly.

'We can't do that,' Sæbald complains, his eyes bright in a face smudged with ash.

'We have no choice. We can't linger here, and all of us together will certainly draw attention, but if we go in what, four groups of four or five, we should be able to skirt the open area.' As I speak, I'm becoming more and more convinced that it's the solution.

My aunt nods her head.

'It's the only way,' she confirms, and somehow, her words settle the rest of my warriors, even though she merely reiterates my decision. I shake my head at the realisation and face them all. A collection of warriors greet me. Some of them look terrified, others merely perplexed, but the majority have a stubborn cast to their faces that I've come to recognise only too well.

'Lyfing, Hereman, Eahric and Wulfstan, you go first.' There's a building we've just skirted, and I grin. 'Go in there, and grab something, anything, and carry it as though it's yours.' Hereman winks at me, as he strides to the open doorway, pausing to ensure there's no one inside before he enters. He emerges carrying a wooden casket, no doubt containing someone's treasures. They'll be pissed off when they discover that gone. Lyfing goes next, appearing with a sack that makes no sound.

'Flour,' he confirms, running a smudge of the white powder over his face. He looks little better than a badger now, all black with a line of white over his nose. I grimace but quickly turn back to the rest of my men.

'Gardulf, Icel, and I will go with my aunt. Wærwulf, stay with us. Ordlaf, Ordheah, Goda, you go next, and then Sæbald, Leonath and Gyrth. We move quickly. Aim to re-join the shadows around the wall, to the far side of the pond as soon as possible.' I don't stop to consider why they're not using the water in the pond to quench the fire. In a panic, no doubt everyone has forgotten of its existence.

Already Hereman, Lyfing, Wulfstan and Eahric are walking towards the open expanse. They're knocked by others, clasping their valuables as they go, but they manage to stay together well enough.

Gardulf, Icel and Wærwulf hurry into the house, and then Wærwulf passes a platter into my hand, and I look down, noting the shimmer on it.

'A plate?' I query.

'Might be valuable,' he murmurs, while Icel leads the way. He's flung a cloak around his shoulders, and hunkers down, no doubt to hide his height. I wish I'd thought to do the same. My aunt has been given a pot to carry, the edges of it etched with symbolism I can't quite see, but the light from the braziers that have been lit to light the path, flash over it, revealing what look to be jagged teeth and leering snouts.

The open area is rapidly filling, and people dash hither and thither, their eyes filled with terror, and then I hear a voice that makes me want to hurry my steps, but I know I can't.

I risk a look over my shoulder, and Jarl Guthrum emerges from the gloom as though he were the very beast on the pot my aunt cradles in her hands. He's surrounded by men blackened by soot and greyed by ash, but I can still see their glinting weapons easily enough. They've not lost their shimmering edges.

'Keep moving,' Wærwulf urges me, even as Jarl Guthrum addresses the crowd. His words thrum with rage, as though thunder overhead. The only thing that saves us is, no matter Guthrum's evident rage, not one person stops what they're doing to even glance at him. A small sobbing child rushes to my aunt, gripping her skirt, and instead of shooing the child away, my aunt gathers them into her arms, head down, pressing on back to the darkest depths of the shadowy area beneath the wooden walls.

It's growing lighter, but it's far from daybreak, not that anyone has slept that night. My aunt stumbles, and I reach out and steady her, and at the moment, the sobbing child, held in my aunt's arms, looks at me, confusion on their face. I try a smile, aware it'll be more like a grimace, and the child's mouth opens. I wince, fearing what will come next, but Wærwulf is at my side. Words buzz between the two of them, and Wærwulf's soft laughter has the child closing their eyes, reassured.

Not for the first time, I wish I could speak the language of my enemy. I can detect the flow of the words, but not always the exact meanings. I'll need to remedy it, as my enemy are making their intentions well known in the size of the settlement they're building.

The open expanse seems to go on forever, but eventually, I can sense the walls above my head once more, and stop, glancing back to see how Gyrth and the others are faring. My eyes are immediately drawn to Jarl Guthrum. He moves through the area, men to either side of him, and they turn men and women towards them with rough hands, not caring if in the process, all that they carry is tumbled to the ground. I wince as a woman is sent flying over the back of a dropped wooden chest, and she shrieks in pain. A man rounds on Guthrum, only to encounter Guthrum's fist, which has him falling backwards, to land on the woman he thought to protect.

Gyrth was the last to leave the house from which we took almost everything they owned. He hurries now, but I can see that Jarl Guthrum's men are scything through the crowd in their frenzy to find my aunt.

'Hurry the fuck up,' I murmur beneath my breath, while Hereman leads the rest of my warriors onwards, Icel and Gardulf with my aunt and the small child we've temporarily borrowed.

But it's becoming increasingly busy now. Gyrth, Leonath and Sæbald have to dodge others attempting to run away from Guthrum's fury. Quickly, Ordlaf, Ordheah and Goda hurry past where Wærwulf and I wait for the last three men. My hand hovers over my seax, but there are only two of us, while Guthrum has over thirty men seeking my aunt. If it comes to a fight, I'll be better off trying my luck over the wooden wall and falling the vast distance into the river.

Sæbald manages to get a family between him and one of Guthrum's men, but Gyrth isn't as lucky. In horror, I watch Gyrth being grabbed and turned around by an entirely bald hulking warrior, in all of his battle wear. I don't breathe. I can't look. Not Gyrth. But the Viking raider merely glowers at Gyrth, and then thrusts him to the floor. The enemy must be a beast to pick up Gyrth as though he were no more than a straw doll. Hastily, Gyrth regathers his feet and resumes his onwards journey. I bite my lip. Should he come straight towards me, the foeman might see him moving with more purpose than someone fleeing the flames.

But Gyrth is no fool. He staggers one way, and then another, ducking low as though to pick something up, but in doing so, allowing the eyes of the crazed Viking raider to move over the backs of others. Only then does Gyrth redouble his efforts to get to me.

'Bloody hell,' he gasps, as he and Leonath arrive at the same time. Gyrth looks white beneath the layer of ash, and I can see where sweat has broken out on his forehead, for all its still cold.

'Come on,' I urge him, and we're once more on our way. I just can't see that we have much further to go to reach the quayside. Surely, Grantabridge can't have grown so huge over the winter months? Quickly, we're swallowed up by the orderly rows of buildings once more, the glow from the fire receding even more, although it makes it more difficult to see. Only then, do I collide with Sæbald, where he's come to an abrupt stop.

'What is it?' I demand. Ahead, I can't see the rest of my men or my aunt. We've become separated once more, and that makes me fucking uneasy.

'Can you hear that?' I shake my head, only then I do hear it, and a grin touches my cheeks.

'That's Beornstan. I'd recognise him anywhere.'

'Aye, my lord, it bloody is,' Sæbald confirms, a smirk on his face.

'Where's it coming from?' I query.

'In there.' And Sæbald points to what can only be termed a cage. My mouth falls open in shock, and then I catch sight of a very human shape moving amongst others slumped in sleep, or worse.

'What the fuck?'

'They've caged our fucking men,' Sæbald growls, moving forwards without thought.

'Wait,' I urge him. The cage, because that's what it certainly is, is halfway down a row of what must be workshops. The tang of fire and worked metal is ripe in the air, and I wonder why there'd be a cage amongst the workshops. Wouldn't they have been better served to keep my men prisoner alongside my aunt?

'It'll be for the moneyer,' Wærwulf informs me in his gruff voice, his words coming from behind me. Slowly I begin to understand. We must be in the trading section of Grantabridge, and my warriors, or at least Beornstan, have been kept captive in the cage usually reserved for precious metals and goods. I must assume, as I glower at it, that the building isn't yet complete. It lacks a roof of thatch and enclosing sides of the wood, and it's open to the elements. For now, it's merely a cage of crossed wooden beams and posts, and no good to anyone, unless they want to keep good fucking Mercian men captive.

'We have to rescue him,' Sæbald urges me, advancing as though to do just that. His usually clean-shaven face is fuzzy, and he scratches at it irritably. We've not had the time of late to tend to our personal needs.

I'm not going to argue with him, but first, first, we need to ensure my aunt makes it to safety from her captivity, and only then can I return for the rest of my missing men.

Chapter Twenty-Three

'We'll come back for him,' I advise Sæbald in a harsh whisper. But he shakes his head, eyes wild, unheeding of the danger we're in, here, inside the bloody Viking raider settlement of Grantabridge, with its tall wooden walls cutting off all chance of escape until we reach the riverside gate.

'I'm not fucking leaving him,' Sæbald responds in an angry growl, aware that if he speaks too loudly, he might just give away our location to the prowling men of Jarl Guthrum. Leonath has returned to our side to determine the delay. His eyes peer at me in the darkness, his empty hand urging me to hurry up, his lips open to reveal his missing front tooth.

'Beornstan,' Sæbald murmurs to Leonath before I can order him back to the rest of my men. 'Caged,' Sæbald snarls furiously. I know then that I'll be unable to force him onwards towards our chance of escape. I'm far from surprised. If I wasn't trying to protect my aunt, I wouldn't leave my men either, and certainly not if they were fucking caged.

But there is the matter of my aunt. She can't fight her way out of here, unlike my warriors, and she's been a captive for too long already.

'Go and release them,' I urge the pair. It's better if I just order it than they just go off on their own. 'I'll send two more back to help you.'

'No need, my lord,' Leonath bows slightly. 'It's just a matter of opening the cage, and then we'll follow. Take Lady Cyneswith to safety. That must be your priority.' I hate to hear my decisions laid bare before me, but Leonath's right in what he says. It's not as though I've not just been thinking about it.

I bite my lip and look once more at the chaos we've caused inside Grantabridge. There are buildings ablaze, flames leaping high into the black night sky from thatch roofs and wooden-built buildings. The sky is lit so brightly now that it could be daytime. The screams of those still trapped by the advancing flames, and those desperate in their attempts to escape, can be heard over and above the shouts of Jarl Guthrum's men, seeking out whoever rescued Lady Cyneswith from her captivity. Those shouts are coming closer, the screams as well, and even the flames aren't taking their time in forging a path through so much combustible material. For a moment, I'm reminded of the fire at Torksey, and of the grey-shrouded men appearing from the aftermath. I shake the image clear from my mind. Now isn't the time to relieve old memories. Now is the time to move and get my aunt free from Grantabridge and fucking Jarl Guthrum.

'Do it, and be quick about it,' I encourage them. 'Remember, the river gate.' Sæbald is already advancing towards the cage, dashing from the shadows of one building to another. 'Follow him,' I order Leonath and resolutely turn my back on them, even though it goes against everything I believe. I hope all of my missing men are held inside that cage. It's bad enough that I've lost two men already beneath Viking raider blades. I don't plan on allowing more to fall to their bloody harvest.

Hastily, I angle towards where the remainder of my men have gone, slipping between the rear of buildings that have so far not been engulfed in the encroaching conflagration, with the settlement-enclosing wall at their backs. Goda furiously summons me on as he waits for me. His eyes are red-rimmed in the terrible light, and his beard is filled with ash as he batters at it, adding yet more dust to the cloud that envelopes us.

'What is it now?' Goda demands to know as I sprint to his side, mindful of where I place my feet over the uneven surface, but his gaze stays behind me. He must be seeking out Leonath and Sæbald.

'They've found Beornstan.'

His lips compress unhappily. 'And the others?'

'I don't know. Sæbald and Leonath will release him and check for the others.'

'You won't aid them?' There's a sharpness to his tone I don't appreciate. I feel stung into replying.

'I said we'd return when my aunt was safely out of Grantabridge, but Sæbald was having fucking none of it.'

'Stubborn bastard,' Goda confirms, but whether he agrees with my decision or not, I'm unsure. And then, I realise, I don't know if he means bloody Sæbald or me. But, together, we resume our escape route, following the retreating backs of the rest of my warriors.

As we move further and further around the edge of the settlement, it grows quieter and quieter until I realise I can hear the stone I kick tumbling into the darkness around me. My breathing's grown ragged, my breaths shallower as I try not to take in too much of the cloying smoke. I take a deep breath to calm myself, hand over my mouth to keep as much of the smoke out as possible. Anyone left on guard duty will surely hear me if I don't get myself under control or burst into a fit of coughing. Ahead, the gloom is more complete; behind, all is still chaos, with the horizon glowing bright with the reds and yellows of leaping flames.

We pass the wooden walls and posts of buildings, and it's impossible to know if Viking raider men, women and children rest inside, content that their homes are in no danger of falling prey to the flames. Abruptly, we're at a different building, this one shallower and longer, and I can hear the movements of agitated horses. This time, I'm the one to stop abruptly.

Ahead, I've caught sight of the comforting shapes of Icel and Hereman, escorting my aunt between them, and I know she's as safe as possible while inside an enemy encampment. Those horses, I know, will belong to my men, and more importantly, they're Mercian horses. I want them sodding back. I think of Haden. I'd rescue him. I have bloody rescued him from the ministrations of my enemy, and I'll do so again. I'll do the same for my men's horses. Hopefully, I'll even discover my aunt's horse amongst them.

'The horses,' I urge Goda, and he nods quickly, just stopping himself from colliding with me, understanding before I need to say anything else. I'm glad he holds his tongue and doesn't berate me for thinking of the horses but leaving Sæbald and Leonath to rescue my missing men.

'This way,' and I begin to creep along the side of the stable, avoiding the jutting-out wooden poles that support the building's walls and roof. The roof here doesn't hang low to the ground as else-where but stops just above where I can reach my arm. The thatch smells damp, and I appreciate, all over again, just how fierce the raging fire must be to ignite such damp material in the east of the settlement. We've been bloody lucky so far. The fire has caught, we've found my aunt, and now we need to find a means of escape. I just need my luck to last a little longer.

I pause at the open doorway, hand on my seax, ready should one of the bastards try and stop me from retrieving my stolen horses. I can hear hooves moving over the wooden floorboards and the outraged nickers of one horse to another, for while the fire might feel as though it's distant, the smell of smoke is present. Every so often, a swirl of smoke-filled air covers everything, and the air is hazy and filled with a strange glow. The horses know they're in danger, even if none of the Viking raiders has realised just yet.

'Follow me,' I urge Goda.

'Aye, I will,' he confirms, gripping his seax, his face set in a line of determination. I know he's thinking of his horse, Magic, safe on the far side of the River Granta. He knows he'd risk his life for the animal. The horses are just as much a part of our fighting force as our fellow warriors.

As one, we step into the stables, looking everywhere to ensure no one guards the animals. It's dark inside, making it just about impossible to see anything beyond the frightened eyes of the horses as one kicks a stable door. They know we're there.

I rush forward, eyeing my aunt's mount with relief. The animal looks at me, head back, preparing to offer a shrill neigh, but I stop her, reaching out to run my hand over her long nose.

'Hello, girl,' I murmur softly, and her fear subsides. 'Are the others here?' I query softly, but Goda has made his way along the row of half-doors and doesn't hear me. The place smells only faintly of horse manure. Our enemy has chosen to care for the animals they stole in the raid that netted them more than just my aunt and warriors.

'There's Beornstan's horse.' I tell myself, moving away from my aunt's horse. 'And those of my dead men.' I growl softly, revenge and vengeance on my mind. From somewhere far away, I hear the Viking raiders shouting one to another, their cries harsh and guttural. I could dash from here and satisfy my need for retribution. But no. I must rescue the horses, just as much as I must save my men and aunt. 'Ah, hello there, Cuthbert,' Goda murmurs, making his way towards me.

How I've missed Wulfred, Cuthbert's rider, and his foul mouth. Now there's a man who knows how to swear his way out of anything. He'd have made short work of our current predicament, his words cutting to the bone, laying bare all we faced, and doing it with a wry smirk. His faith in what we do has never dimmed. I hope it hasn't now that he's been held as a captive by our enemy.

'The horses are all here,' I query, taking a quick count of those I can see.

'Aye, my lord, they are,' Goda confirms. These horses all belong to my warriors and my aunt. There are no unknown mounts that I can see, and now they follow my every movement as I reach to open stable doors and encourage them to exit their confinement. Not that they need much encouragement, as they eagerly walk free.

And then, from outside, I hear rushing footsteps, where before, there was only angry shouting, and look to Goda. He's also heard; that much is evident in the way he stills, pushing between two horses to free himself should he need to fight. On silent feet, the two of us merge into the shadows close to the door, hoping we won't be seen before we can kill the fuckers.

If I wouldn't stop for my men, I shouldn't have stopped for the bloody horses, but I have, and now, with just the two of us, we need to fight off our enemy and rescue the horses as well. And, I realise, not only that, but we need to find a way to corral the horses from the stables without being seen by more of the jarl's men who are specifically searching for us. Quite how we're going to bloody accomplish that is beyond me.

'In here,' I hear a voice that's almost quieter than a whisper and grin, and not just because they speak in the language of the Saxons.

'Beornstan,' I quickly step from the shadows as Sæbald and Leonath pull their seaxes from weapons' belts, only to visibly relax their warriors' stance as they sight me,

'Fuck's sake, Coelwulf, you nearly got stabbed through the neck,' Sæbald complains, his words a harsh whisper, showing more his relief at not stabbing me than anything else.

I glimpse Beornstan, hoping to find a smile on his face for being rescued, but his face lacks such an expression, and I realise, as I glance behind him, that there's only him. Where I consider, are the rest of my warriors?

Beornstan stinks of shit, and his face is a welter of bruises and two black eyes, the wound on the side of his face, gained on the Welsh borderlands earlier in the year, had only just healed and now it bleeds freely once more. What have the fuckers done to him?

'My lord king,' his tone is formal, although his words are lisped through a split lip, and perhaps a swollen tongue as well. Chocolate noses his way forwards, and Beornstan does reach out to run his hand along his horse's shoulder; more of a welcome than I receive. I should have gone for him. I should have been the one to release him from that bastard cage.

'It's fucking good to see you,' I mutter, wanting to embrace him, but aware that he's not going to appreciate it. He's as prickly as a boar.

'Aye, let's get the bastard horses and get out of here,' Leonath confirms, something in his voice assuring me that now isn't the time for a reunion between me and Beornstan. I consider what's passed between them? What words have they shared? But there's really no time.

'The other men?' I ask, just to be sure, as Sæbald moves amongst the horses with Goda at his side.

'Not with Beornstan. He tried to escape. The fuckers caged him with no food or water for the last week, but only after a hard beating. He's been living on rainwater. He doesn't know where the others are. But he says that Osmod and Ingwald definitely still live. The others, he's not so sure about as he was blindfolded when he was captured and slung over his horse like a sack of flour. He thinks the same happened to the others.'

'Fuck,' I curse, reaching for my aunt's horse again. 'We can't sneak ten horses out of the stables,' I murmur, unease creeping along my spine.

'No, we can't. We'll just have to be brazened about it and ride them. If anyone asks, then we gallop for it.' Sæbald offers his advice, and I find myself meeting his wide grin.

'That's even more shit than my idea to get inside Grantabridge,' I argue, just because it feels good to hear my men's voices.

'Aye, my lord,' his lips turn upwards as he speaks. The flicker of his eyes illuminates a well-worn face, complete with its scars won in battle. 'And we can all see how fucking well that's going.'

I shake my head, smirking all the same. None of this is going as I planned. My force is split. My aunt is hopefully somewhere ahead of us, perhaps even already through the river gate and over the bridge the bastards have built over the River Granta. And while I've found Beornstan and my aunt, and the horses, I've lost Rudolf and Cuth-walh, so I've really gained very fucking little. Apart from the bloody horses.

'Right, we could do with Wærwulf to speak his magic and ease our passage, but as he's not here, we just fucking go for it. I'll lead, on my aunt's mount, and take Jaspar as well. You should all have two horses each. Ride one, and lead the other. If someone questions us, just ignore them, and head for the gateway over the Granta. If it gets nasty, I want Beornstan and Sæbald to make a run for it to the gate. The riderless horses should follow, and the rest of us will defend your backs.'

As plans go, it's fucking poor. We need to hope that people are either sleeping or too consumed with what's happening with the fire to think much of ten horses being led away in a place where horses are a rarity. I can't see that we'll escape without a bloody fight. If we're seen then Jarl Guthrum is bound to put my other men, under a stricter guard, but I'll have to think about that when it happens. For now, I need to free my aunt's horse and hope that Icel, Hereman and my other warriors can do the same for my aunt.

Emerging into the greyness of the night, dawn seems to be chasing our heels, as I urge my aunt's horse onwards towards the west, Jaspar eager to follow her, his reins in my hands. I know it's far too quiet here after the noise and panic closer to the fire. I understand that the sound of hooves passing over the clearly marked street, lined with its wooden drainage system, will arouse suspicion, but I hope not enough that someone will actually fucking stand before us and bar our passage.

At least from the back of my aunt's horse, I can see more. Not enough to see over roofs but enough that should someone emerge with a sharpened blade, flashing in the moonlight, from a door or street, I'll see them before they can attack.

Beornstan still hasn't said anything to me. He rides just behind me. Goda has the task of coming last, but it doesn't really matter where we are. All of us could be easily threatened by someone walking from their home, or just running up or down the street in search of more buckets for water. I did notice, with a wry smile, that all the buckets in the stable had gone. Someone was tasked with guarding the animals, but they must have abandoned their post to help contain the fire. They'll be in the shit when they get back, and all the horses are missing.

I'd quite like to see that, but not as much as I'd like to escape from behind Grantabridge's walls. My men, left behind with the horses on the other side of the Granta, must be wondering what's kept us. I certainly didn't consider we'd be gone for so long, or that we'd need to find a new means of escape different to the one we used to get inside.

The sound of the horse's hooves echoes in the smoke-hazed air, and yet, no one comes to question us. There's no hint of iron emerging through the smoky air. Ahead, I finally manage to catch sight of the gateway we've been looking for. And beyond it, I can sense, rather than see, that my kingdom of Mercia is waiting for me, if I can just get through the bloody gateway, and over the sodding bridge, without being seen.

The closer we get, the more I tense, my aunt's horse trying to fight me as my instructions for her to walk slowly, confuse her. The smell of the smoke is getting ever stronger, and she wants nothing more than to gallop from the place.

This is too easy. I can't see that fucking Jarl Guthrum will have given up his hunt for us so soon, and yet I can't hear the shouts of his men anymore. The Viking raiders must realise there are Mercians here, inside Grantabridge, come to rescue my aunt. Surely? How else would she have managed to escape and kill the seven guards tasked with protecting her?

On seeing the gate ahead, a break in the darkness of the encircling wall, I spot something that makes my heart leap. Icel and Hereman, with my aunt between them, scuttle through the open gateway, Ordlaf and Gardulf, standing with bloodied seaxes, no doubt having killed the men on guard duty there. My aunt's horse nickers in welcome, my aunt pausing to look back at us, and I'm just about to spur the animal on when a mass of heavily armed Viking raiders swarms across my path, emerging from behind two abandoned carts to either side of the main thoroughfare.

The horse bucks and twists, and while I fight her, I'm forced to relax my grip on Jaspar. He ploughs through the mass of Viking raiders, as though they weren't there, at a gallop. I watch from the corner of my eye as he forces the Viking raiders to jump aside, one of my foemen falling beneath the hooves with a wet crack. It seems that Jaspar has taken the first kill in this fresh, encounter. I'd smirk if the situation wasn't so fucking dire.

By the time I have my aunt's horse again under control, Jaspar has followed my aunt and most of my warriors through the unguarded gate beating any of Jarl Guthrum's men who think to intervene. No doubt, Edmund and the Mercian ealdormen are there to ensure they're not apprehended again by the Viking raider warriors.

But now my heart stills, my breaths shallow, for none other than that pestilent bastard Jarl Guthrum leers at me from beneath his distinctive warriors' helm, the sharp beak of an owl mirrored in the flame-shimmering nose guard, his exposed arms flashing with their owl inkings. In his hands, he holds both a seax and a dirty, ash-covered Rudolf, who'd twist free from such a tight grip; only the bastard holds a similarly engraved seax settled against Rudolf's exposed pale throat. The edge of the blade reflects the flames that leap from roof to roof behind my head, as though the flames are as eager to reach the westward facing gate as I've been.

Fuck.

So close, and yet it seems I must fight my way to bastard freedom, and in the process, ensure that Rudolf lives, against all of the bloody odds stacked against me, and my few men, and horses.

Chapter Twenty-Four

'He told me you would come,' Jarl Guthrum menaces, his words harsh and heavily accented. His face is illuminated by the glow from the distant flames.

'Who?' I gasp, but I have my suspicions.

'Your enemy, Bishop Smithwulf. He is keen to see you dead.'

'Fuck,' I mumble under my breath, pleased that at least my aunt and the vast majority of my men are free, only to have that relief proved short-lived.

'Your aunt will not get far. My men are to the far side of the River Granta.'

From close by, I hear the shriek of a horse in distress, and the unmistakable sound of iron on iron, but if my ealdormen have heeded my call for arms, I can't see that Jarl Guthrum will be successful.

'You have caused much damage, and must pay for it, as well as paying the price of murdering my sister,' Jarl Guthrum continues, but my eyes are fixed on Rudolf's. Rudolf is blackened with soot and dirty with ash, and I can see where he's been badly beaten, but he still grins at me, despite one of his teeth missing. Damn the boy. He has far too much trust in me to get him out of this.

I hold my tongue, assessing the situation quickly.

Jarl Guthrum has a force of at least twenty-three men, there might be more hiding one behind the other, and they block my path to the gate. But I'm still mounted, as are Goda, Sæbald, Leonath and Beornstan. And while Jarl Guthrum is confident that my aunt won't have her freedom for long, the sound of the fighting has quickly faded. That either means my aunt and warriors are safe, or they're captive already. I don't see that having happened.

So, choices, despite Jarl Guthrum's words. But these choices are all limited by Rudolf's current predicament.

And then Jarl Guthrum barks a command in his own tongue, and the remainder of my missing men appear from the shadows of a building. Ingwald, Cealwin, Eadfrith, Wulfred, Osmod and Oda all have a seax at their throat, held there by Viking raider bastards. My warriors look bruised and battered, but all show relief at seeing me mounted on my aunt's horse. The beast has calmed, but I can feel her quivering beneath me. She's far from settled. She might make the next decision for me, as I try and calm her by rubbing her shoulder with my hand.

My men all live, and that pleases me, despite our current situation.

'Hail,' Wulfred calls, wincing as the blade must nick his neck as he speaks.

'It's fucking good to see you all,' I confirm loudly, hoping my voice shows none of my unease. We're right royally fucked, and yet, I still trust that this will somehow sort itself out in our favour.

In front of me, and unbeknown to Jarl Guthrum, who does seem to have been woefully forgetful at having men actually stand a guard at the gate, I see some of my warriors slipping back inside. I could curse the lot of them, but when did bloody Icel and Hereman ever listen to a fucking word I said? I just hope that means my aunt is safe. I hope it also means that Jarl Guthrum's men, sent over the River Granta to trap us, are all dead.

And then I see Edmund as well, and it takes all of my willpower not to growl an order at the three of them. They need to stay outside Grantabridge, not willingly come back inside.

The greyness of dawn is quickly lifting. More and more of the force I face is coming into focus. I thought there were just over twenty men, but with those holding blades to my warriors' necks, there are more like thirty of them. And so far, there are no more than eight of us, although, we also have the horses as well. But the horses aren't Haden, or even Billy and Samson. Those horses would think nothing of running at our enemy if we told them to. I can't see that my aunt's horse would be quite so willing.

'You killed my aunt's hound,' I direct at Jarl Guthrum into the sudden silence, countering his words about his sister. I did kill her, outside Northampton. I'd kill his other sisters and brothers as well should they come to Mercia. 'I would have the hound's wergild, he was as good as a man. You can get the coin for me now. I'll take your fucking silver.'

The jarl startles at my words, and a wash of confusion covers his face, as the man next to him quickly mutters something in their own tongue. I imagine Jarl Guthrum is seeking clarification on what I just said. The man, tall and with a matt of red braids descending from beneath his helm gives a yelp and bark, as though to confirm the words. Now Guthrum glowers at me, tightening his grip on the seax blade held at Rudolf's neck.

'You demand the wergild for a hound?' Guthrum asks, carefully enunciating the word hound.

'He was a king,' I confirm, enjoying the jarl's evident confusion, even as I try and think of a bloody way out of this. My men are well and truly caught, and I don't know how the fuck to get Jarl Guthrum to release them. And, I'm entirely outnumbered as well. The fire continues to rage behind us, and it would be folly to try and escape that way when so many of the inhabitants of the settlement are desperately trying to rescue their possessions. And yet.

No, I drop that thought. I need to work out how to release my men from the blades at their throats. I try not to watch just what

Edmund, Hereman and Icel are doing, and to ignore the fact that Gardulf has now joined them. They should have run for it when they had the chance.

'A king?' Jarl Guthrum queries.

'You didn't know you killed Wiglaf, king of Mercia?' I retort. I just need the Viking raiders to drop their guard. My men might have their hands bound behind their backs, and blades at their throats, but they'll still know to escape when an opportunity presents itself. I need to manufacture that opportunity.

'He was a hound,' Jarl Guthrum barks, tightening his grip on the seax, so that Rudolf lets out an involuntary squeak.

'He was named for Mercia's king.' I don't let Guthrum know how much my aunt hated the damn bastard king who ruled with that name. That's entirely irrelevant.

'Then I have killed one of Mercia's kings,' Jarl Guthrum finally rallies, he and his translator still clearly perplexed as to why I'm saying such. 'And I will claim the life of another before today is at an end.' Fuck. I didn't need to hear that. 'The bishop said you would not be able to leave your aunt as my captor. He is a wily old fox, and certainly your enemy. No, my lord king, you can submit to me, give me and my fellow jarls full control of Mercia, and I will let your men live. Or you can all die here, and we will still rule Mercia.'

I'm reminded of my aunt's words. Jarl Guthrum's ambitions haven't diminished, no matter what befell him at Repton. He must think the loss of that stronghold is just a temporary problem. It seems Bishop Smithwulf is content to let him and the other jarls believe that. I grimace. I can detect the hand of that bastard, King Alfred, in this. Any chance to save his own kingdom, and he'll take it, even if it puts his neighbours at risk.

'I decline,' I confirm, meeting Jarl Guthrum's eyes easily. As when we met at Repton, he must think he has some control over me, for all, it was Jarl Halfdan who ruled that day. Since we last met, Jarl Guthrum has allowed his dreams of what he could claim from Mercia to make him believe the feat accomplished already. I recall that Goda was a prisoner at Repton. He was beaten and bruised by them. I'm sure Goda hasn't forgotten that. He won't want to repeat that experience.

'You are trapped, Coelwulf. You must do as I say, or your men will die?

'Hum,' I reply as though I'm considering his words. Behind him, and again, I'm still unsure how he can't realise what we're doing, my warriors are starting to advance. Jarl Guthrum might hold a blade to Rudolf's neck, but Icel slips from shadow to shadow, seax in hand, eyes focused on our enemy. Edmund, Gardulf and Hereman do the same. I've seen other shadows as well. My men, who should be rushing to freedom, are instead, coming to my aid.

I hold my fury in place. The biggest problem is Rudolf. The other Viking raiders will drop their captives as soon as they realise they're under attack. But I know that Jarl Guthrum won't do that. And Rudolf is unarmed, and has only his sense to keep him alive, and against sharpened iron, that's not going to do him any fucking good.

'I don't truly think I am,' I reply. 'I have my horse,' I indicate the animal beneath me. 'And my men have their horses, and the exit is only just behind you.' I shouldn't draw attention to it, not when I'm aware of my warriors' intentions, but I must distract the hulking bastard. A glint in Jarl Guthrum's eye is caught by the first of the new day's light, and I incline my head towards him. I can see the bastard thinking through my words. He must sense that all is not as he suspects. Either that or he honestly thinks I'm just bluffing.

And then he turns, just a little, his eyes seeking out the comfort that his men stand at his back, and that's all I need.

Rudolf, alert to everything, lifts his elbows and thrusts them into Jarl Guthrum's chest, even as I rush forward with my aunt's horse, a seax in each hand. If I rode Haden, I'd know what I plan would work, but this is not Haden, and the horse has been ridden by my aunt, and not used in anger. Still, she's all I have.

Jarl Guthrum's distracted for too short a time as his men's cries call him back to my actions. Behind me, I perceive that my other warriors have quickly realised my intent. I can hear horses rushing to a gallop, even in the confined space. But Jarl Guthrum's grip tightens around Rudolf's neck, even as I draw level with him. Guthrum hardly seems to feel the impact of Rudolf's elbows. He bends, just a little, as though to ward off the continuing attack, and the seax dips away from Rudolf's neck. I turn my aunt's horse, and kick out, relying on Rudolf to duck down from Guthrum's arm so that I can kick the other man squarely in the face, and not Rudolf.

My foot hits home with a satisfying crunch, even as my aunt's horse refuses my commands and instead lashes out with her back legs in frustration at being roused to a gallop only to be ordered to stop once more. Men shout and roar, but my intention is merely to gather Rudolf to my side, and escape the place.

A shrill neigh and I fear for some of the horses, and also for my men.

I reach for Rudolf, but he's not where I thought he'd be, although Guthrum stands his ground. My enemy is quick, but not quick enough. Before he can regather his strength and position, I feel Rudolf slipping onto the mount behind me. He stinks of smoke, but at least he's still alive.

'Go, Coelwulf, bloody go,' Rudolf encourages me, and I would do that, but Guthrum isn't as caught off guard as I'd like. There are men closing around us, more and more of them. There's almost no time to move, and although I thrust a seax into Rudolf's hands, there are too many men all trying to attack me and the horse.

The animal shrieks in pain. I glimpse Guthrum as he slashes into the animal's foreleg, a great burst of blood covering him, which he spits aside, and I've fucking had enough.

'Now,' I urge the horse, and she does her best, kicking out with her back legs and her front ones, as she tries to cleave a path through our enemy. I'm stabbing and hacking, cutting indiscriminately through gloves, hands, and necks, jabbing through eyes and almost losing my balance, but still, we're trapped.

A sense of claustrophobic panic threatens to engulf me but then one voice rises above all others, and in its wake, a silence deeper than the grave rings out. Our enemy falls back, leaving my horse screaming in pain, and she's not alone. I glance to Goda, Sæbald and Leonath as well as Beornstan. We're all still mounted, but the horses have been poorly used. I feel my aunt's horse stagger at my weight, and Rudolf and I dismount quickly.

'Take her,' I urge him. 'Take her to my aunt,' I order my old squire, and Rudolf, a slash of marron at his neck, two bulging blackening eyes, with his clothes covered in ash, and one sleeve burnt to above his elbow, does as I say as a line of our enemy opens up in front of us.

I spare a thought for the horse, as she limps painfully onwards, Rudolf's soft voice encouraging her, and then I turn to face my enemy, and the man behind him, who holds the fate of everyone here in his hands. For Edmund has Jarl Guthrum in his thrall, a seax blade now held at his throat, and Edmund looks about as fucking likely to listen to reason as a hound bloodied on the hunt.

Chapter Twenty-Five

'**G**et out of here,' I call to Goda, Sæbald, Leonath, Beornstan and the other men who were held captive. I meet the eyes of Oda, Eadfrith, Cealwin, Wulfred, Ingwald and Osmod as they hurry to follow my bidding. I drink in the sight of them, noting the wounds, those that limp, or hold arms close to their side. Even Osmod, usually slower than a bloody snail, hurries away.

The Viking raiders will do nothing while Jarl Guthrum is threatened by Edmund. Their eyes seem to burn into Edmund, their hatred easy to see, but Edmund doesn't fucking care. He stands proud, his lips furrowed in fury, his eye on me, just daring me.

I force myself not to gloat at this impossible reversal of our fortune, or to call my thanks to Edmund. I was trapped, completely exposed, and now I'm not. And, as everyone there takes one breath, and then another three or four, stillness ripples out from the centre where Jarl Guthrum is Edmund's prisoner, mirroring a pebble thrown into a river.

Edmund has Jarl Guthrum before him, while Icel, Hereman, Gardulf, and Wærwulf move amongst our enemy, removing their weapons, and throwing them in a pile at the feet of their jarl.

Guthrum's face is fixed in a grimace of both pain and fury. Edmund has pulled Guthrum's helm free, to grip the bastard's hair tightly, exposing our enemy's throat for all to see. I watch Guthrum's Adams apple bob against the edge of the blade.

Already, a thin line of ruby glimmers there, as the light from the sun grows in intensity.

The Viking raiders are uneasy, all eyes on Guthrum. From beyond the gate, I hear hooves over the wooden bridge, which means the horses are safe. I wince to listen to the continuing shrill cries of the wounded animals. I hope my aunt's horse will recover from Guthrum's cut.

I also grimace as I see Rudolf slip back through the gate. I didn't tell him not to come back, but I sure as shit didn't expect him to do so. He was out of Grantabridge, as safe as I could make him, and now he's fucking back.

Rudolf carries another seax alongside the one I gave him. No one looks his way, all attention on what's going to happen now.

I'd like nothing more than for Edmund to slide his blade through Jarl Guthrum's throat and end his life here, and yet I also know that's not the answer.

Jarl Guthrum has already been humiliated by the might of my Mercians, and yet his ambitions are rampant. So rampant, that he's forged an alliance with bloody Bishop Smithwulf, and I don't for even a moment, think that it was Bishop Smithwulf's idea.

'Tell me," I demand when I can breathe easily once more, 'Did Bishop Smithwulf seek you out?' I need to know what forces are at work against me and Mercia.

Silence greets my question. I turn to the man who translated for Guthrum once before, but the man holds his tongue, stubbornness in the cast of his ugly face, even with a blade at his throat now that Wærwulf holds him captive. I'd allow the edge to be lowered, but there's no point. I know obstinacy when I see it.

Wærwulf's words rumble, no doubt repeating my question, but still, Jarl Guthrum offers nothing further.

What to do with him? If he offers me nothing, then perhaps I'll kill him, but I'd sooner set him afloat with his hands tied and hope he makes it to the Whale Road and returns to his beleaguered kingdom to inform people they shouldn't return to Mercia again. And yet?

Only, I hear a scuffle of footsteps, and turn to face Rudolf, a broad grin on his battered face as he holds Bishop Smithwulf immobile before him. He's tied the man's hands together, but Smithwulf has the freedom to walk and speak. Still, his attempt to walk upright and with his usual poise is woeful, as his head flickers from me to Jarl Guthrum. I can hear the thoughts spiralling through his mind, as he licks his lips nervously. Everything has come undone for him. How then, will he try and spin this?

'My lord, my lord king,' the bishop's unctuous voice oozes, quickly recovering its poise. Damn the man. 'God be praised, you've come to rescue me, and your most revered aunt.' I focus on Bishop Smithwulf. It's evident he's not slept much during the night, but equally, he shows no sign of harm. I know the Viking raiders have no compunction in murdering the Christ God's priests, as they call them. The fact that Bishop Smithwulf still lives tells me all I need to know about that man's loyalties. Yet, and my aunt would remind me of this if she were still here, he is consecrated as one of my God's priests, and more, one of his bishops. I might not like the fucker, but should anything happen to him, my name would be forever tainted with that.

'Indeed, my lord bishop. Tell me, how did you come to be here?' I'm sure that now isn't the time for conversation, and yet, I need to know. And if in finding out, Jarl Guthrum escapes Edmund's confines and slaughters the bishop, then that won't be my fucking fault. And then, we can kill Jarl Guthrum in retribution.

'I was captured, of course,' the bishop attempts, but I shake my head, denying those words.

'Try again, bishop,' I urge him. Rudolf stands to the right-hand side of me, the bishop in front of him. Jarl Guthrum and his men, face me, as do those of my warriors, headed by Edmund, who've come back to aid me. I know only too well that outside the gate, the rest of my warriors must be waiting for me, alongside my aunt. I'd sooner be out there, but I need to know the truth.

I focus on Edmund, and he lifts his chin higher. Wærwulf exudes calm, for all he has the man in his grasp who can speak both our language and his own.

Icel, Hereman and Gardulf have spread themselves amongst the jarl's men, now that they've taken every weapon from them that they can. I'd feel confident, but I appreciate that at some point, the people of Grantabridge will realise what's happening. How many of them must be warriors? How many of them will think to defend their jarl? But, all the same, I need to know how this predicament has come about.

'My lord king,' the bishop gabbles, bowing his head. He has no answer to my questions. None that will present him in a good light.

'He came to us,' the man beneath Wærwulf's blade offers, his eyes filled with contempt. 'He came to us and promised Mercia to the jarls provided we aided him in bringing about your death.'

Bishop Smithwulf shakes his head at the words, his thin tongue worrying at his lips. But we all know the truth. Wærwulf lowers his guard a little, but the man takes no notice of it.

'Jarl Halfdan has pledged his support as well,' the man continues. 'He'll return to Mercia as soon as news of your death reaches him. They say he'll go to the kingdom of the Irish, but he will not.'

'And the other jarls?'

I'm aware that Anwend is missing, and so too is Oscetel.

'They aren't here, at this time,' the man confirms, and then clamps his lips closed, a growl of fury from Jarl Guthrum bringing his words to an end. The man is belligerent. He doesn't seem to care what his jarl thinks. I take it to mean the man's loyalty is to another.

'Take him away,' I urge Rudolf, indicating Bishop Smithwulf. I'm prepared to allow my aunt and the other bishops to determine what punishment Smithwulf should face for what's happened here. A flicker of panic over Bishop Smithwulf's face, as Rudolf encourages him to walk towards the gate, and then everything happens far too quickly, and the momentary moments of triumph evaporate as quickly as they've come.

Bishop Smithwulf staggers forward and then stills. I watch him, perplexed by what he's doing. And only then see the bloom of magenta that explodes from his chest. His lying mouth opens and then closes, a torrent of blood erupting from it as Rudolf shrieks and skips backwards.

I turn, as all of us do, mouth open in shock, and there, on one of the roofs, smoke rising behind them, is a figure I don't recognise, illuminated against the backdrop of the flames, and in their hands, they hold a bow. Quickly, they add another arrow to the bow, but I'm already ducking, as yet another arrow strikes home, slicing through the man that Wærwulf held tightly.

A flurry of words erupts from Jarl Guthrum's mouth, as a dull thud assures me that the bishop's body has finally tumbled to the floor.

I rush forwards, towards Rudolf, gripping his arm tightly, as I hurry to Edmund's side. He's not released his grip on Jarl Guthrum, even though some of the others have escaped the confines of Icel, Hereman and Gardulf as they try and retrieve their weapons. Icel reacts quickly, menacing with his blade, ensuring he stays between the Viking raiders and their collected weapons.

'Don't fucking kill him,' I urge Edmund. Jarl Guthrum's captivity might be just what saves us, as more and more arrows fall with unnerving accuracy at my feet, and thunk into the ground, landing with a wet squelch of mud. It could be far, far worse.

'I won't fucking kill him,' Edmund glowers. 'Not until I'm bloody ready,' he continues, and now I hear another sound, one I didn't want to hear. Somehow, the bastards have closed the gate that would have allowed us to escape, and we're trapped inside Grantabridge once more. This time, there are only seven of us. Seven of us, to beat back the menace of Jarl Guthrum and his warriors, and all we have on our side is the might of our battle-craft, and Guthrum's apprehension.

Only then, we fucking don't.

Chapter Twenty-Six

Edmund doesn't so much as cry out, as slowly collapse. I watch it, not realising what's happening, while Hereman, Icel and Wærwulf scramble to grab shields from the mass of lost Viking raider weapons.

Edmund's mouth opens and closes, a parody of what happened to Bishop Smithwulf, but he recovers and stands his ground. Jarl Guthrum, his back to Edmund, doesn't even seem to notice what's happened.

Edmund shakes his head, denying what's happened to him, and I snap down on my cry of horror. The fucking archer has somehow skewered Edmund, while all around, the Viking raiders who were so pliant under our triumph, now heckle and hunt for weapons, any weapon. Those who stood between us and the gate might only be weaponed with pieces of discarded wood or forks used by those who farm to till the soil, but they glower at us. And from the far side of Grantabridge, where the archer stands, I can hear the rushing footsteps of others.

So close. So, fucking close, and now we'll fall, here.

And Edmund.

I can't bear to look, but I know that I need to. Not Edmund. My aunt will fucking kill me.

Not Edmund.

But Edmund continues to stand his ground, using Jarl Guthrum to shield his body, and indeed, before we can close any further, the jarl lets out a huff of pain. He glances down, and I see a blade protruding from his foot. I turn to the archer, thinking it a poor shot, but there's someone else on the roof behind the man, and my eyes open wide on seeing Cuthwalh fighting the archer. A punch is thrown and then another. I gasp as the pair tangle together, the bow entirely forgotten about as Cuthwalh attacks the bastard Viking raider.

'What the fuck?' Hereman has noticed his brother's condition, and his words are soft, and filled with deadly malice. Gardulf isn't slow to realise it either.

But we have the jarl.

'Order your men to allow us to pass,' I breathe into the bastard's face. With the archer out of the way, if only for the time being, we can make our escape. If we use the jarl and just remain calm. From outside, I'm aware of a rumble of outrage. The rest of my men have realised what's happening. But I can't see that they'll gain entry. Not now.

'We need to get fucking out of here,' I seethe through tight lips, when Jarl Guthrum doesn't immediately reply.

Edmund nods, but the movement is so small as to be barely seen.

'I will not order my men aside,' Jarl Guthrum murmurs, a smirk on his fat lips. I'd punch the gloating expression from his face, but I don't. I don't need to do more to imperil us, not when I have only seven men inside Grantabridge, and my horses and other warriors outside.

I think of my aunt, and notice that Edmund's lips are turning blue, although his hold on the seax at Jarl Guthrum's neck stays firm.

Hereman has rushed to Edmund's side, standing to the side of him so that no one sees Edmund's injury. We need to tread carefully.

Everything is too finely balanced. We can still escape. We must escape. But Edmund.

Fuck it. Edmund will not die. I won't allow it, and certainly not because of some bastard's arrow. Men should die in hand-to-hand combat, not from such a cowardly weapon.

Hereman shakes his head at me, his face pale. Fuck. Edmund must be very badly wounded if even Hereman reacts in such a way.

'Tell them this,' I urge Wærwulf. If Jarl Guthrum won't stand aside, then I'll force my enemy to do so.

'Aye my lord,' Wærwulf rumbles, but before I can say more, my attention is caught by the fight taking place on the roof. The struggle grows more and more frantic, and then between one blink and another, both figures are tumbling to the ground, locked in a bitter struggle. I briefly close my eyes as both tumble from the roof. The sound of both bodies hitting the ground draws the eye of everyone, and I can't think that means either of them still lives. I'll mourn Cuthwalh when I have the chance. For now, this is our opportunity to live through this.

'Order them to stand aside from the gateway, or I'll kill their jarl,' I instruct Wærwulf. He relays my message, and some of them begin to move, eyes filled with loathing.

'Move towards the gate,' I order my men, my back to Jarl Guthrum, focusing on those who would attack us from the eastern edge of the settlement, while Icel and Rudolf look to where we want to go.

A cry of pain ripples through the air, as though to prove my point, as I pull the arrow free from Jarl Guthrum's foot, where he's been impaled to the ground by it.

A rumble of unease from the rest of the Viking raiders, menacing us with whatever they have to hand, but we begin to move off. I think we might just stand a fucking chance of this working, no matter the words that Jarl Guthrum uses to counter my command.

'He orders them to attack. He says it doesn't matter if he dies, as long as you do as well.' Wærwulf informs me.

'Bloody charming,' I mutter through tight lips. I don't look to Hereman, Gardulf, or Edmund. I just pray that the three of them manage to cover Edmund's wound. Should the jarl realise his captor is weak, he'll try and duck away from the blade at his throat. If that happens, we'll stand no chance. It'll descend into hand-to-hand combat, and I only have five men capable of fighting.

Again, I hear the rumble of fighting men from beyond the gate, and although I hear the crashing of something heavy hitting the wooden door that blocks our exit, if all the Viking raiders don't step aside, I can't see how my men will manage to get inside to aid us.

Abruptly, I slither on the wet guts of the dead bishop, and just manage not to sink my hands into the ooze that covers his chest. The bishop looks strangely serene, a smirk on his lying lips, and I feel no pity for his death. He brought this upon himself. What did he think would happen if he united with the enemy of the Saxons? The enemy of Mercia.

'Let us through, and we'll release your jarl,' I call this time. The Viking raiders are growing more and more belligerent as they crowd ever closer to us.

There's a gap into which we can move, that takes us close and closer to the gate, but a line of our enemy still holds in place there. We've moved away from the pile of discarded weapons, and first one man, and then another, darts forward to grab that which they've lost. I menace forwards, hoping to prevent more from following them, but it does little good, not until Hereman adds his spear to the pile. It lands with a loud twang of wood on metal, and four men, all in the process of getting weapons, startle backwards.

'Fucking stay away,' I urge them, while Jarl Guthrum continues to bellow his fury. His words are sometimes choked, sometimes not. I can imagine that Edmund's grip must finally be slipping.

I risk looking behind us. A gaggle of Viking raiders faces outwards towards the gate, ready to defend it should it fall, but we're getting closer and closer to them, and we need them to move aside.

I risk looking at Edmund. His hand is steadier on the seax than I thought it would be, but his face is growing paler and paler, and I'm aware of a steady running sound, as though water off a drenched roof, and I fear it's Edmund's blood.

Wærwulf keeps up a running commentary on Jarl Guthrum's exhortations to his comrades, but no matter how much Guthrum urges them onwards, none of the Viking raiders has yet determined to take the risk that their lord might die in any attack on us. From beyond the closed gate, the sound of iron on wood intensifies and I hold out half a hope that one of the ealdormen might have arrived, with his reinforcements, and that the gate might just open as soon as we reach it.

But we're running short on time.

Hereman's spear throw has only deterred the Viking raiders from reclaiming their weapons for so long. Now, more and more of them are risking darting forwards to get them, but in so doing, those who stand behind us are also realising they could get their weapons. As more and more of them rush away from the thundering noise of my warriors outside the gates, I'm hopeful that we might have the opportunity to forge a path to the gate.

'Father,' the gasp from Gardulf distracts me. Gardulf never names his father as such.

Edmund stumbles, the seax blade fluttering to the ground, landing upside down, impaling Jarl Guthrum's foot once more with his strangled cry of pain. The jarl thinks to take advantage of the lessening of Edmund's grip, but even as weak as he is, Edmund still holds the man captive with the arch of his arm around his neck. While Hereman props up his brother, Icel is there, with his seax, and he takes full command of Jarl Guthrum, preventing him from gripping the seax, and using it to fight his way to freedom.

My heart thunders too loudly in my chest.

I've been in some fucking fights in my life, but this, well, this is the one that's proving the hardest to live through.

'Coelwulf,' Edmund's voice is weak, so, so fucking weak, and I meet his eye. The green light is dimming within it.

'Stay the fuck alive,' I rumble at him, stabbing forward at the same time to raise a slicing cut on the arm of a man who thinks to try his luck. The man dreams of the battle glory for winning free his jarl, but I'm not going to allow that to happen. I never imagined when I told Edmund to stay the fuck alive when we parted ways, that my words would come to have such meaning.

My foeman comes at me again, and this time, I stab into his belly through the thin padding of his byrnie. The man startles backwards, almost taking my seax with him. And more of them are coming. They must sense our weakness, and yet, we're so nearly there.

'Tell your men to fucking move, or we'll gut them all and display their heads over your own damn walls,' Icel informs Jarl Guthrum. I smirk. Icel really doesn't like the fucker.

But still, Jarl Guthrum refuses to convey those words. It'll be a stalemate, and that's no good for me. Time is pressing. We need to escape from here before Edmund draws his last breath. Only with my aunt's help, will Edmund live.

And then, a sound I needed to hear rips through the air, while at the same time, Icel increases his grip on Jarl Guthrum's neck so that the limping fool is silenced. Guthrum's commands abruptly stop, and so does my fear that we'll die here. For the gates have been breached once more, and now, we're all surrounded by my Mercian warriors, the majority of them mounted, led by Turhtredus and Wulfsige, with Ealdorman Ælhun's men, Ælfgar in the front line with them.

Abruptly, I sag, grateful that Icel has hold of Jarl Guthrum, for Edmund is on the ground sagging between the figures of his son and his brother, still inside Grantabridge, and I don't know what to fucking do.

Chapter Twenty-Seven

I rush to Edmund's side, my mounted warriors ensuring the Viking raiders can get nowhere near us as they surge into Grantabridge. They block the way more entirely than a river in flood.

'Edmund, Edmund,' I call, my words choking as I realise that his chest hardly moves, the bloom of blood down his side, an indication that the archer was one hell of a lucky fucking bastard.

'Get my aunt,' I call to Rudolf. Rudolf, eyes wide and frightened so that he reminds me of the small child I first encountered, scurries to do my bidding. I see him dash, one way and the another, but I'm gripping Edmund's hand, willing some strength to show in it.

'Fucking bastard,' I exclaim but I don't know who I'm talking to anymore.

Icel must relieve himself of the burden of Jarl Guthrum, for he shoulders his way to Edmund's side, knocking me as he does so.

Gardulf is sobbing, the sounds of a child, broken, broken, broken, while Hereman trembles, as he sobs on his knees beside his brother. I've never seen Hereman in such a state before.

'Move. For fuck's sake,' Icel complains. He rips Edmund's byrnies and tunic aside, and all I can see is a mass of red. So much blood. Surely one man can't bleed so much. Surely, there's no one alive with so much blood inside them.

I don't hear the words of Ealdorman Ælhun, or any of his men. I don't know where Jarl Guthrum has gone, and I don't fucking care either. I've already lost Siric and Eadberht in this shit show, and probably Cuthwalh as well. But not Edmund. Never Edmund.

I'm not aware of Icel moving away, until he returns, and roughly thrusts me aside so that he can see more clearly how wounded Edmund is. I want to tell him to stop. I've seen wounds like this before. I know what it means.

My warriors gather around us, blocking the sight of Edmund on the ground from everyone else. A hundred horses arses face us, ensuring the Viking raiders can't get close, but I'm only vaguely aware of it all.

Icel holds layers of clean cloth against the wound, and Edmund's eye flutters open as he hears the acerbic voice of my aunt. I don't look, but I see her feet come into view, and then she stops. I don't want to, but I look up and see her face. She doesn't look at me, only at Edmund, but the sorrow on her face tells me that I'm not wrong.

'Icel,' her words are suddenly soft, as she lays both hands on the huge man's shoulders. 'Icel, please stop,' she urges, her quiet words spoken with composure and years of experience.

But Icel doesn't heed her.

'I need hot water. I need pigs gut, warm water. Bring it to me. Moss and vinegar to stem the flow of blood.' Icel beckons behind him, as though someone might just be standing there with what's needed. But no one other than him is moving, or even speaking. Not my aunt, not Hereman, and certainly not Gardulf, who wails like a small child. Rudolf is silent. Like my aunt's soft word, it does more to speak of this tragedy than anything else.

'Edmund,' I try once more. I need to meet his gaze one more time. I need him to know, after all we've been through, all of our arguments, all of our aggravation with one another, that he was my friend, that it was worth it. That without him, I'd never have been able to fill my brother's position when he died. That he's saved Mercia for future generations. But Edmund doesn't hear my words. His chest rises feebly, and with every beat of his faltering heart, more blood gushes across his chest.

'Edmund,' my aunt speaks now. Her words persuasive. 'Edmund, my love,' and my heart breaks all over again. All these years, I've known, of course, I've bloody known of their love for one another, but to hear it laid bare now, is too much. Too much.

At her words, Edmund's eye flickers open, the light so dim as to be almost gone. Now she holds his lifeless hand in hers. Icel has moved aside, accepting the inevitable, and pulling Gardulf closer, so that Gardulf rocks against him, his cries quieter now, more sullen, his entire body trembling, but his hand rests on his father's shoulder.

'Hereman,' I urge the huge man close, so that he sits beside me. He shakes his head, eyes wild, blood from his brother's wound smeared over his face, to merge with the ash of the fire so that he looks half crazed, and he shakes his head, the words of denial not able to get past his dry lips.

'My love,' Edmund's words are little more than a whisper on the wind. I glance to my aunt, and she smiles through her tears, her face bruised and battered from what the bastard's did to her, and yet she's beautiful in that moment. I've never seen it before. I've never seen beneath the façade of her position, the rigour of her conviction that her family would one day rule Mercia again.

'All will be well,' Edmund smiles, and it's a thing of beauty. I think he can't feel the pain of his wound, and I hope he feels only the love and regard from all of his family, his lover, and his friends.

'All will be well,' she repeats. 'You can sleep now, my love.'

'I can,' he confirms. 'Gardulf, Hereman, look after each other,' he murmurs, his eye almost rolling back into his head, but a sharp sob from Rudolf brings him back to the here and now.

'Coelwulf, you fucking bastard,' he gargles, and his gaze flicks towards mine. 'You're a fine king of Mercia. You've made me proud,'

Edmund murmurs. 'Fight on. For me, and my family, and for the son your brother left behind.' His eye closes and his chest stills, and I don't even hear his words, not in the face of my sorrow and my grief. Not Edmund. Never Edmund.

'My lord king,' the words come from far away, and I almost don't catch them.

'My lord king,' and Ealdorman Ælhun is becoming more insistent. 'There are more of them coming,' he urges, and it seems I'm to have no time to grieve for Edmund. These bastard Viking raiders are far from done with us.

Chapter Twenty-Eight

I cel roars to his feet, rousing me so that I abruptly hear the sound of battle.

'My lord king,' it's Goda who speaks, his words etched in pain. 'We must leave here,' he beckons for me to stand as well. My aunt, eyes closed, murmurs soft words and I imagine she's praying for Edmund's soul, but now really isn't the time.

'We'll move him,' Goda assures me, and I appreciate he's found two cloaks, and with the aid of Sæbald, Gyrth and Wulfstan, the four men mean to move Edmund's cooling body.

'I'll do it,' I snatch the cloak from him. A sad smile touches his lips but he nods in understanding.

'Then, my lord king, do it quickly, for there are Viking raiders on the River Granta and we need to be gone from this place.'

I look around me. Ealdorman Ælhun and some of my warriors are mounted, and they're being hard pressed by the Viking raiders who think to fight their way to Jarl Guthrum's side.

'Help me,' I rouse Hereman and Gardulf from their grief as well, even as Icel, weapon raised, stalks his way to the Viking raiders, fury in his every action, as he forces aside two of the horses to face the bastard Viking raiders. I'd worry for him, but Icel isn't going to die today. But he will wreak terrible vengeance for what's happened here.

My aunt is the first to realise my intent, even as Rudolf hovers, unsure what to do with himself.

'Get Jethson,' I urge Rudolf. 'He'll assist us,' and now Rudolf pushes his way through the gate, thronged with Mercian warriors, and I know he'll bring me the stead. What Jethson will do when he understands his task, I just don't know.

My aunt and I carefully roll Edmund's lifeless form one way and then another, as a further sob hiccups from Gardulf, the movement making it appear as though Edmund still lives.

Hereman labours to help us, ensuring his brother is covered, no sign of his mortal wound showing. But Edmund's face remains uncovered, and it takes all of my resolve, to cover it, shutting him off from the light for one final time. Edmund lived to see another dawn rise, but only just.

I look up then, hoping to find Rudolf returned to me, but the horse is that of Ealdorman Ælhun's.

'My lord king, there are more, on the river. We must hasten from this place.'

'My thoughts turn to Cuthwalh. I can't leave him, not here, where the enemy might sever his head from his neck, and hold it aloft on the end of a spear for all to see. I swallow. Standing, resolved. Once Edmund is on Jethson, I'm going to find Cuthwalh.

'We'll prevail,' I caution the ealdorman. 'How many men do you have?' I ask as an afterthought.

'Enough, my lord king. And the people of Northampton are here as well. They hold the bridge for us, and ensure none of the Viking raiders can come ashore on the western side of the Granta.'

'We're not alone then, and we still have Jarl Guthrum?'

'Yes, my lord king. He remains our captive.'

'Good,' I confirm, only for Icel's roar of defiance to ring loud and clear. I startle, hand to my seax, hoping my words haven't betrayed me. And as I watch, a man I never thought to see again, staggers through the mass of horseflesh and warriors.

'Cuthwalh?' I call, and he must hear his name. He looks up, a smirk of triumph on his face, as he catches sight of me in turn, and the joyful expression slides from his face.

'Help him,' I urge Wulfstan, and Wulfstan dashes to the older man's side. Cuthwalh is a balm for my troubled heart and yet, it's not enough.

Rudolf finally arrives with Jethson, the horse's eyes wide to have been led through piles of corpses. I reach over and run my hand over his nose.

'Calm, my friend,' I urge him, even as Hereman lifts his brother, not even straining at the action.

The familiar weight settles over Jethson, and he quietens. I only wish it were Edmund alive and bitching about the shitting mess I've made of all this. But it fucking isn't.

'Take him,' I urge Hereman and Gardulf, reaching for my aunt, and taking her hands to lift her to her feet. She staggers against me, and finally meets my eyes. She doesn't cry but the grief there is deep. I feel I can see all of her laid bare before me. How much I've never seen. How much she's never wanted me to see. I nod, swallow my tears.

'Go, quickly. Take him from here, and I'll find you shortly.' She wobbles, and Rudolf slides his way between her and Jethson. I watch as they exit the gate, an honour guard of my warriors to either side, heads bowed, and then I turn, towards my enemies.

I'm going to fucking kill all of them.

Chapter Twenty-Nine

Wærwulf is at my side, Gyrth shadowing me, as we emerge through the retreating line of Mercian warriors to face the Viking raider bastards.

One loses an eye before he can blink, and another his hand, seax included, before he can land a strike against me. And on it goes. The Viking raiders have found some stones but not enough.

My movements are sure, precise, my intention to inflict as little suffering as possible, but the bastards must all die.

My blade shimmers in the dull light of the new day, running with the lifeblood of my enemy, of the men and women who've brought the life of my most trusted warrior to an end.

I stab and slash, punch and kick, elbow and menace, teeth in a rigour mortis grin, as I bare them for all to see.

I see the horror on the faces of some, others bellow in fear, while one or two piss themselves even as my blade stabs into their open mouths, slicing open their bellies, and jutting upwards into exposed armpits and across necks festooned in beards and the trinkets of their religion. No one will save them. No one.

And still they come. I'm aware of Wærwulf and Gyrth at my sides. I'm vaguely conscious of more of my allies joining the fray, and I can just hear the strident orders of Ealdorman Ælhun as he directs his warriors to battle against the coming shipmen, but I have only one intention.

I will kill every last fucker. Every last one.

I taste blood, sweat, my tears, unaware I'm even crying as more and more die. A woman runs at me, spear extended, and I duck aside, bring my body alongside hers when she runs past me, and as she comes to a belated stop, I knock her nose with the back of my head, twisting the spear from her grasp. She screams, mouth open so that I can see inside her body, but my blade slips between her teeth and she judders and stops.

A youth, no older than Penda, presses me, his gaze focused only on me, his intention clear in the way he holds his body tight. I can't deny he's been taught well, but he dies all the same, screaming as blood from his slit throat joins the mass on the ground, so much of it, the soil can't drink it in, and I can feel the sticky substance every time I meet another attack.

I knew there were many of the Viking raiders inside Grantabridge, but so many come against me, I realise I've underestimated how many of the bastards have made the place their home.

I slash, and roar, fight and cry, stab and punch, anything, anything, to stop me thinking about what's happened here.

I'm conscious of a voice calling to me. It seems to come from far away, but it's insistent, summoning me, even as I stand, heaving much-needed air into my body as I seek out my next target, but there's no one left.

'Where the fuck are they all?' I bellow, my voice echoing back from the emptiness of the vast open area we only so recently made our way through.

'I think you fucking killed them all,' Rudolf offers, his attempt to fill his voice with his usual infectious enthusiasm bringing tears once more to my eyes.

I round on him. I need to kill. I need to sate this need inside me. If I stop, then what will I be?

I lick my lips, tasting salt, and iron and sweat. Chest heaving, I look down and see my arms are covered in blood, my gloves slick with it, my seax festooned so that it's impossible to see the blade.

Frightened eyes stare at me from the faces of children, and babes, old men and women. There are few of them, and they're all ash covered, eyes rimmed in red from their night of no sleep, and from the slaughter they've witnessed. Some cry, some sob, others are stony-faced. I've made many enemies today, and I don't fucking care.

'Leave this place,' I roar, pointing to where I know the quayside is. All is peaceful there now. Ealdorman Ælhun and his men must have dispatched the new arrivals. And now, well now, I'll give the weak and the old, the young and the infirm, the opportunity to leave here.

'Take only what you can carry. Should you ever return, I'll personally seek you out and slice open your throats.' Wærwulf mirrors my words in their tongue, and those assembled wince, and cower, and then scream with terror. My tone was enough, Wærwulf's words have merely reinforced their cadence.

'Now,' I roar, and Wærwulf again gives voice to my words, and some startle to do as I say, others standing still, terrified.

I turn to Rudolf. If I look as he does, then I'm far from surprised.

He stands tall, his byrnie shimmering wetly, his face, already a welter of bruises and ash, now congealed with the burgundy of a winter's morning. His eyes are stark, from his filthy face, and blood pours from his body to mingle with that on the ground, and yet he does not bleed.

Chest heaving, I realise I stand amidst a pile of broken and life-less bodies. I kick one aside, stride to Rudolf's side, the rest of my warriors following in my wake.

We've killed all the bastards, and now, I'll let some of them go. I'm not a man to kill babes and those unable to defend themselves. And, I must still contend with the instigator of all this, Jarl Guthrum, and perhaps others. I'll see who Ealdorman Ælhun has apprehended, and then, well then I must think of my aunt, and my lost brother, the man who made me who I am. The man I'm broken to be without.

Edmund.

Chapter Thirty

I walk from Grantabridge weighted with more than just the loss of Edmund. I've changed beyond all measure in the short amount of time I've been trapped behind the walls of the Viking raider settlement.

I barely even hear the crash of broken and burned timbers falling to the ground in my wake. Grantabridge is finished. That should give me some joy.

There are bodies and the dying surrounding my path outside the walls. I feel as though I walk from night to day as I finally take a huge gulp of air clean from the taint of smoke. There's a Viking raider ship slowly sinking into the flow of the Granta. There are bodies there as well, some who hadn't managed to even make it ashore, others who've died falling into the water. All of them bob as though lifelike with the flow of the water.

There is one Viking raider ship that's still water-tight. Onto that, those who yet live, are crowding. I watch them from my place on the bridge. I consider where the young child is that clung to my aunt's skirts. I ponder if they yet live, and if their parents are dead. I find that while I sorrow for the child's loss, I can't help but be grateful that my enemy have been killed.

Perhaps, now, finally, they'll leave Mercia's shores.

'What will you do with your prisoner, my lord king?' It's Ealdorman Ælhun who makes the query. I turn from watching my enemy to meet his keen gaze. He's smudged with ash and blood, the two merging together to make him appear as though he's stepped from the depths of Hell, his eyes red-rimmed from the veil of smoke and raging fires that still coat the settlement.

'You have my thanks for coming as requested,' I murmur. 'I trust you've not lost any men?' I find it surprising that my voice can be so steady, when I'm aware that my hands shake. I've sheathed my blades in an attempt not to show how badly.

'It's my honour, my lord king, and yes, my men have either all survived, or have wounds that will heal quickly, God willing.'

'That pleases me,' I confirm. And silence falls between us. It's broken only by the terrified conversation of my enemy. The children look lost, the surviving women don't look much better. There are few who've lived through this slaughter. I can feel the blood of their dead parents on my skin, and in my hair. It itches as it dries, but I can't sorrow on a singular level for any of them. I remember little of those I killed in my rage. Now, I feel spent but also fired up, my belly a gurgle of hunger, sorrow and triumph. I fear I might even be sick.

'What do you suggest?' I question, focusing on the immediate problem, breathing deeply to steady myself. Behind me, I'm aware of people removing the lifeless form of Bishop Smithwulf. He doesn't deserve an honourable burial, and yet, I'll ensure he receives one. I can't let it be known that I was betrayed by one of my supposed allies. He'll have to be remembered as just another victim of the aggression of Jarl Guthrum.

'He's a valuable hostage. He could be used against the Viking raiders. Jarls Oscetel and Anwend were absent from Grantabridge, as I understand it, but I'm sure they still have their sights set on reclaiming the place.'

I grunt my agreement. Jarl Guthrum is a problem I could do without.

'Where is he?'

'I've taken command of him, my lord king,' here the ealdorman stumbles over the words as though embarrassed to have been caught out arranging it.

'It's for the best,' I confirm. 'He should remain our captor for the time being. I won't have him killed, but neither is he free to go as he pleases. I'll need time and the advice of my witan as to how to proceed.' My words sound hollow, but for once, I feel I'm speaking sense. I'm thinking clearly about Jarl Guthrum. Not that I fucking want to. I would kill him, but Ealdorman Ælhun is correct. Jarl Guthrum is an exceedingly valuable hostage. I do need counsel on how to proceed with him. Certainly, I won't have him beaten, and tied to a chair, bound and gagged, as my aunt had done to her. I'll show the bastard how reasonable men conduct themselves.

'My lord king, it would be my honour to ensure Jarl Guthrum is kept as a captive.'

'Then you have my thanks. Ensure he's treated well. I won't be accused of underhand tactics with him.' My words are almost without substance, so quietly spoken.

'Of course, my lord king.' The ealdorman bows from my presence, but I'm not truly aware of what he's doing. I still watch the people of Grantabridge as they hurry away, under the watchful gaze of my blood-stained warriors, and those of Ealdorman Ælhun's. These survivors are fearful, and they're right to be so. They're not welcome here. A pity their families didn't realise as much. What illusions must these jarls create to entice men and their families across the Whale Road? I wish I knew, and then I could deploy the opposite tactic. I could ensure they know that all they'll receive in return for their welcome is a blade to the throat.

Rudolf joins me. He doesn't speak, but I'm aware of him at my side. His presence is a comfort. Haden is still hidden away, with Hemming and Wulfhere. I must send someone to bring back the men

245

I've left further along the Granta, entirely masked from sight by the thick band of impenetrable trees that stretch along much of this side of the river bank. It took us over a day to make the journey around the woodlands to the other entrance to Grantabridge. If my men haven't yet realised that we've won, then I'd be surprised. Even now, I imagine they're rushing back here. But, all the same, there might be those who thought to escape the inferno by taking their chances in the river. I left only four men behind and all of our horses, including Haden.

Rudolf's gaze focuses on the survivors of our fight as well, and I'm aware that while I'm bloody and ash-stained, Rudolf is even more so. One day, I'll ask him how he burned a settlement to the ground, but today isn't that day.

Icel is the next to determine his task finished, and come to my other side. I turn and meet his face. Where he's removed his helm, his face is merely skin-coloured, but his chin is as blackened and bloodied as Rudolf, his normally grey beard, almost pink with blood and ash. We must look a sight for any who think to cast their gaze our way. His byrnie shimmers with the blood of the dead, his eyes slightly unfocused. He's seen things here today I imagine he never thought to see. Or perhaps, he hoped to never see them again. Icel remains, as he has always been to me, an enigma. A man I think I know but who constantly surprises me. I hope, for now, he'll not be flippant and offer me some trite reminder that whatever has happened here, he's always gone one better than me.

Hereman's arrival is not unexpected, especially not with the vibration of the bridge, as he takes each step. I don't lift my head to meet his gaze, but Rudolf moves aside, and Hereman stands closest to me now. I'm overly aware of my heart thudding, of his breathing, heavy and laboured beside me. We rescued my aunt, but at what cost?

Gardulf's arrival surprises me. He moves lightly, a testament to his youth and slighter build, but also to how he's chosen to become a warrior. For Gardulf, being swift is his greatest asset. Unlike Icel,

Hereman and myself. We fight with our strength and skill. Gardulf has yet to acquire that, but he will. If he continues to fight, I can't see how he'd stop now. He has vengeance to seek. We all do. Icel moves aside to allow him to rest beside me.

Slowly, the rest of my warriors join me, even Tatberht, who must have made his way here from Northampton with Ealdorman Ælhun and his men. Tatberht looks old, and bowed by his wounds, grief and sorrow. Tatberht, just like Icel, has seen many men die in his long years. Ælfgar is there as well. There's no need for a bigger force now, and yet, they'll come, of that I'm sure. I summoned them, as Mercia's king, and no doubt, they've made their way here as soon as possible, and yet, Edmund is still lost to me.

I find then that I miss Pybba's presence. He should be here, to offer words of sorrow, to just be with us, but he isn't here. Pybba has had his own adventures to overcome. I hope as I told Rudolf, that he's finally fully recovered from his illness and injuries gained at the hands of the Viking raiders.

I consider other battles, where I've joyfully called my men to order afterwards, scanning them to ensure their injuries aren't life-threatening, that they'll live to fight another day. I think back to that day, which seems as though it were a lifetime ago when I first encountered the Viking raiders who'd been sent by the Repton jarls to kill me. On that occasion, I lost two men, Athelstan and Beornberht, and since then, I've lost yet more, Oslac, Hereberht, Eoppa, Siric, Eadberht and now Edmund. If I had died that day, fighting the enemy Viking raiders, rather than lived, would my men have survived? Would they have lived even if Mercia had been overrun by the Repton jarls, or would they have felt compelled to continue Mercia's fight to remain Mercian?

If I'd died that day, then there would have been no one of a royal lineage to rule Mercia. If I'd died that day, then I would not have had to endure the death of my comrades, and it wouldn't have fucking mattered, not at all.

My mind reeling, I remember Edmund's dying words to me, and

accusingly, I look to Icel. He doesn't meet my eyes, and I consider if he's biding his time, waiting for me to ask the question.

Only then, my aunt joins us. She stands tall, erect, her baring as regal as ever. She would have made someone a fine queen, had she been allowed to rule Mercia. Her bruises reveal themselves in their entirety, and she makes no attempt to hide them. She's as much a warrior of Mercia as the men who join me along the expanse of the bridge that crests the River Granta.

'Icel,' her words are cool, and Icel turns to meet her gaze. There's some resignation on his face, but he doesn't avoid her look.

'Tell me the truth of Edmund's final words. Did Coenwulf have a son?'

'Aye, my lady, he did. But Coenwulf never knew of the boy's birth.'

'And yet you've kept this secret from me, all these years?' Her voice is colder than ice.

'Aye, my lady. For the good of all involved,' Icel responds. There's iron in his words, and I'm surprised by his obstinacy. 'The child has been provided for, as your nephew would have decreed.'

'And yet, not at Kingsholm?'

'No, my lady. We thought it best.'

'We?' Her eyebrows rise.

'Aye, my lady. Edmund and me. We two who knew of the boy's existence.'

A deadly silence falls between the two of them. Icel, the old bastard, has reminded my aunt that while she might wish to lay all of her anger at his feet, her lover was as equally involved.

'Tell me, where is the child, the boy?'

'My lady,' his words are softer now. 'The mother was told, should anything befall her, that the boy should be sent to find Lord Coelwulf.'

I turn, aghast, the memory of finding the boy in the stables at Worcester astounding me.

'Æthelred?' I gasp.

'Aye, my lord. That was the name she chose for the boy. She didn't wish to curse the child with the name of his father. Not after what happened to him.'

I nod. I see it now. The boy, the youth, the reason I didn't banish him from my side – I'd seen his like before. And now, I'm amazed that I didn't recognise him at the time.

My aunt's expression is stony, but her eyes blaze, and I know what her next words will be, for I'm thinking of them as well.

'Then the royal line of King Coenwulf and King Coelwulf, both the first of their names, and King Coelwulf the second is far from at an end. My lord king, you must fight on. It seems, you have an heir after all.'

Chapter Thirty-One

Northampton

I meet the eyes of my aunt, and hers are free from tears, but not sorrow. Not for the first time, I wish I had her strength. Her expression softens, and a half-smile plays at her lips. She must read my thoughts, as so often the case.

'He wouldn't expect such sorrow,' she croaks, and in those words, I hear the pain not revealed by her expression.

'He wouldn't expect it, no, but he has earned it,' I insist, my voice little more than a discordant bark. I feel as though I've not spoken since yesterday. Now, Edmund is buried beside Siric and Eadberht, and I'd sooner have him at Kingsholm, but my aunt was insistent that Edmund should be interred here, in Northampton, and as soon as possible. Hemming and Wulfhere with the horses, and Eadulf and Osbert only just made it back to Northampton in time.

My head pounds, my chest as well. But now, here, in the shadows of the hall inside Northampton, I feel I can finally relax, free from the staring eyes of others, who, it seems, never expected to see their king mourn such as this.

My aunt nods, a solitary tear sliding over her cheek, unheeded.

'He was a good man,' she murmurs, but then shakes her head, and coughs to clear her throat. 'He was a bastard hard man to love,' she tries instead. 'A hard man to care for, and an even harder man to call a friend.'

My aunt and I aren't alone. Hereman is here, Gardulf as well, while Icel is a menacing presence just beside me. None of us are happy, but I think we all have different reasons. We mourn a lost member of my war band, but to all, he was someone different.

'I hardly knew him,' Gardulf whispers. He's young, and one day, his grief may leave him, but equally, it might not. I made enemies when I slaughtered the Viking raiders inside Grantabridge, but they have also made an enemy, of Gardulf. He'll never forgive them for taking his father from him.

'He was proud of you,' Icel offers, when no one knows how to respond. 'He was a hard man, but you made him happy, and proud,' Icel offers. His words rumble too loudly, and yet, they startle me for an entirely different reason. I never realised that Icel appreciated or understood anything about Edmund.

'And you,' Icel continues, looking to Hereman. 'You were his brother, and he loved you, for all he never once showed it.' A faint smile plays around my aunt's lips at the words, offered with a lack of compassion but with sincere honesty.

'And you,' Icel rounds on me. His eyes are hard, his face showing no softness, for all I thought he spoke to soothe us.

'I hated the bastard from when I can first remember him, to when he forced me to resume my brother's ealdordom,' I confirm. I despised Edmund for much longer than that, but perhaps now isn't the time to admit as much.

'We all did,' my aunt murmurs, and now I feel a smirk breaking through the frown of my sorrow.

'Even you?' I query.

'Aye, even me. I never had any regard for his father, and Edmund knew as much. He learned from a young age how to infuriate me.'

'Edmund's father?' I question. I mean, I know he must have had one.

'You won't remember him,' Icel interjects, his tone forbidding. A look passes between my aunt and Icel and they both fall silent. Just another secret to be kept from me. Sometimes, I feel as though I must have walked through my previous life at Kingsholm blinded, for there is much I didn't know and seemingly, never will.

"*A man of the Hwicce,*
He gulped mead at midnight feasts.
Slew Viking raiders, night and day.
Brave Athelstan, long will his valour endure."

The words start slowly, and I turn, furious and perplexed to know who speaks Edmund's words, today of all days.

"*Beornberht, son of the Magonsæte.*
A proud man, a wise man, a strong man.
He fought and pierced with spears.
Above the blood, he slew with swords."

I breathe deeply, through my nostrils, aware that my aunt is as tense as I am. I came here to be away from the gaze of all and to mourn as I know I needed to, and yet Rudolf, damn him, has begun the scop song that honours my lost warriors.

"*A man fought for Mercia.*
Against Viking raiders and foes.
Shield flashing red,
Brave Oslac, slew Viking raiders each seven-day."

My aunt's hand grips mine, while Hereman stands, as though to round on our young comrade, and yet Icel pulls him aside, soft words exchanged so that Hereman rests more easily.

"*Hereberht was at the forefront, brave in battle.*
He stained his spear, and splashed with blood
A thousand and more before Halfdan's men
His bravery cut short his life."

I'm aware that Rudolf is the centre of everyone's attention. All of my warriors, aside from Pybba, are here today to witness Edmund's burial. All are saddened, but some are grief-stricken, whereas others merely mourn a man who stood at their side in the shield wall. But,

Rudolf, God-damn him, reminds all that Edmund is merely one of many. And we've mourned them all. Each new loss is a reminder of what we fight for.

"A friend I have lost, faithful he was,
After joy, there was silence
Red his sword, let it never be cleansed
A friend I have lost, brave Eoppa."

I want to stop him, to have him never speak the following words, but it seems, Edmund had composed his next two verses even while we were fighting to find my aunt. Edmund honoured our lost men, even when he thought the love of his life was gone from him for all time.

'A blood bath and certain death for his foes
Brave Siric's bravery will endure forever
Although he was slain, he slew
And he will be eternally honoured.'

A soft sob erupts, no doubt Leonath or one of Siric's especial allies.

'Swift in the struggle
It grieves me to leave brave Eadberht
He was foremost in battle
The enemy feared him, and in turn, he shamed them.'

My aunt is crying now, uncontrollably. She's lost so much, and Siric and Eadberht died in defence of her. Once more, I'm filled with rage for what's happened to my warriors, to my family. To Mercia. And still, Rudolf hasn't finished. His voice rises and falls, lifts and lilts and I think, perhaps, Rudolf should have been a scop and not a warrior.

"Sturdy and strong, it would be wrong not to praise them.
Amid blood-red blades, in black sockets.
The war-hounds fought fiercely, tight formation.
Of the war band of Coelwulf, I would think it a burden,
To leave any in the shape of man alive."

The hall falls silent, as the last of the words dies away, and I feel once more tears running from my eyes, and I don't care. A man should grieve his friend. A man should grieve for that person who made him a man. It saddens me to know that Edmund will not be here to mourn any future deaths amongst my warriors. His scop song is at an end.

I think no one will speak further, but then Icel stands. He's a giant, as always, but seems shrunken at that moment, and as he lifts his voice, to give form to his words, I feel myself sobbing, as Rudolf watches on, wide-eyed, no doubt fearing Icel's wrath for having so spoken.

I once thought Icel lost to me, as Edmund is now. And Edmund thought Icel was lost and blamed himself for that as well, and gave Icel words they shared together only once, and only because Icel badgered Edmund until he told him. Yet Icel knows them, and now, he gifts them to Edmund.

'Bitter in battle, with blades set for war
Attacking in an army, cruel in battle
He slew with swords, without much sound
Edmund pillar of battle, took pleasure in giving death.'

Silence greets such an acclamation, and I'm aware, I don't know how to own Edmund's loss, not yet, and I never want to, but one day, in the future, I'll have no choice but to fucking do so.

Cast of Characters

Coelwulf's Warriors

Æthelred – a youngster adopted by Coelwulf's warband

Ælfgar – one of the older members of the warband

Athelstan – killed in the first battle in The Last King

Beornberht – killed in the first battle in The Last King

Beornstan – one of Coelwulf's warriors

Cealwin – one of the older warriors from Kingsholm, first appears in The Last Shield

Coelwulf – King of Mercia, rides **Haden**

Cuthwalh – one of the older warriors from Kingsholm, rides **Aart**

Edmund – rides **Jethson**, was Coelwulf's brother's man until his death. Brother is **Hereman**.

Eadberht – one of Coelwulf's warriors

Eadulf – one of Coelwulf's warriors

Eadfrith – one of the older warriors from Kingsholm, first appears in The Last Shield

Eahric – one of Coelwulf's warriors, rides **Storm**

Eoppa – rides **Poppy**, dies in The Last Horse

Gardulf – first appears in The Last Horse – Edmund's son, rides **Kermit**

Goda – one of Coelwulf's warriors, appears from The Last King onwards, rides **Magic**

Gyrth – one of Coelwulf's warriors, appears from The Last King onwards, rides **Keira**

Hemming – son of Beornberht, a young warrior from Kingsholm, rides **Perry**

Hereman – brother of Edmund, rides **Billy**

Hereberht – dies at Torksey, in The Last Warrior.

Hiltiberht – a squire

Ingwald – one of Coelwulf's warriors

Icel – rides **Samson**

Leonath – first appears in The Last Horse, rides **Petre**

Lyfing – wounded in The Last King

Oda – one of Coelwulf's warriors

Ordheah – one of Coelwulf's warriors

Ordlaf – one of Coelwulf's warriors

Oslac – one of Coelwulf's warriors, dies in The Last King

Osmod – one of the older warriors from Kingsholm, first appears in The Last Shield

Penda – first appears in The Last Horse – Pybba's grandson

Pybba – loses his hand in battle, rides **Brimman** (Sailor in Old English)

Penna, his daughter

Beca, his granddaughter

Higuel, his daughter's father-in-law

Rudolf – was a squire at the beginning of The Last King, rides **Dever**

Siric – first appears in The Last Horse

Sæbald – injured in The Last King, but returns to action in The Last Horse

Tatberht – first appears in The Last Horse, normally remains at Kingsholm. Rides **Wombel**

Wærwulf – speaks Danish, rides **Cinder**

Wulfstan – one of Coelwulf's warriors, rides **Berg**

Wulfhere – grandson of Tatberht, rides **Stilton**

Wulfred – one of Coelwulf's warriors, rides **Cuthbert.**

The Mercians

Bishop Wærferth of Worcester

Bishop Deorlaf of Hereford

Bishop Eadberht of Lichfield

Bishop Smithwulf of London

Bishop Ceobred of Leicester

Bishop Burgheard of Lindsey

Ealdorman Beorhtnoth – of western Mercia

Ealdorman Ælhun – of area around Warwick

Ealdorman Æthelwold – his father, Ealdorman Æthelwulf, dies at the Battle of Berkshire in AD871.

Ealdorman Wulfstan – dies in The Last King

His son – (fictional) dies in The Last King

Werburg – (fictional) his daughter

Ealdorman Beornheard – of eastern Mercia

Ealdorman Aldred – of eastern Mercia

Lady Cyneswith – Coelwulf's (fictional)Aunt

The Northumbrians

Archbishop Wulfhere of York

King Ricsige of Northumbria

Viking raiders

Ivarr – dies in AD870

Halfdan – brother of Ivarr (above)

Guthrum - one of the three leaders at Repton with Halfdan

His sister, who dies outside Northampton

Oscetel - one of the three leaders at Repton with Halfdan

Anwend – one of the three leaders at Repton with Halfdan

Anwend Anwendsson – his fictional son

Jarl Sigurd – dies in The Last King

His wife

The royal family of Mercia
King Burgred of Mercia

m. **Lady Æthelswith** in AD853 (the sister of King Alfred of Wessex)

they had no children

Beornwald – a fictional nephew for King Burgred

King Wiglaf – ninth-century ruler of Mercia

King Wigstan- ninth-century ruler of Mercia

King Beorhtwulf – ninth-century ruler of Mercia

King Coelwulf II– ninth-century ruler of Mercia from AD874 (the main character)

Coenwulf – his older brother, died 10 years ago

Lady Cyneswith – his aunt

The royal family of Wessex
King Alfred of Wessex

m.**Lady Ealhswith**, a woman of the Mercian royal family in AD864

Æthelflæd, their older daughter, born c.866

Misc.

Wiglaf and Berhtwulf – the names of Coelwulf's aunt's dogs, Lady Cyneswith

Wulfsige – commander of Ealdorman Ælhun's warriors

Kyred – oathsworn man of Bishop Wærferth of Worcester

Turhtredus – Mercian warrior

Eanulf – Mercian warrior

Places Mentioned
London – more strictly the twin settlements of **Lundenwic** (a market site) **and Londinium** (Roman ruin) **at this time**

Gainsborough, in north-east Mercia.

Northampton, on the River Nene in Mercia.

Grantabridge/Cambridge, in eastern Mercia/East Anglia

Gloucester, on the River Severn, in western Mercia.

Worcester, on the River Severn, in western Mercia.

Hereford, close to the border with Wales, on the River Wye

Repton, important Mercian mausoleum. St Wystan's was the name of royal mausoleum.

Gwent, one of the Welsh kingdoms to share a border with Mercia.

Powys was one of the Welsh kingdoms to share a border with Mercia.

Gwynedd, one of the Welsh kingdoms to share a border with Mercia.

Warwick, in Mercia.

Torksey, in the ancient kingdom of Lindsey, part of Mercia

River Severn, in the west of England

River Trent, runs through Staffordshire, Derbyshire, Nottingham and Lincolnshire and joins the Humber.

River Avon, in Warwickshire

River Thames, runs through London and into Oxfordshire

River Stour, runs from Stourport to Wolverhampton

River Ouse, leads into the Cam/Granta, runs through Bedford (Bed's Ford)

River Nene, runs from Northampton to the Wash

River Welland, runs from Northamptonshire to the Wash

River Granta/Cam, runs from Cambridge to King's Lynn (East Anglia)

River Great Ouse, running from South Northamptonshire to East Anglia

Kingsholm, close to Gloucester, an ancient royal site

The Foss Way, ancient roadway from Lincoln to Exeter

Watling Street, ancient roadway from Chester to London

Icknield Way, ancient roadway from Norfolk to Wiltshire

Ermine Street, ancient roadway from London to Lincoln, and York.

Historical Notes

AD875 is one of the rare years for which we have some information about King Coelwulf II. In this year, he issued two charters, number S215 and S216 in the Sawyer system of categorising Saxon charters (don't worry if that means nothing to you – as with all things Saxon, nothing is very easy and there are a number of different methodologies used to categorise the surviving charters). But, if you visit the Electronic Sawyer (https://esawyer.lib.cam.ac.uk/about/index.html#) and type in the charter numbers, you will be presented with a summary for both charters, as well as its surviving text in Latin. You'll also be told where the charter can be located and where it might have been translated in text or source books (if it has been).

Both of these charters are concerned with Worcester. In S215, Coelwulf exempts Bishop Wærferth of Worcester (he was a real person although he is entirely fictionalised in this book) from the burden of feeding the king's horses and their servants in return for liturgical services, and the bishop gives Coelwulf a piece of land in Gloucestershire for a four-life lease, with reversion to the bishopric in return for 60 mancuses of gold. In S216, Coelwulf gives St Mary's Minster, Worcester, a grant of 6 hides at Overbury, Worcester. Both of these charters survive in only one instance and in the same manuscript, London, British Library, Cotton Tiberius A. XIII, ff. 119-200. This manuscript contains 158 different charters, ranging from the seventh century to the very beginning of the eleventh. I'm sure that the historical Coelwulf would have issued more charters, but alas, only a very few survive. But their survival does show that Coelwulf, regardless of what the Anglo-Saxon Chronicle has to say about him, was an accepted king, with the authority to conduct transactions with the heads of the bishoprics in Mercia.

It's worth considering why these two charters survive. As with all things not dug up from the ground, there has to have been a reason for both of these charters to be filed away in Worcester's scriptorium, or wherever they were kept. The most usual explanation is that these two charters were important at a later day; they proved the ownership of the land, and they proved that it was accepted at a certain point in time. If we think of the Domesday record, which lists land ownership in 1086, it often references events at the time of 1066 as a means of justifying the situation in 1086. The same would have been happening with these pieces of land in Worcester. It's highly likely that King Coelwulf II was doing the same in other places but that, unfortunately, these records have not survived. Perhaps for entirely the opposite reason – someone didn't want the status quo to be maintained. All of the charters contained in Cotton Tiberius A. XIII are concerned with Mercian landholdings, and if I dig deeper, no doubt all reference Worcester in some way. The date at which the charters come to an end is not entirely concurrent with the end of Mercia as an independent kingdom, but it is not actually that many years away from it. It extends about fifty years over the usually given date for the beginning of England as a kingdom, as opposed to the smaller kingdoms before then.

Grantabridge/Cambridge. There is some debate about the naming of the river. If you ask a local, you might get very different answers. However, Cambridge/Grantabridge wasn't a new site at this time. There were ruins there that any settlers could have built upon, and not to give too much away, they obviously did in at a future date as well.

While writing this book, I discovered a new non-fiction book, *After Alfred: Anglo Saxon Chronicles and their Chroniclers 900-1150* by Pauline Stafford. This, to me at least, feels as though it's the work on the actual writing, and survival of the complex source known as the Anglo-Saxon Chronicle, that I've been waiting for throughout the 20 years that the author has been working on it. She has articulated, much better than I ever could, the way that the ASC should, and can be used. 'The political context we think we know is itself constructed from the debatable sources we seek to test.' (pg 2, After Alfred).

For the matter of Coelwulf, named as the 'foolish king's thegn' in the ASC, Stafford highlights that his name only appears in the B and C versions of the text, which closely mirror one another, but aren't an exact copy one from the other. B and C are not the oldest versions of the surviving manuscripts; this is version A, which is itself, a copy of a now lost, earlier text.

This means that the addition of Coelwulf's name as 'the foolish king's thegn' wasn't written down in the form that's been preserved for us until the end of the tenth century (B text), and the middle of the eleventh century (C text). What I'm trying to say here is that even these details are not contemporary – they may have been written over a hundred years later, or over a hundred and fifty years later. To put it into context, that would mean I would be writing about something that happened in Victorian England. (I will note here, that Pauline Stafford believes B and C may have been copied from an earlier, now lost, version of the chronicles.)

This is of great interest to me, and the reputation that Coelwulf II has since endured. While, I make no bones of the fact that my 'Coelwulf' is entirely fictional, I began this series with the express purpose of examining the reputation he has acquired. I feel this distinction is essential, and I hope that future research will reveal more and more of the real Coelwulf. I will keep you informed.

On a final note, the study of the past, contrary to what we might all believe is not written in stone. I am always learning new information, and delight in doing so. I am not alone in doing this. While writing in fiction allows me to play with some events, there are many non-fiction writers also re-examining this time period, and it needs to be recognised that 'facts' are very rarely, actually 'facts' (see the quotation above from Pauline Stafford)' Max Adams is writing excellent non-fiction about this period, which is highly accessible to non-specialists, and there is a huge growth in the topics under discussion, and how new readings of sources and archaeological finds and advances are helping us to understand more and more about what was actually happening. Or to put it even more clearly, why we know what we know about the ninth century.

Meet the author

I'm an author of historical fiction (Early English, Vikings and the British Isles as a whole before the Norman Conquest) and fantasy (Viking age/dragon-themed), born in the old Mercian kingdom at some point since AD1066. I like to write. You've been warned! Find me at mjporterauthor.com. mjporterauthor.blog and @coloursofunison on twitter. I have a monthly newsletter, which can be joined via my website. Once signed up, readers can opt into a weekly email reminder containing special offers.

Books by M J Porter (in chronological order)

Chronicles of the English (tenth century Britain)

Brunanburh

Of Kings and Half-Kings

The Second English King

The Mercian Brexit (can be read as a prequel to The First Queen of England)

The First Queen of England (The story of Lady Elfrida) (tenth century England)

The First Queen of England Part 2

The First Queen of England Part 3

The King's Mother (The continuing story of Lady Elfrida)

The Queen Dowager

Once A Queen

The Earls of Mercia

The Earl of Mercia's Father

The Danish King's Enemy

Swein: The Danish King (side story)

Northman Part 1

Northman Part 2

Cnut: The Conqueror (full-length side story)

Wulfstan: An Anglo-Saxon Thegn (side story)

The King's Earl

The Earl of Mercia

The English Earl

The Earl's King

Viking King

The English King

Lady Estrid (a novel of eleventh-century Denmark)

Fantasy

The Dragon of Unison

Hidden Dragon

Dragon Gone

Dragon Alone

Dragon Ally

Dragon Lost

Dragon Bond

As JE Porter

The Innkeeper (standalone)

20th Century Mystery

The Custard Corpses – a delicious 1940s mystery (audio book now available)

The Automobile Assassination (sequel to The Custard Corpses)

Cragside – a 1930s murder mystery (standalone)

Acknowledgments

Once more, I must thank you, my readers, for taking this journey with me into the past. Writing about Coelwulf, Haden and the men, women and horses who make up this cast of characters is an absolute pleasure, and I feel really honoured that you, my readers, want to read about their exploits.

As ever, thank you to my cheerleaders, EP, AP, MP, JC, MC, ST, CS, and AM. And to Shaun, my cover designer, who is so patient with me. Coelwulf will return. In 2023.

Printed in Great Britain
by Amazon

37352882R00155